Sophie Schwarz
Married With Tv
My marriage with Juergen Schwar.

CH00670743

Dear Jeremy

get well soon

Sophie

October 24th, 2024

insta: the sophie schwarz
sophie-schwarz@outlook.de

Married With Two Men

My Marriage with Juergen Schwarz

and

James Parkinson

by

Sophie Schwarz

Bibliographic Information of the German National Library:

The German National Library lists this publication in the German National Bibliography; detailed bibliographic data can be accessed online via http://dnb.dnb.de.

Translation: Sophie Schwarz
I have translated this to the best of my knowledge and abilities and kindly ask for your understanding should any errors have occurred.
Photos and Cover Design: Jan Reichmann
Publisher: BoD · Books on Demand GmbH, In de Tarpen 42, 22848 Norderstedt
Print: Libri Plureos GmbH, Friedensallee 273, 22763 Hamburg
ISBN: 978-3-7597-5170-6

Contents

Juergen

How should Juergen sleep after a day like this? "It is easy for Mummy. She can go to bed whenever she wants, not when someone tells her to", he muttered. "And it hasn't been exciting for her. It was not as it had been for me. I know everything about racing cars. I was so thrilled. Why do I already have to be in bed?" Juergen had received his good night kiss, but the light of the Berlin August sun was still finding its way through the curtains, and in his ears he could still hear the roaring of the racing cars that had run over the Avus. At last today his mother had been willing to go with him to a motor race. How much had he been longing for it.

How fast the cars had been, much faster than he had imagined in his wildest dreams. The moment he had seen them, they were gone again, just to reappear an instant later. If his mother hadn't looked after him so well, he would have run directly onto the racetrack driven by his enthusiasm. And then the roaring of the motors – was there a sound more beautiful in the whole world? Mummy had been of a very different opinion. For her, it had been far too loud. For Juergen, it could have been even louder. The noise was still humming in his ears and there he wanted to keep it forever.

"When I'm grown up I will become a racing driver", he thought and closed his eyes. Then he saw himself running over the world's racing tracks, sitting in his own racing car, wearing a racing suit and a racing driver's helmet on his head. Of course, he was leaving every other driver behind. No one would ever be able to be better than he was when he would run through the curves, and nobody would be faster on the straights. He would be the only one to be able to make a car perform this way. And seeing the checkered flag in front of him and hearing the spectators celebrating his victory he finally managed to go to sleep, happy and waiting eagerly for his splendid future as a racing driver. And the evening sun was still peeking through the curtain and shone onto his blissfully smiling face.

His decision was made. He would follow this path, no matter what might happen. He only had to hold on for a couple of years, and then it would become true. Carefully he saved his pocket money so that he was able to buy the magazine "Sportauto". He almost devoured it and couldn't wait for the arrival of the new one. He began to collect knowledge. Everything he wanted to know about cars, racing drivers, about every single race on the globe. This knowledge he knew for sure, would be needed when he would sit behind the steering wheel of his racing car. And he wanted to be prepared. If only it wouldn't take so terribly long.

James

How should James sleep after a day like this? He had sneaked into his father's office and watched and listened secretly to how his father's patients told him about their sufferings. Some people James knew as they came frequently to his father, or he met them on the streets of Hoxton. Some he did not know at all. They talked about their pain and showed their injuries and ulcers. Oh, and they even told his father about what was happening on the toilet.

At some point his father discovered him. He did not scold him as James had feared, but his father allowed him, to stay in the office hidden in a corner. James only had to promise him not to utter a single sound and also never to speak with anybody else than his father about the things he heard and saw there. James was only too happy to do so, and he was not only proud of the fact that not even the slightest sound came out of his mouth, even when watching and hearing funny or terribly disgusting things, but also that he did not have to vomit when his father had to put on the scalpel. On the contrary. He was enthusiastic and completely fascinated. He would have loved to get so much closer, to be able to see everything in detail. But his father had said that people wouldn't want that and that he was still too young for it.

The time his father had allowed him to stay in the office passed too fast, and he was sent back to his mother. And now he was lying in his bed, and the London August sun searched her way through the gaps in the curtains as he went through every single moment of his time at the office in his mind again and again. He wondered if he one day could do what his father did himself—helping people and making them whole again.

His decision was made. He would become a doctor when he was grown up like his father. Until then he would sneak into the office very often and he knew that he would have to learn an awful lot. It was best to start as soon as possible. He began to paint everything he observed in the office. Whenever he had the chance, he secretly borrowed one of his father's books to learn and see everything he could not recognise from his hiding place in the office.

Sophie

How should Sophie sleep after a day like this? She saw the sun of the Austrian village shining through the curtains and heard the adults' conversations echoing up from the terrace. It was easy for adults. They could stay up until it was getting dark or even longer. Every day she was sent to bed at seven o'clock. Good night prayer and a kiss, and then Mummy said: "Sleep well", and closed the door. But Sophie's skin was still burning in her face. She had been in the snow, in the middle of summer. Every year they spent three or four weeks in the Austrian Alps, but today she had been on a glacier for her very first time. Daddy had secured her with a mountaineering rope and had led the way. "If the snow can bear my weight, then he can carry you little chamois easily", he said and started to walk. Even now lying in her bed her feet still seemed to try to hit Daddy's footprints in the snow.

So much had she seen today. Chamois climbing the rocks. An eagle circling high above the peaks. And then all these wild berries. She had stuffed hands full of berries into her mouth. At some point, it had become rockier and rockier, with no more trees and only tiny flowers growing between the stone until the first patches of snow appeared. How bright it had been on the glacier. She had to wear her sunglasses and had to apply a lot of sun protection crème. There had been silence, complete silence, interrupted only by the crunching of her shoes in the snow and the cry of an eagle until they finally reached the summit. She never wanted to leave again. Mountains as far as the eye could see, snow-covered giants in front of the blue sky.

But there had been even more. Further down in the meadows, so many flowers had bloomed in every colour. She had learned that many of them were medicine, that the blossoms, the leaves, and even the roots could be used to make healing teas, ointments and all kinds of essences. All this the farmer's wife had told her on whose farm they were staying and she had given her dried lime blossoms and a jelly made of fir tips. "If you freeze very badly in winter and have the feeling, that the Sniffles Man has pinched into your nose or the Cough Witch has blown at you, then your Mummy should brew you a cup of tea with one tablespoon of the lime blossoms and a teaspoon of the jelly. Then you go to bed and you will see that you are completely healthy again the next day." With shining eyes, Sophie took the treasure that was now standing next to her on the bedside cabinet.

She thought, "When I'm grown up, I will discover the world, the whole world with all the mountains. And I will make people healthy again with herbs."

Her decision was made. She would become a world explorer and an herbalist. In her dreams, she saw herself standing on mountain peaks and sailing the seas and heard herself speaking in all languages. She would have to learn and read an awful lot to achieve this. Tomorrow she would start. She closed her eyes and went to sleep while the evening sun of this hot August day shone onto her bed.

Chapter 1

"Hello, I am Juergen."

"Hello, I am Sophie."

"The cold Sophie?" (Remark: in Germany, the Cold Sophie is the last of the so-called Ice Saints on the 15th of May)

"Do not forget, Sophie brings the summer", I answered and smiled at him.

Juergen paused. Then he smiled also. I could see very clearly that he liked this answer and that he wanted to know more about me. And so it was.

"Who are you?"

"Sophie."

"Yes, Sophie and you bring the summer," he said almost impatiently and went on to ask: "But who and what are you besides being beautiful?"

Oops, this man was straight. But who was he? Before I asked him this question, I answered his first. "Do you want the usual brief introduction – marital status, children, profession, hobbies? Okay then – living apart, divorce in progress, two delightful teenage children, a daughter and a son. And I mean delightful literally, they are simply great, at least most of the time. At the moment, I am building my professional restart after previously putting everything into the marriage and the children and forgetting myself and my dreams. I have a dog, a pony, a tom cat and canaries. My hobbies are…" Juergen interrupted my torrent of words. "Sophie, come with me to the airport, now. We will fly to Vegas." "Why?", I asked completely astonished. "I don't even know you." "Because I want to marry you, immediately, as soon as we will be there?" "But…" I didn't get any further because Juergen took me into his arms and kissed me. "I will never let go of you again. Let us fly and marry, now."

I wanted to ward him off. What did this guy think he was doing? I didn't like it at all to be taken by surprise and be kissed right away. Then I perceived something that made me hesitate. It was barely noticeable, but it was there. Perhaps I was a far more exciting woman than I had previously thought, and I could make a man tremble with a few words. But I couldn't believe that either. This was something completely different. Something, that I didn't like at all. How on earth could I tell him my suspicion? A suspicion that, should it be confirmed, would pull the rug from under his feet far more than a flight to Vegas.

Juergen looked at me questioningly as if he was expecting a violent reaction to his kiss, a slap in his face, or a severe scolding. But I wasn't thinking about the kiss or the fact that he had been very brash with it, to put it mildly. Instead, I took a step back and looked into his questioning, hopeful eyes.

"Juergen", I said in a gentle, questioning voice. "Have you been to a doctor recently?" "Why do you ask?" he wanted to know with caution in his expression, almost as if he feared being caught doing something forbidden. "Because I think you need to be examined very thoroughly. I have just realised something that raises a suspicion in me. But I do not want to say more about it."

Suddenly Juergen became very serious. There was no more humorous twinkle in his eyes, no cheeky smile. In a very calm and matter-of-fact voice he asked: "What do you suspect?" "Juergen, please, you must talk about this with a doctor. I am certainly not going to tell you anything else about it. It is only a suspicion. You should get a thorough examination." "What do you suspect?" And there it was again, the smile as if he was planning a prank. This confused me because we were talking about something very serious. "No comment", I said.

"Sophie, I went to the doctor long ago and am still going. He only needed much longer for the diagnosis than you did and far more devices." "You should have just taken him into your arms and kissed him. This would certainly have helped," I said, trying a joke, although I didn't feel like laughing at all.

Juergen laughed heartily and then, being severe again, asked again, "Come on, speak up now. What do you suspect?" "And you are really and seriously informed and in treatment?" "Yes, honestly, for many years. Ok, your suspicion?" Juergen now asked more urgently and with a slight trace of impatience.

I would have to express my suspicion. This took all my courage. I looked into Juergen's eyes and said the words, that barely wanted to leave my mouth: "Morbus

Parkinson, the Shaking Palsy as James Parkinson himself named it." "That's right. I am absolutely impressed. And? Does this change anything for us?" A slight nervousness crept into Juergen's voice, and I could feel his tension. But why was he already talking about us?

"No, I'm still not going to Vegas with you and I'm not marrying you either." "Thank you", Juergen said and took me into my arms again. "Thank you for giving me a chance."

Chapter 2

Morbus Parkinson. Why didn't that bother me? Why didn't I run as fast as I could away from Juergen? I did not need a man with a chronic illness that did not promise an easy life after everything I had already been through. If such a diagnosis comes into your life when you have already been in a stable relationship for a long time, you get through it together. At least this was what I believed in. But I only knew Juergen for a couple of hours. There was still time and opportunity to go separate ways. Juergen would understand that.

"But I can't do that", I thought, and why I could not do it kept me awake most of the night. Why on earth couldn't I leave it at this one encounter? I got to know an interesting person, who I could definitely include in my circle of friends, but nothing else. But why did I know deep down that this was not up for discussion, that on the contrary, it was all or nothing? After such a short period spent together? Things like that didn't happen in real life. This was the kind of thing Hollywood movies were made of. Had it been his certainty, his marriage proposal although hardly knowing me, his fragility that this quiet, fine trembling was showing, or the fear in his eyes that I could reject him because of his illness? I didn't know.

As I couldn't even think about sleeping anyway, I got up and gathered my books on neurology around me. I immersed myself in the book. No thinking, no feelings. Switching to the level of mind. Maybe this would help me although I doubted it. Of course, I knew what it was all about with the Shaking Palsy. It is a neurological disease that causes neurons, nerve cells, to die off in the substantia nigra which is located in the mesencephalon. The task of these cells is to produce dopamine, which in turn is a messenger substance that, among other things, ensures that signals and impulses are transmitted between the nerve cells, the neurons. Coordinated movement is not possible without or with too little dopamine. A lack of dopamine also slows down a person's actions and thinking. The dying of the dopamine-producing cells progresses, which is why the disease continues to worsen over time. However, the disease can also come to a standstill. I was aware of the fact that there was no causal treatment for Parkinson's disease; nothing had yet been found to cure the disease permanently. I also knew that the drugs that were usually prescribed were all associated with serious side effects and had to be dosed very carefully so that people could benefit from their effects as long as possible and be spared the side effects as far as possible.

When that didn't help me, I started looking for solutions. Of course, I wouldn't be able to cure Parkinson's disease, but weren't there any additional ways to give a person having this disease a better quality of life and to slow down the progression of the disease? Why did a person get Parkinson's disease in the first place? As with any illness, there were many more causes than the purely physical ones. How often had I been laughed at for thinking this way. But I knew for sure that it was the case. How often had this approach helped me and other people, even with the most severe illnesses?

I remembered how my thinking about health and illness had been guided towards self-responsibility by the farmer's wife as a child. How much I had learned, got to know, and tried out since then. Medical herbs, hydrotherapy, homoeopathy, the importance of sports and exercise, respiratory therapy, nutrition, psychosomatics, and much more. That had to be possible with Juergen's Parkinson's disease also. Perhaps I could help him. We wouldn't have to be in a relationship for that.
But then I had to find out a lot more about him. Who was he? What had his life looked like until now? What were his dreams? When and how had his symptoms started? What other illnesses had he had? What had his childhood been like? What on earth had he actually been doing in and with his life before he came across me and proposed to me?

I was sitting between all my books and looked out of the window. The day was slowly drawing in when suddenly the phone rang.

"Do you have time on Tuesday?" It was Juergen calling. "Good morning to you too. You are very early", I answered. "Good morning, sorry. I haven't slept all night, so it hasn't sunk in yet that another day has begun. Anyway, do you have time on Tuesday?" "Yes, but why?" "Well, if you don't want to marry me in Vegas, I thought I could at least come and visit you." "Juergen, you are living in Ludwigsburg. That is not just around the corner from Oberhausen." "I know, pretty much just over four hundred kilometres. So do you have time on Tuesday?"

He was persistent, I had to give him that. I smiled to myself and said: "Yes, I can arrange that." "Great, but I had hoped for a little more enthusiasm on your part. I will let you know when I arrive and then we will go for something to eat. I have already chosen a hotel. I'll book that now because I don't want to go back on the same day. That would be almost eight hundred kilometres. And maybe there might be time for a breakfast."

"I have children. There won't be any breakfast, I will have breakfast with them. But we also need to talk about your Parkinson's disease." "Yes, of course, I wanted to ask you something about this anyway." Juergen took a short break. Before he continued, I heard him taking a deep breath, as if he had to overcome himself to ask the following question. "Do you want to help me?" I also hesitated for a moment. I hardly knew Juergen and was sure this question wasn't only about a few tips. This question included so much more. A yes would mean making a commitment that was much closer than a wedding in Vegas. That meant taking responsibility and not disappointing the trust placed in me. And again, I hardly knew Juergen. How should I be able to commit to this now? Finally, something inside me said yes, and I replied to Juergen, "Yes, I will try."

Juergen breathed an audible sigh of relief. "Then everything will be fine. But you can always change your mind. I don't want to commit you to anything." "I know." I did say that, but I knew that I would try everything and wouldn't give up at some point, no matter what our relationship status would be.

"See you Tuesday," Juergen said. "See you Tuesday," I answered, slowly and thoughtfully putting the phone away. What had I just done? What was I slipping into? But it felt right, right, and good—until Tuesday.

Chapter 3

James Parkinson was a casual acquaintance of mine long before he came into my life very intensively with Jürgen. He was the son of a doctor and a doctor himself, born on April 11th, 1755, in Hoxton, which was still a pretty good part of my favourite city of London at that time. One day earlier, on April 10th, 1755, another important man in my life was born – Samuel Hahnemann. He also was a doctor, the son of a porcelain painter in Meissen. I've never been there so far. He founded homoeopathy, which has enriched my life and saved it. But back to James. He discovered the Shaking Palsy, which in modern times is known as Parkinson's disease. I often wonder whether this honour would please the humble fighter for social justice James.

James lived in exciting times. It was the so-called Georgian era, the era of the Industrial Revolution, and the founding of the scientifically based modern surgery by the Scottish physician John Hunter. James had studied with him among others. James Watt invented the steam engine, the American War of Independence took place, Napoleon lost at Waterloo, Josiah Wedgwood invented porcelain for the masses, agriculture was reformed, the so-called common land was banned, and London grew and grew and grew. More and more offices and warehouses were built also factories and by and by the public gardens in Hoxton, where the hurried city dwellers had been able to relax a little, disappeared. They were replaced by factories and tenement blocks that were soon bursting at the seams. More and more people had to share the inflated rents to at least have a roof over their heads, albeit in completely filthy flats without proper sewage systems. A hotbed of disease, vermin, alcoholism, hunger and crime. The workhouses brought to us by Charles Dickens came into being. The surgery James had taken over from his father, which had previously looked after the illnesses of a fairly well-to-do patient base, was now at the increasing centre of hunger, misery, poverty, crime and the famous Hoxton madhouses, places of absolute horror.

As a Hoxton-based doctor, James was responsible for one of these madhouses, the Holly House. It was considered exemplary, which is not at all surprising as James was a committed advocate for people's rights. He also tried to improve the situation of individuals in the madhouses with all the means at his disposal. Not only did people with severe mental disabilities end up in the madhouses, but it was not uncommon for unwelcome relatives to be deported there. With the right amount of money, it was relatively straightforward. James also noticed people there who were shaking all over and had uncontrolled saliva running out of their mouths, but who showed no signs of mental disability and therefore didn't belong in one of the madhouses. But who should take care of them? And he wrote his famous treatise "The Shaking Palsy".

Chapter 4

"Good morning most beautiful Sophie. I want to make my way to you now, but I don't even know your address. Sophie in Oberhausen is not accepted as an address by my navigation device." This was how a cheerful Juergen greeted me on my mobile phone on Tuesday morning. In fact, it was almost midday. I gave him my address.

"But Juergen, I have children. You can't just pop in here." "Are you not allowed to receive friends? Then I have to rescue you from your captivity." Today he was in an excellent mood. "Of course I do. But I'm a bit more careful with friends who want to run off to Vegas with me. That might be a bit much for the two of them." "I don't have any children, so you are the expert. If that's what you mean and you think it's right, then I will call you when I am approaching, and you can tell me where we are going to meet. Is this better for you and your offspring?" "This is how we do it. I appreciate your understanding. See you later." "I am glad that you're receiving me at all", said Juergen. I could tell from his voice that he was really relieved that I wasn't backing down after all. "See you later. I am looking forward to seeing you."

This man had the talent to overwhelm me very charmingly. There was always a smile in his voice, which magically found its way onto my lips and resistance was impossible. I also had to admit that his persistence was flattering to me.

The day took its usual course. I made my way to the forest with my collie dog June. I loved these daily walks in the woods with June. They were most welcome breaks in a stressful everyday life, an opportunity to let my mind wander. More and more often my thoughts wandered to Juergen, to Parkinson's disease, and to the question of what was happening to me and my life right now. I was content, indeed happy, to be free with my children and my animals. I didn't need a man, at least not in the moment. But Juergen seemed to see this in a decidedly different light.

Just as I emerged from the forest, my mobile phone rang. "It's me, Juergen," he said very cheerfully. I discovered that there is a takeaway not far from your house. I am there now. As you know, I was born in Berlin and am practically obliged to eat every Currywurst that crosses my path. Do you know where I am right now?"

I laughed. "I can imagine where you are. You can only be talking about one take-away. That's also where we go when we're hungry for French Fries. And how am I supposed to know that you were born in Berlin? You haven't told me this fact yet. I think the city is terrible, by the way." "A matter of opinion, I don't think it's great either, even if the removal of the Wall has done it a lot of good. I don't go there often anymore. But what kind of woman are you if you didn't immediately have researched who I am and where I am coming from? Very unusual." "I am a very special woman, anything but ordinary." "I've already come to the same conclusion. When can you be here, and should I leave you some Currywurst? I would make that sacrifice for you in a heartbeat. Or would you even like your own sausage?" "I'm just coming round the corner from the forest with June. Give me five minutes. And I've already eaten – the sausage is all yours." "Wonderful. But who is June?" "My dog. The greatest and most beautiful in the whole world. If she doesn't like you, you can leave immediately." " I certainly won't have to. She will love me."

I approached the takeaway and saw Juergen sitting at a table in front of it, visibly enjoying eating his Currywurst. What happened next still amazes me today. Although all tables were occupied, my otherwise very reserved June walked purposefully to-wards Juergen, whom she had not yet met, and lay down under his chair.

Juergen was beaming over his face and said: "Welcome, Sophie; why don't you come sit with June and me? Still speechless, I sat down with the two of them. Slowly all this was getting mysterious.

Chapter 5

Daily phone calls, or to be more precise, several phone calls a day, soon became an integral part of Juergen's and my life. He accompanied me when running in the woods, was there when I went shopping, and sometimes even when I was cooking. The route between Ludwigsburg and Oberhausen became Juergen's favourite one and he often set off completely spontaneously, without asking me, only to announce in a good mood on the way. "Hello, my sun, I will be arriving in Oberhausen in about three hours. When can I take you out for dinner?" "Juergen, today I can't." "There is no such thing, you can reorganise everything." "Today is a good example of the fact that you can't reorganise everything. As much as I would love to do it and as much as I love spontaneity – with two children, work, animals and further education, I'm not as flexible as I might like to be." "No chance?", Juergen asked. "Oh Juergen, everything needs some planning at the moment. In between, I also need some time for myself. You're making me completely dizzy right now." "That's good, then you can't think about everything. If you would reflect everything, you would probably send me and my Parkinson's away." "Is that your fear? Believe me, if there was any danger of this, I would have told you on the very first evening. I knew I was getting involved in a very special menage à trois with you AND James Parkinson. Just give me a little more time and space to plan." "I'll think about it. But what can I do now? I'm already halfway to Oberhausen and booked my hotel." "Have a nice evening on Oberhausen. Tomorrow morning, we can have breakfast together. I can manage that." "You can't be serious", Juergen said almost indignantly. "I am completely serious. There is no other way. I invite you to breakfast." I was so sorry that I couldn't make this evening together possible, but I had told him often enough that we would have to make arrangements. "Then it is what it is, but I don't like it." "Me neither. But I'm looking forward to our breakfast."

We learned more about each other with every conversation. Juergen was a journalist, and his great passion was motorsports. Of course, as a child, he had dreamed of becoming a racing driver. "But the dream was over when an ophthalmological examination revealed that I lacked three-dimensional vision", Juergen told me one evening as we sat together in a cosy atmosphere after dinner. "I knew then that I was not an above-average bad tennis player who rarely hit the ball, despite all my dedication to this sport, but that my eyes made it almost impossible for me to play better. But it was also a hard blow for me because it also meant that I could never become a racing driver. There was nothing else I could imagine as a career – I wanted to be a racing driver and of course win the races, all the races, because I was so sure that I would be the best. And now that shouldn't work at all?" Even after so many years, Juergen still had tears in his eyes, which he quickly wiped away. "You didn't see that, have you?", he said somewhat ashamed. "Was there anything to be seen?" I asked, stroking his head before leading the conversation out of the sad realms.

"So then you chose a profession that brought you as close as close as possible to the race track", I assumed. "It wasn't that easy because my parents wanted me to have a proper job. After having passed my A-levels by a friendly twist of fate, it was agreed that I should study law. My parents decided that the legal profession was proper and solid. I was asked rather less about this." I looked at Juergen in disbelief. "You studying law? I cannot imagine you studying law. How did you get through it?" "With the help of a lot of excellent beer", Juergen answered laughing. But the sadness in his eyes belied his cheerful reply. It must have been a very difficult time for him.

"When I had achieved the Bachelor of Laws and imagined a lifetime of legal work ahead of me, I couldn't think of any that could give me any pleasure at all. Not a nice thought. Of course, I dutifully applied for a legal traineeship. At the same time, however, I also applied for a journalistic traineeship at the Stuttgarter Motorpresse. After all, the newspaper Berliner Tagesspiegel had already published articles written by me during my school days. A child's play, that's how I see it today, but I was very proud of it, so I thought that if I didn't give fate a chance, it couldn't save me from a lifetime on the legal treadmill either. So I stood in front of the mailbox with my two applications, the one for the legal and the one for the journalistic traineeship. I made a promise to myself to accept the offer I received first in response to my applications, no matter what family dilemma it might create. That was my plan. And simultaneously, I let the two applications disappear into the belly of the mailbox. I'm only realising just now that I hadn't thought for a moment that I might receive a rejection for both applications."

"I know, you're a journalist now, but that could have come about in different ways. Which application won the race?", I asked, impatiently waiting for the outcome of the story.

"The Motorpress of course. Fast cars, fast reactions. They invited me to Stuttgart and my heart did somersaults with joy. Now it was just up to me to prove that I deserved this chance. I still had self-doubts, but don't you always have them as a self-critical person?"

"And what about your parents? Was their placet still so important to you even in your mid-twenties?" "That's a good question. We always had our problems, my parents and me. But after all, they supported me throughout my university years and didn't want to harm me. Their world was like this. I knew for sure that if I got the journalistic traineeship, nothing, absolutely nothing in the world would stop me from accepting it. But I also wanted my parents to understand me, I didn't want to go to Stuttgart in a fight. I don't like arguments. I absolutely don't like arguments."
"I can understand that very well. Me neither. But a cleansing argument is better than a lazy compromise. How did your revelation conversation go?"

"There was none – my parents were on holiday at the time of making the decision", Juergen answered. And this twist of fate in his past still brought a smile to his face. "I sat down and wrote a letter to them explaining the situation and asking for their understanding that you have to accept once-in-a-lifetime opportunities. My bag was packed for the trip to Stuttgart for the job interview I told them. I would keep them informed about the course of events and hope that they will be happy with me. I wished them a good holiday and I really meant that sincerely." "Cleverly solved, you could say." "But what else could I do in the pre-mobile phone age? The appointment was soon, I couldn't reach them by phone, but I didn't want to hide anything either. They could see that I had both written and sent the letter before I left for Stuttgart. In short – I travelled to Stuttgart, survived the whole introduction and selection procedure, and was immediately in the middle of the world of my dreams. Farewell jurisprudence, farewell Berlin, you walled-in city. The world was finally my home." His whole face was beaming and I almost thought I could see all the journeys that had made up his life and work passing on his forehead.

Chapter 6

"Good morning, Sopherl." Who else but Juergen would call so cheerfully first thing in the very early morning? "Good morning", I answered far more tired. "Did I wake you up? Sorry, but you know that sleep is completely overrated." "Oh, you ignorant one, your brain needs a break too." "No, you forget, I have my dopamine pills, you don't need to sleep with them. But I won't give you any", he laughed. "I am very happy you don't", I yawned. "I find a few hours of rest extremely pleasant." "You're not a journalist. Do you know what can happen anywhere in the world while I slumber unsuspectingly in Europe? I have to be able to react immediately." "Does that mean, that no journalist in the world goes to sleep?" "The good ones very little."

How had I learned, I thought, and dug around in my brain that was still half-asleep for the psychosomatic explanations of Parkinson's disease. Right, it was control, always wanting to have control over everything and everyone. I asked Juergen: "And what makes you interrupt my beauty sleep so rudely?" "I would like to ask you if you can take the coming weekend off." "I must think about it and organise myself. I can tell you in the evening." "Earlier would be better." "I will try. Why the rush?" "I've found a nice hotel and I should confirm it soon. I want to show you something near the hotel."

My curiosity was aroused. "What is it?", I asked immediately. "I will tell you when we get there. Don't worry; nothing bad or anything that might be offensive to a true lady like you." "I'll take your word for that. Are dogs allowed in the hotel?" "I didn't ask about that. Isn't it completely natural that you can take your dog with you to a hotel? I always assumed that. In fact, I've never even thought about it." "Unfortunately not. Travelling with a dog has its own problems." "Couldn't June stay with your children and your ex-husband …" Juergen didn't finish his sentence because he knew that he was touching on a very sensitive subject for me. "No, I have already explained it to you. I got June as a traumatised dog, full of fears. Even though she loves the children and gets on very well with my ex-husband, I promised her I would never leave her behind. She trusts me. And I do not betray trust, not your trust either." "Ok, that's okay. I can understand it, and it makes you even more lovable. I never knew a person like you. Do you take care of yourself from time to time?" "I don't know how this works", I said and Juergen understood. "I'll ask at the hotel about dogs, and you'll let me know as soon as you've sorted everything out, please?" "I will, I promise. Until later." "'til later."

Two minutes later I received a text message. "June is allowed to come along." It seemed really important to him, but why?

We arrived at the hotel almost at the same time. Juergen had obviously put a lot of effort into selecting a hotel. "There's plenty of forest for you and June and your running too", he said with a grin and pointed to the forest directly adjacent to the hotel while June greeted him stormily. "Why just for June and me? You are very welcome to join us. We would actually really like that, both of us." "Sopherl, if the good Lord had wanted us to walk, why did he let us invent a car?" I didn't find this sentence at all as funny as Juergen did. "Because humans were created to move and walking is good for us, especially for Parkinson's disease by the way." "I know, they told me the same when I was in the clinic and chased me onto the piste with some cross-country skiing poles, without any snow. I don't quite believe that. It can't be that simple." "Has anyone claimed that walking cures Parkinson's? No one has yet found the miracle cure. But it helps the body to cope better and to minimise the effects. Or don't you want to stay fit and mobile for as long as possible?" "Yes, I do, but there must be another way. Walking always reminds me of those boring Sunday family walks or hiking holidays in the Allgäu or something like that. Thanks, but no thanks." "It wouldn't be boring with June and me." "Maybe, but you can have the fun without me. Speaking of fun – shall we not check in and put this topic aside for now?"

I would not be able to solve this problem now. "He is an adult and responsible for himself. Don't interfere, don't patronise him. His decision, his responsibilities", I admonished myself. "My boyfriend, not my patient. Never treat friends and family." I didn't want to do that. I just wanted to give him some advice. After all, he had asked me for help. And besides, this sentence and his overall reaction annoyed me. How often had I heard similar stupid remarks when people sought an excuse? But now away with these thoughts and I said to Juergen: "Why don't you check in? June deserves a walk in the forest after the journey." After walking a couple of meters, I said to myself, "And I need to cool down while I'm running. After all, I want to have a good time with him."

Chapter 7

"What plans have you made for today?" I was curious and didn't know what Juergen's plans might be about. Many things were possible with him. "I'd like to show my two ladies a bit of the region and then something special. Wait and see." What Juergen seemed so keen to show me was very important to him, as his voice was very serious. He rarely spoke like that. What was it that he wanted to show me?

Our route took us through forests and small villages until Juergen finally stopped in a car park. At first, I couldn't understand why he wanted to park there. But I received the answer to my unspoken question very quickly.

"I spent a few weeks of my life in this rehabilitation clinic. Even if not everything was going well here, I owe it to the people here that I am so well medicated concerning Parkinson's that I can live again, which I could hardly do any more before I came here. Although I was supposed to arrive and check in by ten or twelve o'clock, I didn't reach my destination until late afternoon. In my condition, getting my luggage into the car took me hours. And then I still had to drive here. That was only possible with lots and lots of breaks. The first thing I was told off for coming so late. After all, there were fixed times for this at the clinic. "That was very cheeky of you", I said more cheerfully than I felt. Now, it was clear why Juergen had been so serious in the morning. "Exactly. I then remarked that I was glad to have made it to the clinic at all and asked where I could park my car and, after that, could lay my weary head to rest. 'Why park your car? Surely you don't want to tell me you travelled here on your own by car?' The lady at the reception was completely dismayed. 'How else would I have got here? On foot I wouldn't be here by now.' Her unhelpful reply was that someone could have taken me here, my wife, for example, or I could have travelled by train. The clinic would offer a shuttle service from the railway station. 'I do not have a wife, and looking at my state, how was I supposed to get on a train with my luggage like that? I thought this clinic was familiar with my illness. It doesn't look like that to me at the moment.' I was almost furious, Sophie. I had dragged myself here with the last of my strength, and now I just wanted to sleep. Why this clinic didn't offer a door-to-door shuttle service is still a mystery to me. Not everyone has a family. But that's not so important for now. The lady still didn't give up. 'But you can't drive a car in this condition.' I could only reply: 'I could, and I did. And this is how it went – I drove for ten minutes and then took a break. That's why I'm late now. With the very last of my strength for today, I want to park my car now because it's probably in the way right outside the front door where it is now. And then I want to go to my room.'"

For a moment, Juergen was carried away by the experience of that time, which still greatly disturbed him. He continued: "She finally explained the way to the parking site. Without any support, I unloaded my luggage from my car. Then I made my way to the car park. It took me half an hour to park my car and shuffle back to the clinic. Once there, my details were first to be recorded. I was then handed the house rules and told, still in a reproachful tone, that I would, of course, not see a doctor until tomorrow as I had arrived too late. Finally, the receptionist handed me my room key, told me my room number and floor and considered her task concerning me complete. I asked if there was a trolley or something similar for my luggage, as I had reached the end of my tether. Again, the woman wanted to remind me of my late arrival. But then even she realised that she had now made this issue more than clear and should instead find helping hands without any further comment. She obviously didn't want to risk a collapsed patient in front of her workplace after all. Finally, in my room and on my own, I switched on the television, fell onto my bed and slept so long and deep as I hadn't done for years until, in the morning, a scream of horror woke me: 'Mr. Schwarz, you can't lie on the bed in street clothes, and the TV is far too loud.' Welcome to the Parkinson's jail, I thought."

"And this jail you now want to show me?" "Yes. We can't go there, especially not with June, but we can walk along the grounds. You should know the full extent of what you are getting into with me." "Juergen, I know exactly what I am getting with you and James Parkinson, but I appreciate your open telling and showing me all this. I sincerely thank you for that. But what was it like for you being here? I can't imagine you here. You must have been told exactly what to do and what not to do. How did you deal with this?"

We strolled across the grounds. Patients with varying degrees of Parkinson's disease and multiple sclerosis took advantage of the lovely weather for a walk with or without walking aids, with or without a wheelchair, with or without support.

Juergen had become very serious. There was no sign of his usual smile in his eyes. "Where and how will I end up," he said very quietly and then continued cheerfully: "This is where they tried to introduce me to the joys of Nordic walking. You experienced for yourself how successful they were with it. And here you can look into the swimming pool. I liked that." I tried to imagine Juergen there, taking part in therapies, he who rejected everything that had to do with a healthy lifestyle or looked like physical exercise. Juergen, the lonely wolf who lived only according to his own will in a gymnastics group? But I should not forget how desperate he must have been. And alone. Being on your own is no problem when you're healthy, but when you're ill? Just the description of how he had got here, even if he hadn't gone into detail, said more than words could say.

"Have you got an impression, Sopherl?" Juergen asked after we had round the site. "Then I would like to leave here again. I can tell you everything I have to say and answer your questions, which I assume you will certainly have somewhere else." I agreed with him. Then, his eyes rested on a man who was in a very advanced stage of Parkinson's disease. I saw fear flicker in his eyes. "This doesn't have to be your way, Juergen." I took his hand and held it very tight. "You know, on the one hand, this disease progresses differently in each person, sometimes fast, sometimes slowly, sometimes it stagnates. On the other hand, you don't know what else is wrong with this man. And besides, you're not alone anymore. I am with you."

Juergen looked at me with unspeakably sad eyes. "Sopherl, that was the worst thing here. You come here because you are looking for help, full of confidence but also complete of despair, at the absolute end of your strength. You have been trying to come to terms with this diagnosis for years, giving yourself hope that it won't be so bad for you or that the worst is at least still many decades away. However, the wards and therapy groups are not categorised according to the severity of the illness. No, they are always all together as long as they are mobile. There is the one person who will never be able to achieve what is required, no matter how hard they try, and there is the other one, like me, for whom none of this is of any use because it is so simple that you think they don't take you seriously. For example, I was supposed to put round building blocks into round holes. For some of the mixed bunch, this was an impossible task. I just thought to myself: 'Guys, I haven't got that far yet, and for me, the round has to go into the square anyway.' But nobody understood this hint about football, and nobody was interested in it either. As a result, I didn't go to therapy more and more often. I had only wanted to have my medication adjusted anyway. The neurologist whose patient I was hadn't yet developed the right composition. Otherwise, I wouldn't have needed a whole day for the journey to the clinic."

Juergen shook his head thoughtfully. "You are asked to be positive about your illness, to accept it, and then they come along with a bit of block sorting and Nordic walking and act as if all this was great fun and everything could be fixed with this nonsense. If it were so easy, then I want to know why so many people are in such a bad state and why we need such strong medication. And then, every day, you're with these poor people who can't even grasp the building block because they're shaking so much, who have to wear nappies and have salvia running out of their mouths. They have to sit where they've been put because they can't get out of there themselves. But you are told to stay optimistic and cheerful. And do you know the brochure title they were handing out here?" Now, the sheer anger was written all over his face. "'A better life with Parkinson's', that's the name of this thing."

Back at the car, Juergen paused. "Now you know what to expect. I wanted to show you that. I have this damn illness too. It is part of my life, and I don't know where it will take me. Will it go well? Will I remain stable, or will I first lose control of my body and then of my mind? I don't know, and that scares me. It really scares me. And I can't involve another person in that. And yet, I still want to marry you. And I never wanted to get married. Me? Never. It's all so crazy." So we stood in the car park by his car, looking at each other. June was standing between us and leant alternately against Juergen and me. After a brief silence, because I wanted to wait and see if Juergen wanted to say anything else, I said: "That's what we call living. Nobody knows what is going to happen. No one has control over their next breath, their next step, the next second, anything. We repress this thought, prefer to lull ourselves in a false sense of security and fall prey to the delusion that we have everything under control. We only suppress these facts, which would drive us crazy if we had them constantly in front of our eyes. An illness, no matter what, an accident, all that robs us of this illusion. We can keep our blinkers on and maintain the life lie of having control over our existence until we are forced to realise the truth. I think it is better to admit these facts, accept them and discard the lie about our ability to control everything. No matter what happens in my life, I must learn to cope with it. Am I poor or rich? Am I single or in a relationship? Do I have children or not? Am I successful or not? Am I healthy or ill? What I make of it is my task. A crazy journalist who, to top it all off, has Parkinson's in his rucksack has been laid at my feet. What can I do with this now? I didn't order it like this. Shall I return this parcel to the sender? Or do I accept this parcel, unpack it, get to know the contents, and find out with you whether we can get along with each other and cope with life's tasks? Sending back is for cowards. I've never been a coward. And even if I don't understand many things in life, I have realised that it is better to accept gifts."

"So you're not leaving my life now that you've seen everything here?" Juergen looked at me in complete disbelief. "Why should I? Juergen, I knew all this. It is part of my job to understand this and many other illnesses in all its facets. I haven't seen or learnt anything I didn't already know today. Let's find out how to lead a better life with Parkinson's. What do you think?" "That heaven has sent you. And you really don't want to go to Vegas with me?" "Oh, Juergen", I laughed and chased him around the car. "Let's leave here quickly – this is not your future. But also be thankful. These people here have made your and our future possible with their medication. They made some mistakes but obviously knew how to find the right medication. And now let's go, I am hungry, starving in fact." "And when do we unwrap the presents that we are supposed to accept?" asked a completely relieved Juergen as he started the car and drove slowly out of the clinic parking site.

Chapter 8

It was early in the morning. The day dawned sluggishly. The sun battled heavily with the smoke from countless coal fires and factory chimneys. It was cold. James and I buried our hands deeper in our pockets. Today, James wanted to show me the Hoxton Madhouses because I didn't want to believe what he had described. He had told me that some of the houses were run by a butcher from the country who was known for his utter insensitivity towards the inmates of his establishment. He recruited his so-called carers from among the city's well-known thugs and alcoholics. How should I believe that, after all, Warburton, that was the man's name, was also called a doctor? Did you not need any medical training to run a madhouse or, in other words, a psychiatric hospital? I wouldn't say I liked the phrase madhouse at all. Later, after seeing the worst of their kind, this phrase didn't cause any problems for me anymore. But I was referring to the madness that prevailed there and that of the authorities who allowed it and not to the poor souls who were locked up in the houses with almost no prospect of release. James told me that if only enough money were paid, it was easy to make a person disappear into one of these hells. It was utterly unimportant whether there was a psychiatric illness. With sufficient money, each medical colleague was prepared to order the hospitalisation. It was a convenient way to eliminate disagreeable relatives, especially if they stood in the way of an inheritance.

An unimaginably horrible stench greeted us. People were tied to bedsteads into which they had been defecating for days, if not longer. We interrupted the rape of a woman by several warders or carers, as they called themselves, and saw how they beat up other inmates. From the cellars came the cries of the so-called complex cases locked up there or of the inmates who had refused to obey orders, some of whom had not been given a meal for days.

A man was sitting in a corner. A thread of salvia was hanging from one corner of his mouth, and his body shook incessantly. His trousers were full of dried faeces, and he stared at us with a dull look. "This is the Shaking Palsy", James said. "This man isn't insane. He has a disease of his nerves and needs care and treatment. I wrote an essay about it and also gave lectures on this disease. But people like him still end up in the madhouses. I will try to free him."

My face was wet with tears. So this is what Shaking Palsy, Parkinson's disease, looks like in its untreated complete form. James gently took me in his arms and led me out.

"Sopherl, wake up. You must have dreamed something awful. You shouted, and you even wept. What have you dreamed of?" Juergen was distraught and stroked my hair gently. "My sun, you don't have to cry. I am here with you." Slowly, I came to my senses and said quietly: "It's all right, Juergen, you don't need to worry. I don't know what I was dreaming either. Please, hold me." He did, and I fell asleep again.

Chapter 9

We continued to talk on the phone for hours. In the evenings, we spoke on the phone until I fell asleep. Juergen had no regular sleep rhythm and usually only slept for an hour or two between our calls. He was planning our first holiday together. It wasn't going to be anything spectacular. "A dog-friendly trip to the Black Forest. If you like, you can collect me in Ludwigsburg. After all, it's on the way." That's what was agreed.

It was my first journey without my children. A weekend had already been unusual, but a complete week? As much as I was looking forward to the time with Juergen, it was hard to say goodbye to my children. June came with me, but the children had to go to school, and when I asked if we should move the trip to the school holidays so they could come with us, they just grimaced. No, thank you. I interpreted it correctly. Of the 424 kilometres from my house to Juergen's, I cried at least 250. "Well done", I said to myself. "You'll look wonderful for your boyfriend. The anticipation of our time together certainly radiates clearly from your eyes, swollen from crying", I scolded myself after a glance into the mirror. But I knew Juergen would understand. And even if he didn't understand something, he always accepted it.

"Was it that bad?", he asked when I arrived at his house. "I can't comment on that, but I can imagine it. Although most women with children I know are happy to get rid of them for a few days. Should we cancel the trip?" "No, I've done the worst part of it. So awful. But let's go now."

Of course, Juergen wasn't finished yet. I knew him so well by now that I wasn't surprised. Although he always had a packed travel bag in his flat, he usually needed more time for the last few things than he had imagined or planned. In addition, Parkinson's disease does not like any pressure, not even positive pressure like that of a departure.

"Sophie?" "Yes?" "Could you please hand me a pair of black shoes from the shelf? I want to pack one pair of shoes as a reserve." "Of course." My eyes fell on the shoe rack. There, neatly lined up, were three pairs of completely identical black shoes, albeit in different sizes from regular to huge.

"Jürgen?" "Yes?" "Which pair do you want? They all look very much the same but have different sizes," I said with a question mark in my voice. "The one in the middle should be fine", I received as an answer. So I handed Juergen the pair of shoes he wanted and asked: "May I ask why you have the same kind of shoes in different sizes?" Juergen paused. He found it difficult to talk and do something simultaneously, and why should he do that? Why are we doing this anyway? I asked myself at that moment. Then he answered: "Well, since I've been taking these pills, I never know precisely how swollen my feet will be that day. Sometimes I have a slim 8,5, sometimes an 11. I am given diuretic tablets for this. But apart from the fact that I have to sprint to the toilet, they have done nothing to solve this problem. You get used to it, even to the completely brown, discoloured lower legs the pills are causing. But wait a moment; perhaps you have something in your collection of homoeopathic remedies that could help with this."

"It's not quite that simple, but if you want, we can start a homoeopathic and naturopathic treatment. This will take some time, and I must learn more about you. But I can also recommend a colleague because treating your partner can be problematic." "No, please do it yourself. We will have time in the next few days and later, too. I trust you completely. But did I understand that correctly? You were talking about me as your partner?" "Yes", I said, and again, I felt this heavy parcel of responsibility on my shoulders. Why did I take it? It was not for nothing that there was a rule not to treat the partner. After all, there was a lack of professional distance. Homoeopathy is not just giving some lactose pellets. It also goes deep into the psyche, something that is referred to as mental-emotional symptoms. Was my partnership with Juergen already prepared for such an unsparing candour? And how should I be able to relax completely in our relationship if I always had to keep a therapeutic eye on Juergen from now on? This undoubtedly offered him many advantages. He wouldn't have to wait for any appointments; he could put his trust in an intimate person he otherwise trusted and who would also be there for him on weekends and public holidays. Would it be better for me to say no? I couldn't. I saw his distress and knew only too well how much people were left alone with their illnesses and the hardships that resulted from them. And then it was Parkinson's. This disease, the treatment of which required a medication that could trigger hallucinations, addictive behaviour, massive states of restlessness and much more. Or simply swelling feet.

I couldn't refuse to make it easier for myself. It would just be a farce because would it be easier if I refused treatment, my help? There was only one big NO inside me - all or nothing. I could never exclude that part of Juergen if we stayed together. What had I got myself into? It was already an all-or-nothing relationship in its tender beginnings. I was not only with Juergen Schwarz but also with James Parkinson. We made a nice triangle. But I knew there was no going back now. I couldn't, and I didn't want to leave Juergen alone again with everything that was happening and everything that was still to come because this illness has many faces. And I wouldn't have been able to go on living a relaxed life either. Both men were already too important to me. I looked to the passenger seat next to me, where Juergen was waiting cheerfully and visibly relieved for the journey to begin. When I looked to the back seat to check that June was well settled, I almost thought I saw James Parkinson sitting beside her. "I won't be able to get rid of you either", I said to James in my thoughts. And I said out loud: "Then let's get going. Off to the Black Forest." "And off into the future with two men", I thought.

Chapter 10

"I've never driven with you before, but yesterday, you drove your speedster sportily, safely and swiftly through the streets. Where did you leave this driver overnight? You seem so hesitant now, almost anxious." Juergen looked at me questioningly from the side. "You've got me", I said and headed for the nearest possibility to park the car. "It's probably time for a confession on my part", I began, and Juergen turned his full attention to me. He was really good at listening. "I've always loved driving. This independence. No smelly buses, no unpunctual trains. And no more horrible men accosting me at bus stops and following me from the bus stop to my destination. How I looked forward to the day when I would finally have my driving license and a car. I loved my old VW Beetle. He was already 18 years old when I got him, but he was mine; he was reliable and offered me freedom and security. Driving has always been part of my life. As you already know, my father was a car mechanic. I still smell the workshop where he worked in my early childhood in my nose. Cars have always been part of life. As soon as I walked into a garage, I saw my father in front of me and felt a sense of security because he always knew what to do when a car didn't want to work. But from an early age, I was afraid of mountain passes, tunnels and high bridges. I drove my parents crazy with these fears when we were travelling to and in Austria. I was overcome with panic before every tunnel, especially the Arlberg Tunnel. Nobody knew why. Well, and now we're travelling a mountain pass road. I am feeling insecure, and although I know that you have to practise the things you're feeling insecure about doing, I've been avoiding this kind of road. But Oberhausen has no mountain passes, and I was never confronted with them when I travelled."

Juergen was silent for a moment, looked intently into my eyes as if he could find an answer in them and then asked: "And why didn't you tell me all this? I could drive." Horrified, I replied: "No way – it's even worse as a passenger. Then, I don't have the slightest influence on what happens. Besides, I want to get over this. It can't stay like this. I want to practise." "Then we have a task. But you could have told me beforehand. That's not a problem at all."

"I was ashamed." "What for? And anyway – in front of me? Are you kidding? You accept my Parkinson's as if it were a pimple on my nose, and you are ashamed of something that can be trained away? Oh, Sopherl…" He squeezed my hand tightly, and I felt pretty stupid. But how could I admit a weakness when I always wanted to be strong and had always had to be it so far? But it had been easy to do so towards Juergen. I had just explained it the way it was. Nevertheless, I asked meekly: "Do you think less of me now?" "No, absolutely no, Sopherl. It's good that you trust me, and it also makes you more human. What you manage and master all alone – as an average person, you feel small and weak compared to this. Honestly, I'm delighted to be able to help you. Cars and driving them is my speciality." Juergen smiled at me encouragingly. "Then let's get started with the training, shall we?" Still insecure, I replied: "Ok, it's your responsibility."

"Good, you can just ride at your own pace now. You don't have to keep to any minimum speed. Only drive at the speed at which you feel safe. You stop at every passing place so that faster cars can overtake you." "But…" I began. "No, just drive off. I am with you." I realised how good his words were for me. He gave me security. He supported me. That was so beautiful and gave me courage. I drove off. Slowly, like a snail, I crept around the bends. At least, this was how it seemed to me. But there was only praise coming from the passenger's seat. Only when I looked in the rear-view mirror to check whether angry drivers were tailgating me, which was not the case a single time, did I get a warning: "You are travelling forwards, not backwards. It would, therefore, be an advantage if you could also look forward." Of course, he was right, and finally, we reached the summit of the Schauinsland. Relieved, I parked, let the dog out of the car and emptied a water bottle. I felt like a heroine. I had overcome myself and my fears, and at times, it had even been fun, even though I was more than aware that I had been going really slowly.

Then, to my horror, I remembered that if you climb a mountain, you must descend it. So my lesson wasn't over yet. And as if he had read my thoughts, I had probably turned white as a sheet, Juergen said: "Now relax and enjoy your success. That wasn't bad at all for the first time. It's still early, so we should be able to ride up and down a few times today. That should give you security."

"A few times? Today?" I exclaimed in disbelief. "You're the therapist; you should know how important that is. And now, come June, let's go and find a place to play football. I think Sopherl needs a break now." June saw the ball and jumped up at

Juergen. "Of course he's right, " I thought, watching them play. Neither the dog nor the man could stop when a ball was nearby. Their game seemed to have rules, but I couldn't figure them out. You had to be Juergen or June to understand them. It was a perfect moment.

After they had finished their football match, we drove back down the mountain and back up again and... three more times. I became more confident with every run and rarely had to give way to faster riders. With every bend, the ride became more fun. "We'll do that again tomorrow to consolidate it. What do you think?" Jürgen said and added: "I'm proud of you." "I agree with that. I am feeling so good now. Thank you for your patience. But now we have to hurry. Do you remember we wanted to watch football tonight?" And we drove back to the hotel where Juergen learned another facet of me – my passion for football. Did he watch the game, or did he watch me cheer, suffer and swear? "You know exactly what you want and are so full of life. You inspire me. Sometimes, I lost my zest for life over the last few years. But now I only have to look at you, and I'm fine. Heaven must have sent you to me. You are my sun." Then he took me into his arms. I would never forget those words.

Chapter 11

"Do you still want me to help you with homoeopathy and naturopathy?" I asked over dinner in a cosy little restaurant, where we had our meal after another day of driving training and playing football with June. "We haven't got around talking about it yet. Now that I've overcome my fear of mountain passes, it's your turn. But only if you want to." "Of course I want to. And after I have helped you, I feel far better about asking you for help. What do you need? What do I have to do?" Juergen's prompt reply came. "All I need is your entire medical and life history." "You need a lot of time and patience for that." "Don't we have all the time in the world?" and as soon as the words had left my mouth, I would have loved to undo them because a brief but infinitely deep sadness flickered in Juergen's eyes, and he said, barely audible: "You certainly, I don't."

"I see that differently. Living with a diagnosis like yours, not knowing how bad the disease will develop, is incredibly difficult. Feeling how the body tries to evade all control is something that no one who hasn't experienced it can really imagine. How often do I discuss the importance of every single day with my patients and how important it is to lead a healthy lifestyle to maintain a healthy body and soul for as long as possible. Most people take their health for granted and too often treat it recklessly. You've been putting up with all these symptoms for years, and you've gone through it all alone. No partner to help you or with whom you could have shared the problems when everything was getting too much for you. Nobody who cared for you and told you: 'I won't leave you alone, even if it's getting tough.' You have my absolute respect for the way you have mastered your life so far, and I am sure you will continue to do so. Maybe that's why we met, especially at this point, because it was time for you to experience that, too, real love and solidarity."

Juergen was silent for a while and let my words sink in. Then he began. "It comes in waves. I'm not talking about Parkinson's, although he does that too. But now I mean the realisation of what this disease means. That's why I try to enjoy every day when I'm feeling well. There were times when this was different. At the moment, I'm well, very well indeed. It's been like this since I was in this clinic a few years ago. And then you hope it stays this way or maybe even gets better. So, what do you want me to start with?"

"Preferably at the beginning, and I don't mean the day the doctor made the diagnosis, but when you think it started. People usually have symptoms for a long time, but they are often so diffuse that they are not associated with Parkinson's disease. When do you think it started?" I hoped Juergen wouldn't mind my professional tone, but I had to create boundaries for myself. But I didn't have to worry about that. Juergen thought for a moment, then he spoke: "I can't tell you exactly when it started. But I remember exactly when I first thought of the word Shaking Palsy. I was 30 years old and had returned from a rally trip, as I often did. I had already prepared the text on the plane. This way, I could drive straight from the airport to the editorial office to finish it there. The deadline, you understand. That was nothing special but my everyday life, which I loved so much. I was tired, exhausted. A long flight lay behind me. So I grabbed another coke, I don't know how many I already had, and put my legs up on the desk to collect myself for a moment when suddenly my left leg twitched entirely uncontrollably. Only very briefly. I looked at my leg and massaged it a little. At first, I thought it was tension after the long flight. Then it twitched again, this time for longer. And then it crossed my mind: 'Surely you don't have Shaking Palsy?'" Jürgen took a short break, still thinking about the situation back then.

"The leg calmed down again, and I put this unpleasant thought aside. The article was more important. At some point, I went home, fell into bed, and slept. After that, I was at peace, or so I thought, because neither my legs nor hands were shaking again." Juergen took a short break. "It is challenging to describe another problem I had. There was always a restlessness within me, such as in my stomach, something like an inner trembling. That also influenced what I could eat. Some colleagues made jokes about it, for example, about my can of sausages, of which I always had one within reach. The sausages stayed with me for a long time. In general, I ate certain things that I knew I could tolerate without feeling sick in my stomach excessively. I still do that today, by the way. One day, I went to a doctor because I thought there might be a more serious cause for the constant discomfort. I also found it challenging to explain to him what my problem was. But the good man took his time to look at everything and then decided that my problems were my work, my everyday life, my travelling and the resulting constant jet lag. I should take some time off work and

42

also stop drinking coke. Then, the situation would calm down in the foreseeable future."

"You obviously didn't follow that advice, " I said, pointing at the half-full glass of coke in front of Juergen. "Oh, my parents tried to break me of that habit so often. I hope you're not preaching to me about it." "No," I answered, "I won't do that. You are a grown-up and intelligent man. You know that these soft drinks aren't healthy when drinking many of them. If you drink them anyway, you are willing to suffer the possible consequences. But believe me, life doesn't ask for your allowance – you will have to endure them. So it's not clever. But you're not my third child. I certainly don't want to and won't educate you."

"But I don't like any water", Juergen said almost defiantly. "Is life always about what you like? I'm imagining you in a desert right now; all your coke supplies are emptied, and you're about to die of thirst. Then someone arrives with water. Would you send him away because you don't like water and would rather die of thirst?" "But I'm not dying of thirst yet." "Are you so sure about that?" "I have to think about this first." "Ok, and what happened after you visited the doctor?"

"Nothing. The overall situation remained unchanged for quite a while. At some point, phases of heavy heart stumbling set in. That scared me, and for a short time, I even wondered whether the doctor from back then might have been right after all and that I needed a break. I, therefore, had a cardiological checkup and was certified as having an absolutely healthy heart. With a heart like that, I could even become a pilot. That reassured me a lot, even though I preferred to leave the flying to the real pilots. I was advised to do endurance sports, such as running or cycling. You know my opinion on running." "Why should we walk if we have cars or something like that?" I tried to quote him. "Exactly, but I ordered a stationary bike, and when I am at home in Ludwigsburg, I use it every day, really." "That's better than nothing, after all. I think it's good." "Better than nothing? Please, I work myself into a sweat. I deserve more appreciation than that, don't you think?" Both of us began to laugh. We had no idea how life-defining the topic of drinking and exercise would become.

"So you kept travelling the world, wherever the cars went." "Yes, that was and is my life. One day, I thought about taking some time out, returning to university and studying something I would enjoy, unlike law. I was thinking about American studies or something like that. On a holiday alone in the Maldives for Christmas and New Year's Eve, I wanted to consider it. So I got on the plane, the engines were started, the aircraft started moving, and the moment it took off from the runway, I knew that I wouldn't want to give this up for anything, anyone or any study in the world. I closed my eyes and only enjoyed my flight. My decision had been made."

Chapter 12

We spent a few carefree days free of driving therapies and medical history examinations. It was like a tacit agreement as if we had agreed to put the problematic issues aside and enjoy life. And this was what we did. In the afternoon of our last day of travelling, I took Juergen back to his flat.

"Those were very nice days. We should do that again," Juergen said, and his sad look belied his matter-of-factness. That was why I asked: "Are you very sad?" "Isn't that always the case at the end of a beautiful journey? You are sad it's over and curious about what may come." "And what's coming?" "I hope for many other journeys together, and maybe you will marry me one day. But now I understand your refusal to fly with me to Las Vegas. After a week with this dog, I don't want to part with her either. Are you taking good care of her? And June, you take good care of Sophie." He stroked the dog's head gently, and I noticed a slight tremor in his hand.

"Now we just need someone to look after you," I replied with a smile. "I'll have to do that myself because you two ladies don't want to stay." I wanted to start an explanation, but Juergen waved me off. "I know, children, work and other animals. I understand that, but I'm allowed to have wishes and dreams." "Wishing and dreaming are always allowed, " I replied, slowly setting my car in motion. It wasn't easy for me to say goodbye either, but what could I do? "Until as soon as possible", I called out to him from the open car window, and slowly, our hands parted. "Off to the children, work and other animals", I thought with a smile and wiped a few parting tears from my eyes. Yes, it had been lovely days and very interesting ones.

I still had a lot more to learn about Juergen. He had lived in a completely different world, a world that he had only been able to give me a glimpse of so far. I had already received the first ideas for creating an accompanying treatment concept, but I still had a lot of questions for Juergen. This man. How he had stormed into my life and taken up residence there along with Mr Parkinson. And it was good he had done so.

Back at home, I immersed myself entirely in my family. The children had to tell me so much, and my cat Romeo didn't want to stop purring. I had never imagined travelling without my children. Of course, I had realised that this day would come at some point, and the timing had been right, not too early or too late. And yet, it had happened so quickly. They had just been babies. In the middle of my thoughts, the phone rang.

"I just wanted to know if you arrived safely," I heard Juergen's now so familiar voice. "Yes, I did. I wanted to let you know, but the welcome was much more stormy than I had hoped." "As you had hoped?" Juergen asked. "Yes, I was afraid I would receive a much cooler reception. I can't go on talking now. Now it's the children's turn. Shall I call you later, and we'll talk again until I fall asleep?" "I like this idea. Enjoy your warm welcome. Until later."

I didn't like having no time for Juergen now, but what could I do? My children came first. I only knew Juergen for a few months. How complicated my life had become. I had never thought I would get divorced. My family and my children had been my everything. Then, my marriage broke up, and suddenly, nothing could be taken for granted anymore. There was no room for a man in my life, but Juergen saw this differently, and so did I if I was honest with myself. But how would that work? What would the children say to Juergen and, above all, to James, who was inseparable from Juergen? I would find solutions for everything, but not tonight. Instead, I did what Scarlett O'Hara did in my favourite film, "Gone With the Wind," and said, "Let's put it off until tomorrow." Later, lying in my bed, I called Juergen while cat Romeo was purring beside me, and June held watch beside my bed.

Chapter 13

Life continued in fullness, and attempts to resolve our relationship had to wait. We continued talking on the phone often, and Jurgen visited regularly but never went to my house. I stuck to my rule: "This is my children's home. No men."

When I told Juergen this rule, he asked with mock concern: "But I am only one man, or are some more men existing?" "But that's not a serious question, is it?" "No, I trust you. But when you talk so casually about men, it makes you think." "You can believe me. You're enough for me. You make everything complicated enough," I replied with a laugh.

"And when shall I get to know the two of them? It should happen sometime, don't you think so?" "When I think it's the right time and it's not the right time now. But please, let us now enjoy the evening. I've been waiting for it so long and looked forward to it so much." "But we don't know each other that long, and we often spend nice evenings and days together", Juergen said with a grin. Of course, he knew that I had been waiting for a concert by the Scottish band Runrig for years, which would perform this day in Oberhausen. I was finally standing in a sea of tartan and Scottish flags, and the concert was about to begin. Time and again, something got in the way when I wanted to go to a Runrig concert. "Not this time", I thought, when Juergen suddenly groaned.

"What's wrong with you?" I asked anxiously. "Nothing special, no reason to panic. My back has been giving me problems for a few days, and I must have just made a wrong movement." "Shall I have a look? Do you want to see a doctor? Would you rather go to the hotel?"

"No, it's not that bad, and I know how much you were looking forward to the concert. I'm fine again now. Let's enjoy the evening." And that was what we did. A Scotland evening, a Sophie evening. Scotland was the country that had shaped me so much. Juergen understood me. If not him, the traveller, who else should?

The next day, Jürgen drove back to Ludwigsburg. "You have to come to me soon, at least for a weekend", Juergen urged. It hurt me so much having to reject him repeatedly, but I couldn't put him at the centre of my life the way he wanted me to. "Juergen, you know that it isn't easy. And we're managing it really well." "Yes, but it's quite a distance, and it would be really nice to be closer." "424 kilometres from door to door, to be precise. Of course, more closeness would be great. Do you think I'm feeling differently? You knew from the start that I had children, and my life would be centred here with them for a few more years. Never ask me to choose between you and my children. You would lose that decision, no matter what you mean to me. Nothing and nobody is more important than my children. Please accept this, or we will say thank you for the beautiful time, and that's it." My heart was pounding, and tears were burning in my eyes. I had known that the time would come when Juergen would be unhappy about the long-distance relationship and the clear preference for my children in my life. But I wouldn't leave my children for any man in the world. Maybe ask the children's father to step in for a short time in an emergency. But I knew that Juergen's wish was that I should leave my children behind to live with him. Never.

"Juergen, please imagine your mother had done what you want me to do. Imagine she had gone away with a man, leaving you behind. How would that have been for you?" "Awful, absolutely awful. Even if it wasn't always easy between us. My mum gone, simply unthinkable." "Please don't ask me this again, neither directly nor indirectly. Life will give us a solution; it always does. Please let me know if you can't or don't want to continue like this. And let me know when you have arrived safely back in Ludwigsburg."

I turned away and walked to my car. I didn't want Juergen to see my tears, to see how deeply he had hurt me with his urging. I quietly said to myself, "This dream is over. Take care, Juergen."

As if this conversation had never occurred, Juergen announced his return to Ludwigsburg in the evening. "How's your back?" I asked immediately. I also blanked out the morning's conversation. "It hurts quite a bit. I'll have a doctor look at it tomorrow. He'll probably be able to give me something for the pain. Yes, I know you see it differently. But why should I have it examined thoroughly? I know that I don't move enough and that I have Parkinson's disease. Something always hurts somewhere." "So you don't want any advice from me?" "No, not today. I only want the pain to stop. The driving didn't do me any good. I'm trying to relax now. Don't be angry that I can't talk to you as long as usual today." "That is ok. Please let me know as soon as you know anything more tomorrow", I asked worriedly. "Yes, of course, and now you sleep well too. June and Romeo shall have a special cuddle with you today, even if they can't replace me." I had to smile. "Sleep well, too, if your back allows it."

I didn't hear from Juergen the next day, and my calls were unanswered. This was highly unusual. Juergen had always managed to make short calls or send messages to my mobile if he didn't have enough time for our usual long calls. I felt the same anxiety as the day before. My everyday life demanded my full attention, yet I kept looking at my mobile. Nothing, not even a short message that he would be in touch later. What was going on in Ludwigsburg?

"Stay cool! He is a grown-up man and has got through his life very well without you so far", I tried to reassure myself. Not for the first time, I cursed long-distance relationships. "It's only because of these stupid mobile phones", I continued. "You're always reachable. In former times, you had to wait for the post to be delivered by a mounted messenger. Keep calm, Sophie". So I talked to myself, but the more time passed, the more restless I became. Something was wrong.

Finally, at 4 p.m., the telephone rang. It was Juergen. "Hello, my sun, how are you?" he said with fake cheerfulness. I replied, audibly tense, "I believe you're going to tell me that now."

"I am in hospital. My general practitioner guessed that kidney stones could cause my pain. The man better shouldn't play the lottery. There aren't any kidney stones. I have a broken lumbar vertebra, and please don't ask me how I managed to break it. I have absolutely no idea. They want to operate on me tomorrow. Can you come? I don't trust them and would like your opinion first. I have done nothing that could make a vertebra break. I only write about sports; I don't do sports myself." Still making jokes despite the situation. But I could still hear the deep concern in his voice.

49

"I have to organise myself. Please give me half an hour; then I should be able to tell you whether I can come or not. Many things can cause a vertebra to break. No sports and poor posture are two of them. But we can talk about all this in peace. Please tell them that nobody is allowed to operate on you without me having spoken to the head physician and seen the x-rays." "You really try to come?" Juergen asked, cautiously hopeful." "What did you expect? This is an emergency." "That makes me feel better."

I had reacted spontaneously. But how could I leave him alone in an emergency because who else was there apart from me? Who was prepared to help him and organise things for him? As far as I knew, nobody. The disadvantage of a life of independence, the price for freedom. But maybe it was worth it. I didn't know, and now was certainly not the right time to philosophise. Now was the time to act and to act quickly.

I explained to my children and their father that Juergen was in hospital and needed my help. Juergen had become a familiar name to them as a good friend with whom I had already travelled. "Can you three manage without me for two or three days?" "If a friend needs your help, you must go – we can manage." That was the unanimous answer. "Thank you very much. Ich will keep it as short as possible." "Don't worry about us, and drive carefully." "I promise."

I quickly packed a few things for June and myself and wrote to Juergen: "I'll be in Ludwigsburg in about 4.5 hours. How do I get the house keys? I have June with me." Then, I hugged my children and drove off. Once again, I was in tears and asked myself: "What am I doing here?"

Important notice

Before I continue to tell the story of Juergen and me, I must point out that I am only telling the facts and do not want to take generalised revenge on doctors, clinics, rehabilitation clinics, physiotherapists, and nursing staff. I also do not advise against seeking medical treatment with confidence.

Furthermore, I deliberately refrain from mentioning doctors, clinics, therapists and carers by name. Even if they have brought great pain, suffering and unnecessary changes into Jurgen's life, partly out of negligence, partly out of arrogance, ignorance or other reasons unknown to me, I want to spare them that such mentions could damage their reputation or cause them other problems. I am well aware that such accusations cannot bring insight, but usually only the opposite.

This is why I will describe all treatments, operations and discussions with doctors and therapists as accurately as possible. Anyone who feels addressed is welcome to critically question himself whether he was involved in Juergens's treatment or behaved similarly towards others. I know from my numerous patients that Juergen was and is not an isolated case and that despite all the excellent medical work done and all the wonderful doctors and therapists who are beyond reproach, there are also others, the black sheep, just like in any other profession.

Stopping is very difficult once a mechanism has been set in motion in the medical machinery. Juergen and I learnt that mistakes are not punished, and you are always referred back to the "perpetrators," whose bills are always paid in full by the health insurance companies, even if the patient draws attention to the deficiencies in the treatment and billing. The costs caused by the errors must be borne by the patient or the general public through health insurance contracts, not by those who cause them.

My heartfelt thanks go to all the great and helpful people. I wish there were many, many more of you. Maybe my ruthless honesty motivates some people to make positive changes. I want to pass on Juergen's request to all who are already patients or may become patients: "Ask questions, don't simply accept anything. If you don't know for yourself, find someone you trust who does. Never believe that you can place responsibility for yourselves and your well-being into the hands of others. It belongs to your own hands. And never think that there aren't any other ways. Sophie and I looked for them and found them."

Chapter 14

I found the keys. Unlocking the door to Juergen's flat was unusual; I had never done it before. I felt like an intruder. What was I doing here? Even June went hesitatingly into the flat. "Why doesn't Juergen greet me? Where is he?" she seemed to think. I quickly set up a feeding corner for June and spread out her cosy blanket. So June knew everything was fine, at least for her, because she knew this procedure from our journeys. "I hope it goes well having to go to the hospital straight away and leaving her alone so soon", I thought anxiously, but what choice did I have? Unfortunately, both she and I had to go through that.

On the living room table was an open bottle of Juergen's malt beer and a plate with a few crumbs of his breakfast bread. The feeling of being an intruder overcame me again, and I suddenly realised how much Juergen trusted me. Out of love or out of desperation? Now was not the right time to think about it, so I returned to my functional mode. When I left, I said the usual words to June: "June, take good care of the house. See you soon." Then I stroked the beautiful collie's head and pulled the front door shut with a heavy heart. I took one deep breath. It was 9 pm. Would they even let me into the clinic to see Juergen?

They let me in, and I soon found Juergen in his hospital bed, the usual hospital headphones on his ears, his eyes turned toward the television hanging on the wall. He was startled when I gently nudged him to get his attention, and his face lit up.

"You really have come, my sun. Let me touch you. I can't believe it. You're really here." "I told you that I would come. Didn't you believe me?" I asked gently. "Yes, but then I thought again that it's impossible for you. Where is June?" "Hopefully, she is lying on her blanket in your living room or eating in the hallway. I hope you're okay with me having set up her feeding there." "I agree with everything. You should both feel as much at home there as you can. I am so happy and thankful that you came." He held my hand tightly and couldn't take his eyes off me.

"Now, please tell me in peace what's going on. Or are we disturbing your roommate? He seems to be asleep." "He's okay with it. He is a nice guy, and I told him you might still come. He had a terrible motorbike accident. They had to more or less puzzle him all together again. Creepy. Incidentally, he works for a car racing team. That fits perfectly." "Enough for you to talk about. But please tell me what's going on with you?"

"A lumbar vertebra is broken, that's it. They repeatedly asked me if I remembered anything that could have caused the fracture. Whether I had fallen or had carried something heavy. I only remembered a crate of water that I lifted, but that wasn't heavy. I do that all the time. And you say that water is healthy." "And why do they want the operation? You don't necessarily have to operate a fracture of a vertebra." "They want to discuss this with us tomorrow. I told them I wouldn't decide anything without your advice. An operation on the spine and having Parkinson's – I don't know if I want to take that risk. They have to give me excellent reasons for this."

"Maybe the fracture is displaced or unstable", I said. "Do you have any pain?" "Not much, but I get an awful lot of drugs, although the pain hadn't been bad. Unpleasant, but no severe pain. That's why I don't understand all this fuss. And doesn't a vertebral fracture in the lumbar region cause loss of sensation in the legs, symptoms of paralysis, problems urinating or the like?" "Not necessarily. It always depends on the fracture and what it has destroyed. You can be happy that it's not like this for now, and then we must see how to ensure it stays that way. I'll get you an extra glass of water and prepare a homoeopathic medicine. Is that ok for you?" "Yes, of course. But then you stay with me for a while and hold me tight, right? The shock has got into my bones." "In any case, until I'm thrown out." "My sun, come here into my arms first. You are simply incredible. You just drove off straight away to be there for me. No one has ever done that for me before." "Get used to it and be careful. We don't want to break anything else within you. You seem to be very fragile." "But I can take a kiss."

I rested my head on Juergen's arm and felt my eyes getting heavier and heavier. I didn't want to think any more, not about what was happening back home at the moment, not about what the dog might do alone in an almost unknown flat and least of all about what decisions would have to be made tomorrow regarding Juergen and his lumbar vertebra. No more thinking, just no more thinking – and I fell asleep.

"Sopherl, you have to wake up," it whispered in my ear. I tried to lift my head, but my whole body was completely tense from the position I had adopted to sleep on Juergen's arm. "What's going on?" I mumbled sleepily. "The night nurse has just been here and said you must leave. She's also worried that you could be a patient here tomorrow at the latest, the way you've been lying here." "But it can't be that late." "Well, whatever you call it, it's midnight." "Midnight? Did I sleep that long?" With a jolt, I was wide awake. "June, the poor soul. She needs her walk. Can I leave you alone, and when shall I return?" "The girl needs you. I can manage through the night, and they won't leave you here anyway. Besides, sleeping a bit more after this day would be best. The head physician has announced that he will be here tomorrow morning at eight o'clock. If you could be here to discuss everything together, me asking the stupid questions and you asking the smart ones, that would be great." "Of course. I will be here on time. Don't let anyone do anything to you we haven't discussed beforehand. I'll phone you when I walk the dog." "That's great. Then I walk with you in my thoughts and can be reassured when you're safely back in the flat. Give my love to June. She shall take good care of you." "I'll do that. Until later."

I kissed his forehead, and at that exact moment, I asked myself why I had kissed him on his forehead. Juergen seemed so fragile in his hospital shirt, so only the foreheads fitted.

Quickly, I ran to my car. The dog, the poor animal. How had I managed to fall asleep so soundly? When I unlocked the front door and quietly called out: "Hello, Juni-girl", a very sleepy dog came at me, wagging his tail. I buried my face in the soft fur and whispered: "I am so sorry, so awfully sorry, my girl. Let's go quickly." And then the two of us ladies set off on a midnight walk.

"June and I are on the move now. I haven't the slightest idea where I can go here; it's best if we walk a big circle, then we'll definitely get back to the flat, at least I hope so. The air is perfect for me now; it slightly clears my head." "How has June been all alone in my flat?" Juergen wanted to know anxiously. "Very good. She has slept."

We continued talking about trivial things. Juergen explained where I could find drinks and the washing machine. Eventually, I was back in the flat. "I'm going to feed the dog, and then I'm just going to fall into bed. Don't be angry with me, but I can't go on talking now if I want to hear the alarm clock in the morning." "I believe you. I am so grateful that you came and are here. Sleep well, my sun. I love you."

He had never said this before. He had proposed to me many times. But these three magic words I heard from him for the first time. I didn't know how to react at all. It was too much in one day and then in the middle of the night. So I just replied: "Dream of me. Kiss." And I ended the phone call.

Chapter 15

"Good morning, Mr Schwarz. Let's see what we can do with you." With these words, the head physician stormed into the hospital room and was taken aback when he realised another person was next to Mr Schwarz. "I have to ask you to leave the room as I need to speak to Mr Schwarz", he told me. "One moment, please, Professor …. Good morning to you, too. May I introduce my partner, Ms Sophie Strehlke, who will participate in all discussions and decisions? My dear Sophie", Juergen looked at me. "May I introduce you to Professor…, determined to care for my damaged spine." I said with a friendly smile: "Good morning, Professor… What do Mr Schwarz's findings look like?" He cleared his throat briefly and then explained: "Whatever you want. So, in your case, we are dealing with a fracture of the fifth lumbar vertebra. Unfortunately, this fracture is unstable. This can lead to displacements, which, in the worst case, could even lead to paraplegia. And we don't want this to happen. We don't want that. That's why we want to operate immediately. Today, we are preparing everything; you will speak to the anaesthetist, and tomorrow morning, you will be the very first in the operation theatre. No need to worry. You can go dancing with your wife in a few weeks." He smiled cheerfully at Juergen and me and wanted to slip away.

"One moment, please, Professor…" I spoke up. I would like to see the x-rays, and then you should explain your planned procedure. This is an operation on the spine of a person with Parkinson's disease." The professor turned around and looked at me as if I were a rare insect. "But please, Mrs Schwarz. "Strehlke, Ms Strehlke, please," Juergen interrupted him. "Well, Ms Strehlke, you can trust me when I tell you this. After all, this has been my speciality for twenty years, and I also give lectures on spinal surgery regularly. And besides, X-rays and computerised tomography are not photos." He laughed briefly. "You have to be able to read and interpret them. I don't want to offend you, but that might be too difficult for you despite your commitment to your partner." "Why exactly do you think so?" I asked while Juergen smiled to himself. He knew that arrogance couldn't put me off. "Because I assume that you don't have the appropriate education. You really can entrust your husband to me." "On the one hand, I can understand the X-rays and CT images; I am trained accordingly. On the other hand, the surgeon should explain his planned procedure in detail to the patient and answer all his questions. Otherwise, on what basis should the patient consent to the upcoming procedure?" "Well, I had no way of knowing that you are a colleague of mine." He slowly realised he had made a mistake in his tone and behaviour. Please excuse me." "I didn't say that I am a colleague. But I can assure you that I am more than familiar with the musculoskeletal system and X-ray and CT images. So, what shall we do now? How do you want to operate? Please be so kind as to explain everything now." I was still extremely polite, but my voice had become very strict.

The professor struggled visibly to keep calm. "You'll have to accompany me to the nurse's room. But Mr Schwarz is not allowed to walk." "I trust Ms Strehlke entirely; unlike her, I don't know anything about x-rays. So why don't you show her these x-rays? If you both return to me afterwards to discuss the next steps together, that would be wonderful," said Juergen with a winning smile.

"Do you want to follow me?" I wanted, and I followed. The findings on the pictures were obvious. Nevertheless, the risk of surgery in a person who has Parkinson's disease was too significant for me. I was not concerned with the operation as such but with the increased risk of anaesthesia.

The Professor wanted to explain the pictures, but I thanked him and said: "I have seen what I had to see. Thank you very much. We can now return to Mr Schwarz if you don't mind."

Back at Juergen's bedside, the doctor began: "Your wife, no partner, can now confirm my diagnosis, and we can now discuss the operation. We have to stabilise the fracture. To do this, we must immobilise the affected vertebra and include the vertebra above and below with the help of a titanium plate. This will minimally affect the mobility of your spine in future, at least until the metal is removed in a year. But a few days after the operation, we will send you to a rehabilitation clinic, and there, you will learn to deal with it—no need to worry."

Juergen looked at me questioningly. "How do you see it? You don't look as if you approve of these ideas. That looks like a lot of scepticism right now." "You are right, dear", I confirmed. "The diagnosis is correct. But I would choose a conservative treatment because of your Parkinson's disease. That means no operation because I believe that the risk of anaesthesia is too high. In Parkinson's patients, anaesthesia carries a significantly higher risk of permanent postoperative delirium. You can imagine this as a sort of dementia. This is why operations should only be undertaken in life-threatening situations and with careful consideration of your underlying disease. In addition, due to this underlying disease, I believe that the immobilisation of only three vertebrae, should you decide in favour of surgery, is too little. Parkinson's leads to permanent vibrations in your body, even when you appear calm on the outside. I know that. Furthermore, your posture already shows a clear tendency to the forward direction instead of upright. This means this implant would be under significantly higher tension than in a person with an upright posture. If you are going to have an implant, it should include five to six vertebrae and in that case, you would have such a large", I indicated the size of the affected area with my hands, "part of your spine completely immobile."

"How do you envisage a conservative treatment?" the professor was quite displeased. "We can hardly put plaster around the spine." I stayed calm and answered: "I'd better not go into that now. I'm sure you know you can apply immobilisation by an orthosis worn by the patient for a few weeks. This is at the expense of the back muscles, but they can be built up again. A post-operative delirium can lead to a nursing home or worse."

"That is going too far. We don't want to go back to the medical Stone Age. An orthosis has not been commonly used for a long time now. And how long do you want to tie poor Mr Schwarz to his bed? Mr Schwarz, do you like this nonsense, or would you rather trust modern surgery?" "I need time to think", Juergen said. "But Mr Schwarz, the fracture is unstable, so we can't wait much longer. We need to know whether I should put you on the operation plan for tomorrow or not. After all, this is also an organisational question."

I had never seen Juergen's face turn red in anger before. Now was the time. "May I ask you to excuse me, professor, when I set my health above your organisational problems? Yesterday, I received the diagnosis of kidney stones that could be removed without an operation. Now, what was supposed to be a kidney stone has turned into a vertebral fracture, which could leave me paralysed or with dementia.

59

So, it is only natural that I have to think about it and want to consult with the person I absolutely trust. Otherwise, I would be pleased to be transferred to another clinic." All this Juergen said in his usual calm and matter-of-fact voice. This way, he emphasised in this tense situation more than clearly that he, Juergen, had the last word and would not allow further discussions. After a short break, he asked: "Do you have anything else relevant to add, or is the information just discussed the sole basis for my decision-making?" "There is nothing else. Well, Mr Schwarz, I am an internationally recognised expert in this field and have already performed countless such operations. You shouldn't let that drive you crazy." He gave me an unmistakable glace.

"Nothing is driving me crazy. I need some time to think in peace before I decide. Then I will let you know my decision as soon as possible. And if I've understood correctly, it depends on your competence and that of the anaesthetist and the nursing staff as well. Will a neurologist be consulted who is familiar with Parkinson's and also with my medication?"

"No", the professor replied. "This is not necessary. Our head of anaesthesia will know that. He also is a very experienced colleague." "When do you need to know my decision?" Juergen wanted to know. "As soon as possible." "Ok, you can expect it by 1 pm. Thank you very much." "Ok, Mr Schwarz, see you later", said the professor, who was obviously not used to such an apparent contradiction from a patient, and left the room.

"Well, my sun, please explain it all to me again, calmly and for an absolute medical layman. It looks rather bad. Am I between a rock and a hard place?" "No, it isn't that bad, but it isn't pleasant either." And calmly, I explained the diagnosis and treatment approaches to Juergen again, including their advantages and disadvantages and the respective risks.

"Now, what would you advise me to do? What would you do in my place?" Juergen asked after the detailed explanations. "Definitely the conservative option, i.e. the orthosis. The risk of surgery would be too high for me, as there is a safer way. But if you want an operation, then definitely one over five to six vertebrae. The other solution is too fragile; it will not work." "Don't you have to go for a walk with June now?" "Do you want to get rid of me?" "No, not at all. But I must think about all this and decide on my own. After all, I am the one who has to live with what comes out of it. And the dog needs its walk. So why don't we combine the two things? Could you be back at my place around 12.30 pm so I can talk to you before talking to the professor?" "I can manage that. I'll leave you in peace and return here at half past twelve. Is that really what you want?" "Yes, it is." He kissed my hand and said, "Thank you, my sun. You can't decide for me, and you're doing so much for me. Thank you also for your openness. I prefer knowing the risks to staying in some security that doesn't exist. So, it's perfectly fine. I want it that way. Together with you, I can do anything." "See you soon", I said quietly, kissed him and left.

Opening the door to Juergen's flat, I was once again greeted by a very sleepy dog. At least this way, I knew June was coping with the situation without throwing the whole house into turmoil. "First, I need breakfast now. You already had yours, sweetheart. Let's see what I can find." It wasn't much and nothing I liked to eat, but it would work for today. I would have to do some shopping, but not today. Certainly not today. Juergen didn't even have proper tea and milk. Without tea – that was hard.

"June, we have enough time for a long walk as Juergen wants to be alone until 12.30 pm. You won't believe me when I tell you what this professor said. Arrogant, over-confident and impolite. Prejudice doesn't come out of nowhere. But anyway, the most important thing is that he does his job well so Juergen can play football with you again soon, right?" June looked at me; of course, she understood every word. Then we set off to explore the neighbourhood. I would have to ask Juergen where there was a forest or some other piece of nature where I could go running with June. Walking on roads was not enough for June and me. How long would we have to stay in Ludwigsburg? And the professor had also mentioned a rehabilitation clinic. After today's experience with this doctor, I would probably have to stay here for a few more days. I couldn't leave Juergen alone and go back to Oberhausen. I would call my children and ex-husband later to ask if I could stay another week or two. Suppose Juergen decided to have the operation; who knew what would happen? Or even afterwards in the rehab. I wasn't one who unquestioningly trusted others regarding medical treatment. And should he decide in favour of conservative treatment, we first had to think about how and where this could work.

61

And once again, I asked June, "Oh, June, what have I gotten myself into? What am I doing here? You and I don't even belong here. And then he also said he loved me. Why now in this situation? Stop brooding, Sophie; concentrate on the essentials. Wait for his decision and then think about what you want to do next. And get yourself something sensible to eat." This way, I talked to myself and the dog and felt that my thoughts were running in circles, faster and faster, trying to overtake each other. I completely sank into my thoughts.

I had walked on without looking at the surroundings. Where had I ended up now, and, more importantly, how could I return to Juergen's flat? I stopped abruptly, looked around and tried to retrace my steps. "Lost in Ludwigsburg", I thought and resolutely set off on what I thought was the way back. Finally, I recognised a house. But did I have to turn right or left there? I looked at my watch. There was hardly any time left. I decided to turn right, but after several metres, I discovered this decision had been wrong. "This cannot be true", I scolded myself and automatically began to run. I couldn't be late for Juergen. Finally, I was on the right path but kept running. The running helped me. Whenever everything became too much for me and my thoughts began to spin, running helped me. It was the same this time. With each step I took, the inner pressure eased and as if by magic, my thoughts took on the correct order. "First, I make everything comfortable for the dog in Juergen's flat, then I drive to the hospital, talk to Juergen, and then we inform the doctor. After that, I will see what is going to happen."

Chapter 16

"There you are. That is great. You didn't run away." This was how Juergen greeted me when I entered his room. "What on earth makes you think I could have run away? Did you fear I could do so?" I kissed him on his cheek. "A little bit", Juergen confessed. "We haven't planned all this. I wanted to show you the beauty of the world and not a hospital." "Man proposes God disposes. People only believe that they have control over their lives. But let's hear what you've decided." "You will not like it." "Ok, you want the operation." "Yes, but the way you suggested, with the longer implant. That sounds more plausible to me. I know you are afraid of the possible negative consequences of anaesthesia. But I want to leave all this behind as fast as possible and hope it will be fine. I had no problems after the kidney stone operation a few years ago." "Ok, your life, your body, your decision. I want to point out that the risk of negative consequences of anaesthesia increases with age and the amount of medication you take. But of course, I accept your wish and will support you on your way if that is what you want." "I thought you would want to argue with me endlessly. Are there no questions, no 'are you crazy' or nothing like that?" "Why should I? You are an intelligent man. You know the facts. You made your decision. I can't guarantee that my way would be a hundred per cent successful, even if I am pretty sure. But something else, what do you think about the professor?"

"Very convinced of himself. Too much for my liking. But I already know this. It's probably his way to build trust. If it works for other people, that's fine. I have to admit it tends to unsettle me. Someone who brags with his skills and knowledge like that often needs to do it. If he is such a genius, why isn't he in one of the leading clinics in the US or elsewhere? It's strange. But he'll manage. After all, he did a pretty good job patching up this guy in the bed beside me. I have done some research. Do you know how many athletes experience a vertebral fracture, for example, in Moto GP? Amazing. And even more impressive, they are back on their machines in no time at all, and there it jolts a lot more than within my body. I've decided to assume he can do it, even if I don't think he's a genius. But I ignore his chatter-. He must have become chief surgeon for some reason. In any case, it can't be because of his hairstyle, or perhaps hospitals have a casting couch like in Hollywood for the leading roles in the house." Jürgen grinned at his joke, and I had to smile too. "Oh Juergen, please just stay like this", I thought and told him: "Ok, we're thinking similarly about this gentleman. I don't know anything about Moto GP. I'm just learning the secrets of Formula One through you. I go to the nurses' room now to tell them you are ready to tell the professor your decision."

A short time later, he came to Juergen's bedside. "So you have made a decision. May I know what it is?" "I would like to have the operation, as I think that this can considerably shorten the healing process." "You have decided very wisely, Mr Schwarz. I can understand your wife's concerns, sorry, your partner's concerns very well. But one has to stay optimistic. It will be okay. As I have told you before, I have done such an operation countless times, and nothing unusual has ever happened. It won't do so with you, either. I will tell the nurses to prepare you for the operation tomorrow and inform the anaesthetist. He will visit you soon and tell you all about the anaesthetic. We keep no secrets from you, " laughed the professor cheerfully, leaving the room satisfied.

I felt uneasy but couldn't put my finger on it. "Juergen?" "Yes?" "You haven't told him that you want the longer implant." "Oh, I simply forgot that. But he will see this himself tomorrow. And now, let's talk about something else. How is June? How has your walk been?" I was very reluctant to let go of the subject, but Juergen was the boss of himself, and I had done what I could. But the uneasy feeling remained and kept growing within me. Nevertheless, I allowed myself to change the subject. "The walk was exciting. I got lost, and we had to run so that I could be here on time. Can you please tell me where I can go shopping? It looks like I have to stay another couple of days, and you haven't even got a decent tea in your house. Furthermore, June needs her food as well. Is there a forest nearby or at least a piece of nature so June and I can go on our runs?" "Of course," Juergen said, explaining where I could find everything.

"We now have to prepare Mr Schwarz for the Operation. You have to leave now." Juergen and I flinched at the very resolute voice as we had fallen asleep. "Good evening", I replied. "The anaesthetist hasn't been here yet, and I must be there for the discussion." "But that is impossible now. The anaesthetist will be late and can't tell when he will finish the operation and talk with Mr Schwarz. But he will come. Nevertheless, you have to go now. You must follow our rules." "Juergen, I have to participate in the conversation with the anaesthetist." But Juergen said: "I will manage. You can go home. We don't want the nurse to get even more upset."

I realised that any further objections were futile. What was wrong with Juergen? When we were on our own, he asked me so many questions and said how urgently he needed me, and now he almost threw me out of the hospital. This was something else that I didn't understand in this situation, which seemed to me absolutely surreal. "As you wish," I said to Juergen, much sharper than I had intended, and then turned to the nurse. "When will Mr Schwarz be taken to the operation theatre tomorrow?" "At seven o'clock. Why do you ask?" "Because I will be here at six o'clock to calm him before the operation. See you in the morning, Juergen." I leaned over him and gave him a quick kiss. "You can do better than that", he whispered. "Maybe, but not in front of the nurse and not if both of you throw me out. You can call me later. I am off to June now."

"But no visitors are allowed on the ward this early", the nurse called out authoritatively. Already on my way to the door, I turned round again, put on my most winning smile and said to the nurse: "I won't come as a visitor; I will come as the personal bodyguard of Mr Schwarz." Then I looked at Juergen, who was struggling to suppress a laugh. "I agree with you, Sophie. I won't allow anything without the consent of my medical advisor and my bodyguard. See you tomorrow at six a.m., my sun." I kissed him, nodded to the completely dumbfounded nurse and left the room before she could issue another prohibition.

I managed to keep my composure until I reached my car. Having arrived there, I couldn't and didn't want to hold back my tears any longer. Why had he decided to have the operation? Why hadn't he insisted on the larger implant? What if he suffered permanent damage from the anaesthetic? Who would look after him then? As far as I knew, a sister and a father existed in Berlin, but did they already know about the vertebra fracture? What if he died during the operation or afterwards? My car shook from the heavy sobs that shook me. All the tension of the last few days was in this outburst, and I was simply terrified. Again, I reminded myself that we hadn't known each other for long, but that didn't help me either. Feelings are feelings. Wasn't that damn Parkinson's enough? Did it have to be made even harder?

Then I thought of June, who was waiting for me in Juergen's flat. "I can cry there as well, so June is not alone, nor am I," I told myself. Then I wiped away my tears, blew my nose, and drove back to June. Immediately after arriving, we went for our evening walk, a long evening walk. I didn't want to be alone with my thoughts in this flat, Juergen's flat. My children, Juergen, the operation, what on earth I was doing and what was happening to me. It was simply too much. Tomorrow, I would think again, now I was only putting one foot in front of the other, on and on and on. Later, I would bury my face in June's fur and hopefully find some peace.

However, I had barely walked a few metres when my mobile phone rang. Juergen. "I don't know if the nurse will be able to recover from your announcement. In any case, she didn't say anything else. You should have seen yourself—like a mixture of the goddess of revenge and Wonder Woman. Being protected by you feels wonderful." "That's fine", I said. Battered as I was, I couldn't share his enthusiasm. "I'm pretty exhausted and going for a long walk with June to recover." "Do I disturb you? We could go together so you won't feel lonely. If a woman walks in the streets at nighttime alone, it can deter villains when she is on the phone." "You know that I am not alone but that a dog is with me, who defends me? Yes, although she looks simply lovable, she defends me. She has already proved this several times. Furthermore, I am the bodyguard and a mixture of the goddess of revenge and Wonder Woman. Do you believe I am afraid of villains? I think they will be afraid of me."

I automatically adopted Juergen's conversational tone. He was about to have an operation on his spine. I already knew him well enough to know he was afraid of it and hid his fear behind his humour. This wasn't the time for fundamental discussions or for voicing any concerns. Now was the time to strengthen him, to stand by him. "I'll put everything else off until tomorrow", I thought again, just like Scarlett O'Hara.

Chapter 17

The following day at six o'clock, I found Juergen lying in his bed rather pale. He didn't feel comfortable in his skin, so shortly before the operation, that was noticeable, even though he tried to seem confident. "You can still cancel the operation", I suggested to him. "I know", he replied, "but I don't want to do so. I want to be fit again soon and leave this place behind. According to the professor, the operation is the fastest way to achieve this." "What did the anaesthetist say last night?" "The usual stuff and that Parkinson's wouldn't be a problem at all. He said that he has already anaesthetised many Parkinson's patients, and all of them have woken up again, and then he laughed."

I bit my tongue not to say, "The question is, in which conditions?" I didn't like statements like the anaesthetist's at all. They probably were not meant to be malicious and were intended to reassure or cheer up the patient. But I would have preferred a frank, factual conversation to such empty phrases. Well, I hadn't been allowed to be there, and now I had to pull myself together. Juergen needed positive thinking and support.

"That's reassuring", I replied accordingly. "Did you at least threaten him with your bodyguard?" I tried a smile. "Indeed, I did so. Let's see if it is going to help. Otherwise, I wouldn't want to be in his shoes. Even though I haven't felt your wrath yet, I can imagine it can be terrible." "Be glad you haven't experienced it yet. I defend my loved ones like a lioness defends her cubs." "So I am one of your loved ones, then?" "Would I otherwise be here?" Juergen's face was radiant with happiness, but this disappeared abruptly when the nurses came to collect him for the operation. "Please, my sun, give me a kiss now to carry me through the anaesthetic and then leave."

I honoured his wish. It was unspeakably difficult for me to leave Juergen in his current fragility to strangers who had not made me trust them. Walking down the hospital corridor towards the staircase, I straightened my back, took a deep breath, and left the clinic briskly. I drove back to Juergen's flat, where June greeted me and looked at me as if she knew only too well what I was going through. She snuggled to my legs, and I dropped my bags to sit on the floor with her. I finally let the tears that I had been holding back to be strong for Juergen flow freely. June and I stayed like that on the floor for a long time. Then I decided: "Come on, June, let's go for a long walk, just the two of us ladies, and then I'll get us something to eat first." I wiped my tear-stained face, and we set off.

"Mr Schwarz is still in the anaesthetic recovery room; try it again in two hours", the nurse told me when I asked her how Juergen had survived the operation. "This does not answer my question", I told her. "I didn't ask where Mr Schwarz was but how he had survived the operation." "I don't know anything about it. But I know he still is in the recovery room." "Could you please give me the telephone number of the recovery room so I can call them directly, please?" "We don't do that. That is completely unusual. Why is it a problem for you to wait another two hours?" the nurse replied in a very snippy voice. I took a significantly intense breath to prevent myself from exploding when the nurse discovered that her behaviour wasn't appropriate, and she added in a very mild tone as if she wanted to calm a bucking horse or a rioting toddler: "There is no need to worry, they are taking good care of you husband."

This mild tone was the very last thing I needed right now. But why argue? I wouldn't get anywhere that way. So I ended the call and phoned the clinic's switchboard to be put through directly to the recovery room, which worked without any problem.

"Mr Schwarz came through the operation very well and is in the process of waking up. There have been no complications. He can be transferred to the regular ward in about two hours. Because of his Parkinson's disease, we prefer to keep him here a little longer than necessary. I assure you that I will inform you of any abnormalities. But this is not to be expected." I had been put through directly to the doctor on duty, and the calm objectivity with which he answered my questions about Juergen's condition helped me a lot after all the empty phrases and the bitching around. Direct answers to direct questions. This is the way people should treat each other. Another two hours of waiting. I should cook something. Who knew how long I would stay with Juergen in the hospital later on?

After almost two hours, my phone rang. My heart stopped beating for a moment. It was the hospital calling. A nurse informed me that Juergen was now in the regular ward and had asked for me. She wanted to know whether it would be possible for me to come because that was very important to Mr Schwarz. "I set off immediately. How is Mr Schwarz doing?" I asked because the urgency with which Juergen demanded my presence worried me. "Very good according to the circumstances. Still a little tired, but otherwise fine, and that's normal." "Thank you very much. I'm already on my way."

A little more reassured, I made my way to Juergen. When I arrived, the professor was with him to explain what had been done during the operation. "It's good you're just joining us. Good afternoon, " the professor greeted me in a visibly good mood. "Good afternoon, Professor... Hello Juergen, nice to see you awake," I greeted the two gentlemen and asked, full of curiosity: "Let us hear what you have done."

"As I told you, it was a routine procedure for me, and as you can see, Mr Schwarz also underwent the anaesthetic without any consequences." "Not this bragging again", I thought, and Juergen muttered: "It's better this way." "You're right", even the professor agreed. "We decided to immobilise three vertebrae with an implant to give you the most excellent possible mobility in the spine. We will remove this implant and the fastening screws in a year. Take a good rest now. Tomorrow morning, a physiotherapist will come and practise walking with you with the help of a walker. Don't worry; you will only need a walker for a very short time. You can be transferred to a rehabilitation clinic in a week at the latest. After three weeks there, you will feel like a new person. Patients usually get used to this immobilisation quite quickly, and intensive exercise is carried out there much more intensely than could be done on an outpatient basis. You don't have to worry about anything. We will arrange everything for you."

"Shouldn't Mr Schwarz first consider whether this is what he wants? After all, he has just had an operation and where he would like to receive which further treatment, he can only decide after having done some research." I didn't like the role I had been assigned here at all, but I was even less comfortable with how they kept trying to rule over Juergen's head as if he didn't have an opinion of his own. Perhaps it was right for many people to have any decisions about themselves taken away from them, but that should be clarified first. "I will arrange for someone to come and talk to him in more detail. But it is essential that he receives intensive physiotherapy and learns to live with the stiffness of the spine and build up his muscles." "I am more than aware of that. But now I want to know why you decided to favour the smaller implant." "A larger implant was never an option except for you. As I have told you several times, we want to maintain the greatest possible mobility, and I believe that the effects of your husband's Parkinson's disease are not so strong that they could jeopardise the results of the operation." "Let's hope so", I said, although I disagreed. But facts had been created that could be changed no more.

"I am still here," Juergen said. "It is very nice how both of you are talking about me, but I would prefer it if you spoke with me. Today, nothing more will happen, and from tomorrow onwards, I will learn how to walk with the help of a physiotherapist and a walker, right?" "Excuse me, please", the professor turned to Juergen. "Of course, we're talking to you. Yes, what you said is right. This will not be difficult for you. The walker is just a safety measure until you have got used to the implant." "Okay. The rest we will discuss tomorrow. I am hungry and tired now." "These are good news. I leave you and your wife alone, and we'll see us tomorrow", the professor said and left the room.

Juergen and I didn't talk a lot. He was tired from the operation, and I was exhausted from the tension, but I was dissatisfied as well. Within myself was still this strange feeling that something was wrong. And how the professor swept away the Parkinson's. I doubted that he had ever looked at Juergen's medication because this would have taught him that Juergen wasn't in the initial stage of the disease and that you shouldn't underestimate the vibrations. But I decided to think positively despite all the strange feelings.

"What about you?" asked Juergen. "Aren't you glad I've over everything and everything went well? One week here, three weeks in a rehabilitation clinic and then I will be as new, and I can finally begin to show you the world's beauty." "Of course, I am glad. But I don't like he chose the small implant." "No need to worry about that. I am sure he knows what he is doing. He has studied for a long time for a reason. I rather think about our first trip when all this is behind us and you get some time off the kids. California would be great, or New Zealand or..." Juergen fell asleep. I stayed with him until the night nurse asked me to leave the hospital. "Please go home. You can't help him when you have a breakdown out of exhaustion. You have to look after yourself as well and shouldn't sacrifice yourself. You are worth it. I promise to look after Mr Schwarz as well as possible." These were the first nice and honest words I heard in this clinic. Tears came into my eyes, and I couldn't answer; I only nodded and tried to smile. I would thank the nurse tomorrow, but she seemed to understand me anyway. I kissed the sleeping Juergen on his forehead. Home, the night nurse had said. How I had loved to go home, to my children, away from this all. Home.

Chapter 18

June and I allowed us to go on a very long walk in the city at night. I only hoped that I would find our way back without any problems this time because, once again, I hadn't paid attention to the route. To say I was wandering the streets lost in thought wouldn't be right either because, in my head, there was a completely unknown emptiness. Think nothing, no decision, not looking for solutions for anything. The dog and I were simply walking. Anything else was too much at the moment. Later, I fed the dog and forgot to feed myself. I felt no hunger, only exhaustion, and I fell into a dreamless sleep.

As if from another world, I heard the phone ring. I should take the call. It was already light outside. What time was it anyway? "Good morning, Sophie. Were you able to sleep?" "Good morning, Juergen. What's the time? You woke me up, so I think I could sleep. How are you? Sorry, my brain is not yet working correctly." "It is seven o'clock, and it is excellent you could sleep. Me too. The professor will soon come, and later, the physiotherapist to chase me out of bed. I can't believe that I will start walking already today. This sounds almost too good to be true, doesn't it?" Juergen sounded wholly relieved, and I felt so happy for him. "Yes, that sounds great. Do you have any pain?" "No, not at all. They seem to have done an excellent job. I could leave for the next rally right now, but I don't think they'll let me do that. So I'll start with walking." "It is so great that you're feeling so good. That also lifts a burden from me." And it really did. He had come through the operation well. He would go to rehab in a few days, and I could finally go home to my children and my work. I could then visit him in rehab at the weekends. I could get that organised somehow.

"Do you need me within the next three hours?" I asked Juergen. I always need you, my sun. But I could only say yes when you meant I could manage the professor's visit and the walk without your help. Nothing terrible will happen to me. I think you will go on a long walk with June. How is the poor lady?" "She is doing great in this unusual situation. I would love to take her for a run through the woods, then have myself a shower and breakfast in peace. I didn't eat anything yesterday. Would it suit you if I came to the hospital between ten and half past ten?" "That would be marvellous. That's how long I'll be staying here", Juergen said, and you could hear the smile in his voice.

When I arrived, Juergen was standing at the lift with his walker. "Your taxi is waiting for you," he said, laughing. "My taxi?" I looked at him questioningly. "Sit on this thing, and I will drive you." Juergen tapped the walker's seat with his hand in an encouraging manner. "Are you sure?" "Absolutely. Come on, sit down, and then we will go on a sightseeing tour across the hospital ward. They told me to walk a lot, and you won't believe it, just now I like it. Off we go."

As soon as I sat on the narrow seat, Juergen started walking. Our round didn't last long, but we laughed joyfully and relieved. "Just as I said," exclaimed Juergen. "Lead a better life with Parkinson's." Laughing, he drove me to his room, and we started to make plans. But we weren't the only ones making plans. The hospital did so, too, so the following day was spent choosing a rehabilitation clinic. After all, Juergen was given a considerable choice between two clinics. Transport was organised, as Juergen was due to start his rehabilitation in just two days. Three weeks later, the last few days would be nothing more than a memory that would always remind us never to forget how fragile our happiness was. At least, that was the plan.

When I returned to Juergen in the early evening after having fed June and myself, I hardly recognised Juergen. The cheerful man I had said goodbye to earlier that afternoon had disappeared. Juergen looked at me with a pain-wracked expression and moaned: "Please, do something immediately. I can't stand the pain any longer, and these stubborn nurses don't want to give me any more painkillers." "What has happened?" I asked, alarmed. My worst fears seemed to be realised. "Please, please, no", I thought. "I don't know, Sopherl. When I woke up after a short nap, I suddenly felt this pain in my back. I have done nothing I wasn't allowed to do. Even the pain my kidney stone forced me to suffer wasn't as horrible as this." "I'll see what I can do." "Please hurry!" shouted Juergen, and I was already heading to the nurses' room.

"Excuse me, please, Mr. Schwarz is in extreme pain. Could a doctor please look after him?" "No one is available at the moment. The doctor on duty is still in the operation theatre. But I can tell him that he'll check on your husband immediately after finishing the operation." "Do you know how long this will take? The pain is extreme."

"No, I can't. But I think it might last another one or two hours." "Couldn't you ask if you can give him a painkiller until then?" "I could, but he has already been given the maximum level and is not responding. We'll have to wait for a doctor." "And in this beautiful large clinic, only one doctor could feel responsible for such an emergency?" "Well, emergency", she said ironically. "He is here in the hospital and is well looked after." "I agree he is in hospital, but well looked after? He screams in pain." "Some patients are more pain-sensitive and can't pull themselves together. Perhaps you should be with your husband and help him rather than having fruitless discussions with me here." "Wait a minute, you claim that if a person screams in pain while in your care, he should pull himself together more?" "What shall I do?" I took a deep breath. "Please put down your cup of coffee and accompany me to Mr Schwarz", I asked the nurse. "And why should I do so?" "Because it is your job to care for the patients in this ward. What's more, telling him to pull himself together will be more credible and effective coming from you." What absurd theatre play were we in right now? I was stunned, but that didn't help either. Help for Juergen had to come from somewhere. The nurse finally gave in. "I'll give the operation theatre a call." "Wonderful. You find me with Mr Schwarz."

"There is no doctor available at the moment, and the nurse says you've already been given the maximum dose of painkillers." I didn't tell him anything about my discussion with her. "Then see if you can find or steal something somewhere", moaned Juergen. "I would hate to kill you. I don't know what dose you've been given so far. And as they haven't relieved the pain so far, another one won't do anything except cause more problems. Let's do some breathing exercises, and show me your feet." I pulled up the duvet and began to massage the reflex zones of the lumbar spine on the right foot. "And why should breathing exercises help? I need medicine." "Every woman who has given birth to a child can tell you that breathing exercises help." I hated having to be so strict with him. But what else could I do? "Come one, join in – I'm the only help you've got now." He groaned, but then he resigned himself to his fate. The pain didn't go away; at best, we managed to cut the absolute peak of the pain. But I could feel how good it was for Juergen that he no longer felt utterly helpless but could do something himself.

The door opened, and the nurse shouted, "The doctor will soon be here. He has just finished the operation." And she disappeared again. I preferred her disappearing.

Finally, Juergen calmed down, and concentrating on breathing and reflex zones helped me. This allowed me to gather my strength for the next battle because that's how the conversations in this house seemed to me now. Why didn't anyone else complain? Was I that sensitive?

After a while, a completely exhausted doctor came to Juergen's bed and asked him to turn to one side so he could examine his back. Juergen tried to do it in vain. I stepped in. Not again. "Do you think it is a good idea to ask Mr Schwarz to make movements that cause even more pain in the spine? What do you think about an X-ray examination because it is evident that something is wrong?" "You should leave that to me", I was told by the doctor. Despite all my sympathy for his situation, a fuse in my brain snapped. "No, I won't do that because I do not allow you to worsen the condition Mr Schwarz is in no matter why – ignorance, overwork, fatigue." "No, you are going too far. Let me do my job", the doctor shouted at me. I calmly asked him: "How important is your license to practice medicine to you?" "Why this stupid question?" "Because I will do everything in my power to withdraw it from you if you don't arrange for Mr Schwarz to undergo an X-ray examination immediately and leave the treatment to a more knowledgeable colleague. Don't you realise what can happen to the spinal cord during these movements?" "You'd better believe her", Juergen moaned his advice to the doctor. "What she says, she does." "What do you mean by that?" A hint of uncertainty crept into the very young doctor's voice. "You've just had a vertebral fracture operation, and the professor won't have done anything wrong." "Shall I bring Mr Schwarz to the X-ray examination, or would you prefer to initiate it?" I spoke with all my determination. At which university was such a treatment for spine injuries taught? "Enough is enough."

Finally, the doctor would let Juergen be brought in for an X-ray. I accompanied him. And it was clear to everyone that I would not tolerate any contradiction. The whole procedure was indescribably painful for Juergen. Still, after one look at the pictures, it became abundantly clear that my warnings to be careful had prevented even worse things than what was shown. The implant had loosened, and one of the fastening screws had started to move. This caused the pain.

"We will have to change the operation plan for tomorrow. Mr Schwarz needs an-other operation. I will inform the professor. Until then, you are receiving a drip with a drug that relieves your pain." "Is this compatible with the Parkinson's medication?" "I think so." "If you were sure, I would feel better", I said resignedly. That was all I could achieve today; I was aware of that. This hadn't been a skirmish but a full-blown battle.

Over time, the medication began to take effect, the pain reduced to a level that Juergen could tolerate, and he became tired. Sleepily, he mumbled: "Thank you, my sun, thank you so much. Now you have to marry me." Then, he slept soundly while I watched over his sleep until I was thrown out again by a nurse. This time, without any friendly concern for my well-being, I was made to feel clear that someone like me, who demanded and criticised, was not wanted there. I spared myself the trouble of asking what they thought would have happened to Juergen's spinal cord otherwise. It was pointless. Could such things really happen in a German hospital? I looked again at Juergen for a long time. Two operations in such a short space of time. What would his body, already ravaged by Parkinson's, do with it? Would we be able to laugh again as freely as we did at lunchtime? "Please leave now", I was asked again. What was left for me to do? I had to go.

Chapter 19

Again, I was with Juergen at six o'clock in the morning. They didn't like seeing me there again but said nothing about it. I noticed Juergen's high painkiller levels, and he said, "Don't worry, my sun. They don't dare to mess up twice. See you soon." I couldn't think of a suitable response; I was too stunned by what had happened in the last few days and by the way such a vulnerable person was treated. None of this corresponded in any way to what I understood by humanity. I whispered, "I'm with you, and it's going to be okay" into Juergen's ear and kissed him goodbye. Then I watched the caravan of the bed with Juergen and the nurses pushing it until the lift doors closed behind them. I was overcome with emptiness.

"You don't have to call before 2 pm. It will take longer today." I almost replied: "And next time, the whole day", but I bit my tongue just in time. What would such a verbal exchange of blows achieve? Nothing. I just nodded and set off. No one had regretted the mistakes, and I assumed this would not happen either. Many hours of waiting were lying before me. Enough time for a long run and a thorough shopping trip to replenish the non-existent stocks of healthy food. I tried to think practically. Wouldn't it make more sense to rest and relax? But how should I manage that? Not thinking about what could happen in the worst case or the second worst one, not creating self-fulfilling prophecies, and so on - buying food and running. It didn't look like I was going to get home quickly. I would stay at least another week until Juergen could leave this clinic of horrors.

"You see, Mr Schwarz, everything has worked out wonderfully. The implant is now firmly in place. Tomorrow, we'll start mobilisation, which you are already familiar with, and you can go into rehab in a few days. You will soon forget this episode and return to travelling through the world." The professor appeared at Juergen's bedside late afternoon, grinning smugly as if he had just performed a miracle and not dealt with the consequences of his misjudgement. Juergen was exhausted and could hardly keep his eyes open. Two anaesthetics in such a short interval left their mark, but it looked like they wouldn't be permanent.

I couldn't prevent myself from saying: "Let's hope you don't need a third attempt because all good things come in threes." The cheerful, self-satisfied grin disappeared abruptly from the professor's face. "So please, let's stay objective. It's all good now. These things happen." "They happen less often if you work more carefully and consider a person's illnesses when making decisions." "Surely you don't want to accuse me of malpractice. I can prove that I acted to the best of my knowledge and belief. And your husband is doing well now, too." I was prepared for a riot. "Perhaps you should significantly increase your knowledge to spare patients unnecessary double operations in future. And I am sure that you have secured yourself on all sides. But I don't want to start this discussion now. My partner needs all my attention. He is more important to me." I turned my full attention to Juergen so that my back was turned to the professor. He said goodbye with a brief greeting and left us alone, as alone as you can be in a hospital room.

Juergen's recovery was progressing well, and the day of his transfer to the rehab clinic was approaching. "I'll visit you there as often as possible." "Why?" Juergen asked, irritated. "Wouldn't you like that?" I asked, just as irritated. "I thought you were coming with me. I've already organised a small flat for June and you right next to the rehabilitation clinic." I looked at Juergen, stunned. "Why did you do that without even asking me? I have to go back home to my children." "Because I need you." "You will be well looked after there. But my children need me, and I need them, too." Now I was in tears. "You've seen where it leads to if you don't keep an eye on people. I don't know anything about these medical things. I can only do cars. The children have their father. Just a few more days until we know everything is going well at the rehabilitation clinic. Please."

Of course, Juergen was right about himself. For him, I was a safety net, a support. I would have wished the same in his place. But what about me, my children, my life? I needed fresh air and space. I had to get out of this room, out of the hospital, away from Juergen, who was looking at me expectantly. "I have to think about it and to run a while. At the moment, I can't say anything about this; I simply can't. I will come back later." "When will that be?" "I don't know. I won't run away; no need to worry. You made this decision that I absolutely disagree with without asking me, even if I can understand you. Now, I must clear my mind, which I can't do here." "But don't stay away too long because I would begin to worry that you left me after

78

all. I didn't want to harm you. It would be best if you had a break after your days here. I wanted to surprise you. And I need you, my sun." "Please, that's enough now. I said that I would come back. That should be enough. I need some rest now. See you soon." I got up and left the room almost in a hurry. That couldn't be true. He wasn't allowed to rule over me like that. I quickly picked up June and took her to the little forest I had discovered. I needed running, just running, becoming myself again.

After letting off the steam, I dropped onto a tree trunk, exhausted. June laid her head on my legs and looked at me. "Oh, June, my girl, what should I do?" How I would have loved to let out all my anger, all my sadness, drum my fists on Juergen's chest and shout at him why on earth he thought he could rule over me like that. "And what are you thinking, James? Why did you make him so insecure, this strong and clever man? What's in it for you?" I shouted into the forest.

"Nothing," said a calm voice, making me cringe. Now, I had already heard voices. It was getting stranger every day. Nobody could be seen who could own this voice. "You know I'm not responsible for all this." "Who are you?" I asked although I couldn't see anybody. "James, James Parkinson." "But that can't be true." "But you are hearing me. This disease Juergen has, which is named after me, makes people insecure. Suddenly, they need medicine that only a doctor can prescribe. They don't know what is going to happen to them. Try to understand what this means to a free spirit like Juergen." "That is perfectly clear to me. It must be awful. And now he has this fracture of the vertebra on top, and the treatment was anything but simple. This is why I came here. But I cannot stay forever. I have children, I have my job, my own life."

"But you decided to go for the complete package. Are you going to back out now when Juergen needs your help in a difficult situation? After everything that has already happened, do you want to put him in the hands of people you don't know?" "It's not fair, it's just not fair. We've only known each other for such a short time. We just wanted to have fun." "And you will. But it would be best if you stood by him longer, supporting him with your presence and knowledge. He needs you so that he doesn't give up on himself." "That would be nonsense. A vertebral fracture will heal, he will get used to the implant, and if he trains, he will be fit again in one or two months and can come to Oberhausen. And until then, I'll come regularly."

"Juergen and training without a personal coach? Can you imagine that?" James laughed.

I took a couple of deep breaths. "Okay, I will go with him for a few days until he gets used to everything. But then he has to manage without me for some time. We can phone. And if all else fails, I can return to him in a few hours." I felt a weight on my shoulder as if from a hand. That's right, believe me." Then the weight was gone, and it was quiet inside of me. Nobody would believe this – I didn't believe it myself. It was probably due to nervous overload, but it wasn't important at all. Then I was talking to myself – who else should I be talking to here alone? "Come on, June, I'm going to make us something to eat, and then I have to think how to explain this to my children and their father before I return to Juergen."

Chapter 20

"Will you wait for me in the clinic, or shall I call you on arrival?" Juergen was excited. Tomorrow, he would leave the clinic and could make a big step towards freedom and self-determination. He could hardly wait for the farewell to the hospital, nor could I. We had tried to make the best out of the time until his discharge. I had treated Juergen with manual therapies and homoeopathy; we had walked a lot, still using the walker, and we had talked a lot.

"I would drive behind you so we would arrive at the same time", I replied to his question. "But they can't or don't want to tell me when you start tomorrow. What do you think if I leave your flat tomorrow at nine and drive directly to the Black Forest where I move into the flat you rented for us? I will not be allowed to go to the rehabilitation clinic with June, and she has to know that she will be safe at this new place and that I will always return. You know this from our journeys. There have been too many changes for the dog recently. You call me on your arrival. Then I will come as soon as possible. Don't forget to charge your mobile phone." "Are you sure there is no other way? I would feel much better if you were with me." "I would prefer this as well, but our wishes don't count here. You call when you're near the clinic, and I try to be there on your arrival." "Okay, I will keep you informed about where we are during the journey. I am so sorry for making life so difficult for you and June. I've already got so used to you, to the fact that I'm no longer alone, that someone is there for me. I didn't want that before. Sometimes, I almost panic that you could be gone and I could be alone with all this. At the moment, you are my strength." "Nonsense, you are stronger than you believe. Just look at what you have done and achieved in your life. A lot I can only dream about. And how you cope with the diagnosis of Parkinson's. None of this was a weakness. You have only got a bodyguard now." I smiled at him.

"Oh my sun, you are so much more. All this overwhelms me. You know, I've always been afraid of this kind of situation—being at the mercy of others, unable to walk or drive a car. When I went here with my pain, I didn't give it a second thought. If you have health problems, you go to the doctor or a hospital, and it gets sorted out there. And it has always been like this. Okay, they couldn't make Parkinson's

81

disappear, but they gave me medicine, which helped me to get along with it. I never thought that anaesthesia could be more dangerous for me now than it used to be before my time with Parkinson's or that a professor could make such an error of judgment because the facts of the case were not that complicated after all. Somehow, I believed that doctors would make fewer mistakes than other people. Please lower my bed so I can slowly prepare for my beauty sleep." "Of course, let me have a look." I tried to lower the bed, but the technology failed me. Juergen called a nurse. "No problem, I will do it for you", the nurse chirped, and the top part of the bed, which had been set to the highest position, including Juergen, who had undergone spinal surgery a few days ago, came hurtling down with a loud crash until it was stopped by the frame of the bed with a band and a jolt. The shocked Juergen bounced up and down once more before he, like the bed, came to rest.

"Oops, sorry", the nurse said. "I am just a student, and I am not familiar with the beds." "But you already know that human beings are lying in these beds, who partly recover from serious operations? Mr Schwarz, for example, had an operation because of a vertebral fracture. Such actions on your part can have terrible consequences for the patients." Once again, I was stunned. "I only wanted to help." "I honour your intention, but you haven't done so. Why don't you get a trained nurse if you can't do something?" "I didn't think of it." "Please do so in future; otherwise, you might kill someone. More I don't want to say for now. Juergen", I took his hand, which still clasped the duvet tightly. "How are you? Do you have any pain?" "I can't tell you that yet. First, all my limbs are still shaking from the shock." "I believe you are. It's high time we get out of here. All this can't be true anymore. Do you remember the cleaning lady two days ago who looked like the servant of Scarlett O'Hara in "Gone With the Wind"?" I tried to distract Juergen. My attempt worked. Juergen laughed. "Oh yes. She sang something to herself, sprayed a cloth with a disinfectant spray at the room entrance and then wiped the table, the toilet seat, the windowsill and finally, the bedside table with the food trays, all with the same cloth before disappearing again. The look on your face was marvellous. I thought you would never be able to close your mouth again, and that absolute bewilderment in your eyes. Wonderful." And then Juergen remembered another incident that we could laugh about in the meantime, even if you can't imagine something like that happening in a clinic. "You went with me into this ward bathroom to help me shower because I couldn't stand for that long and wasn't agile enough to wriggle into this narrow shower in this bathroom. You had a real fight with the nurses because they hadn't washed me and wouldn't help me shower either. 'At least tell me where I can shower Mr Schwarz myself.' And then you almost stepped in the faeces that were blocking the drain of the ward shower. When you saw the blood on the door handle, your composure was gone for good." Juergen shook with laughter. Well, nothing serious had happened as a result of the bed drama. Otherwise, he wouldn't have been able to laugh so painlessly. It was beautiful to see him so liberated. "You can't say that", I protested. "I didn't rave or shout, and I didn't drop to the floor in anger or hit the nurses with my fists either." "Spitting. You forgot you didn't spit on anyone either." I hadn't seen Juergen this cheerful for a long time. Then, all these unbelievable things did at least one good thing: they made him laugh. "Please let me examine you briefly so I can be reassured that your crash has no consequences." When nothing was found, Juergen relaxed utterly.

"Would you please give me another massage of my reflex zones? They help me so much", Juergen asked. "With pleasure. And afterwards, I go home to June, and we'll see us in the Black Forest." "Okay, but I also want a kiss. I am so tired that I will surely fall asleep during the massage." And this was what he did. I quietly slipped out of the room to pack for June and myself. "Anything is better than this clinic", I thought.

Chapter 21

June and I were back in the car with a few belongings, and all I could think about was that I was heading in the wrong direction. When I contacted my children and ex-husband, they only replied that everything was excellent. They had everything under control. I shouldn't worry about them and should take care of Juergen. "Perhaps you can relax a bit as well after all these years of family work. Just break away from everything," my ex-husband told me. Well-intentioned, for sure, but how should I do it? My children were my life. I only fell in love and was overrun by events I had never wanted. "That's called living", I admonished myself, wiping away my tears. "Concentrate on driving and trust your family. Perhaps it's good for them to realise I couldn't be taken for granted. The advice to relax isn't so bad after all. At least I could try. What music would you like to listen to, June?" I decided on Celtic harp music, as June was unwilling to come up with a suitable suggestion. The weather was fine. I opened the convertible top, and we set off to the gentle sounds of the Celtic harp.

Juergen had chosen an apartment next to the clinic for his two ladies. "I don't want to make it any more challenging for you than it already is. And maybe I can visit you and June there once I'm better. They say I'll be able to walk better than before the operation within a week or two. So Juergen had told me optimistically. I had just settled in and made a cup of tea when my mobile honked. That was my ringtone for Juergen, the man of the cars.

"I've arrived. This time, nobody had any reason to scold me. I was on time and didn't drive myself, so I was very well-behaved." Juergen laughed. But his choice of words made me sit up and take notice. 'scold me, very well-behaved', what had happened to Juergen? When had my rebel turned into a well-behaved patient who was proud that he had obeyed? I hoped this was irony. "Shall I come immediately, or can I first go on a walk with June?"

"Have your tea in peace, and then walk with June. We're still doing the bureaucratic stuff here, and after that, I can go to my room. I have to see the doctor sometime later, who will decide on the therapies starting tomorrow. At the moment, I'm still being wheeled around in a wheelchair so that nothing can happen to me. I think they take excellent care of me here. Get some rest. The last few days have been anything but nice for you. Everything will be fine from now on." I wanted so much to believe Juergen, but it seemed as if the last few days' events had made me paranoid. There was no feeling that everything would be okay now. There was more of a feeling that everything could become worse inside me. But I was probably wrong, and in a few days, Juergen and I would laugh about it. "Well, then I'll be with you in two hours at the latest, and we'll explore the clinic together. Okay?" "Perfect plan. I look forward to seeing you."

Juergen in a wheelchair. The sight of it gave me a stab in the heart. But he beamed at me. "I can also use the walker when accompanied. When I'm alone, the wheelchair is safer for a few more days. Don't look at me like a rabbit looks at the snake. Let's get going." "Come here, I'll help you up, and then we'll both march off." "Do you want to have another ride on the walker? That was funny last time." Juergen asked me. But I didn't feel like it today. "We better don't do that today. It didn't end well last time. I better walk. Let's see what's on offer here."

We explored the entire site. Had I ever seen Juergen walk so much? He was unstoppable and full of anticipation. He was particularly fond of the swimming pool, which we could see from the outside. So, I learned something new about him again. He loved swimming. Just like me. But he favoured the swimming pool; I was happy with any sea or lake as long as the temperature wasn't too close to freezing. "If you like swimming too, we should go to a hotel with a swimming pool on one of our next trips – I love swimming so much." "That's a good idea. Sophie?" "Yes?" "You were talking about our next journey as if it were already fixed. Otherwise, you're always very hesitant because of your children. Has anything changed?" "No, but there will be a future trip; the only question is when. But I don't want to think about that right now. I don't want to think about anything at the moment. Can I get a cup of tea somewhere around here?"

With interruptions to look after June, we spent the rest of the day together. We made plans for what we would do together at the weekend. Juergen couldn't leave the clinic this weekend, so we planned walking routes on the grounds, and I would bring tea and cake. "I'd rather have tea from a flask that this hospital brew", I said to Juergen, who laughed out loud and replied: "If you are so demanding. I think a Coke will do; at least nobody can spoil it." "No comment. But tea is a must. My children once said: cars run on petrol, mum on tea. And they were absolutely right." Juergen laughed, and we enjoyed the completely carefree day.

"When do you have your first therapy tomorrow? At least I want to be there for the first few times and keep an eye on them. After our experiences in the hospital, I no longer trust anyone that quickly." "Now, don't develop a phobia", Juergen gently reprimanded me. "What is supposed to happen during physiotherapy? I have to learn to get out of bed with the immobilised part of my spine and change some movement patterns that are no longer possible with this implant in my back, as usual. I don't need my bodyguard for this. They're professionals here. Take the morning off and come to lunch." My uneasy feeling wouldn't let me rest. "Juergen, please let me be there for the therapy. Not every physiotherapist is equally good, and they should see that you are not alone here but that somebody is watching them. Haven't you learnt anything from your experiences in the clinic? And yes, even when practising such things, things can go wrong if they are not done expertly and correctly." "Sopherl, the professor said, that nothing can happen with this implant. Don't drive yourself and me crazy, and please give me my freedom. I'm not a doddering old man." "I didn't say that at all, and I really don't want to patronise you. But…" "Please stop", interrupted Juergen. "I'll do it on my own tomorrow. There won't be more than this one physio appointment anyway, apart from the nurses treating my wound – it's Friday, so I'll have a rest until Monday. But from then on, things will get going according to the schedule. Don't look so worried, my sun: what else should happen now? I'm so happy that I'm doing so well. Do you think I'm going to let that be changed again?" "Juergen, please. Then why should I come with you? You told me to look after you and watch the therapists. Otherwise, I wouldn't be here." "Yes, but not for every appointment. Enjoy half a day off just for June and yourself."

Nothing could be done about that. He wanted it that way and no other way. And it was true: He was independent and self-determined. I was the last person who tried to take that away from him, but unlike me, he didn't know what could go wrong either. And after everything that had happened so far, which shouldn't have happened, I was perhaps overdoing it. But my gut feeling wasn't getting quieter.

June and I explored the neighbourhood extensively the following morning and enjoyed our breakfast in peace. I had just opened my laptop to start work when my mobile honked. It was a few minutes past eleven o'clock. "Sopherl?" I heard Juergen's agonised voice. "Something is very, very wrong. I'm in absolutely terrible pain. Please come as soon as you can." "Are you in your room?" "Yes." "I'm already on my way."

As an endurance runner, I had never been a strong sprinter, but I ran in a record-breaking time on this day. "My feelings and me. Why didn't I assert myself?" The accusations raced through my head. I arrived in Juergen's room entirely out of breath and with a bright red face. He moaned quietly to himself and didn't even notice me at first. I stepped up to his bed and gently stroked his hair.

"What have they done to you?" "I don't know, Sophie. I was in the treatment room with a very young physiotherapist. There, I had to lie on the treatment table and do exercises." "Can you describe the exercises for me?" I asked Juergen. "Not exactly. All sorts of twisting exercises for the back down here." He pointed to his lumbar spine. "First of all, we wanted to loosen the muscles, the young lady had said. When I told her this was very difficult and painful for me, she replied that this was normal. She said I wasn't used to this kind of exertion, as I had hardly any back muscles, but she would change that over the next three weeks. After this time, my spine would be very flexible, and I would have strong muscles in my back. Before the next appointment, I should take a painkiller. And when I had problems doing an exercise, she bravely reached out for support. "For heaven's sake", it escaped me. "She tried to mobilise the immobilised part of your spine instead of practising with you how to deal with the fact that it is immobile. If you have pain like this, something must have happened to the implant. I will immediately look for a doctor." "It is Friday, and no doctor is here anymore, I was told." "I will find a doctor. Do you want me to help you lie differently, or is it ok for now?" "It's ok", said Juergen unconvincingly. "It hurts the least that way. Please hurry and Sophie..." "Yes, what do you want? I have to go", I asked impatiently. "I want to apologise for blindly trusting again despite the negative experiences. It won't happen again". "I'm sure it will, but that's life. For now, I will try to limit the damage."

With these words, I left the room, closed the door, leaned against it and took a couple of deep breaths to calm down. Then, I began to look for a nurse. Is the staff of a rehabilitation clinic called this way? What sort of nonsense goes through one's mind in such stressful situations. In the nurses' room, I found a woman and a man, both dressed in white coats, enjoying a cup of coffee.

"I apologise for interrupting, but Mr Schwarz has been in much pain since the physiotherapy. He needs immediate help, and X-rays need to be taken at once to check if there was any damage done, as he was utterly pain-free before the physiotherapy. "Today is Friday, and we don't do any X-rays on Fridays. He must have something like sore muscles; he's probably just not used to exercise. We often have that here. It'll be better in a day or two. I can give you a hot water bottle for him. This often helps." "That is very kind of you, but Mr Schwarz isn't suffering from sore muscles. The exercises that were done in the physiotherapy mobilise the spine. Mr Schwarz has a spine that is partly immobilised by an implant, and the correct physiotherapy was meant to show him how to get along with that. I must insist on an X-ray control because there is a well-founded suspicion that this incorrect physiotherapy has caused damage that needs to be dealt with immediately."

"Enough is enough," the man in the white coat said. "You can't come here and tell us what to do. That's not how it works. "And who are you, if I may ask?" I was on the verge of losing my temper; I wanted to scream and hit something. Juergen was in a lot of pain. How did these people react? "I am the ward physician. Now, go back to your husband and reassure him. We won't do any X-rays today, Monday morning at the earliest and only if I deem it necessary."

I calmly picked up my mobile phone. There was no point in talking further, so I had to seek help. The ward physician seemed uncomfortable with this and asked in a harsh but unsettling tone, "Who are you calling?" "Not that it's any of your business who I want to talk to on my phone. But since you are asking, I'll answer you. I'll call an ambulance so that Mr Schwarz can be taken to a clinic immediately, where the necessary radiological and other examinations can be carried out, which you deny him. Then, I will instruct my lawyer to initiate proceedings against you for failure to provide assistance and medical malpractice. After all, you are not even prepared to go to Mr Schwarz to inspect the complaints in person. If you would please let me make my phone calls in peace? Of course, I will leave this room to avoid disturbing you further." I left the room and was bumped into by the ward physician, who sprinted towards Juergen's room at an almost record-breaking speed. Over his shoulder, he shouted to the nurse: "Inform the X-ray department that we are coming with a patient and that they should prepare everything for X-rays of the lumbar spine." I looked at the doctor with wide, innocent eyes and asked: "Can I refrain from calling an ambulance now?" He didn't answer, but his face turned so red that I wasn't sure whether I should call an ambulance for him.

Before the doctor could speak to Juergen, I was already at his bedside and explained, "I have asked Mr., what was your name again?" "Dr...." replied the physician indignantly. "Okay, so I've asked Mr... to take an X-ray of the operation area to be on the safe side so that we know whether the physiotherapy has damaged anything that is causing you so much pain. Is that okay for you?" "I agree with everything. If only this pain would finally stop. You can't give me anything immediately, can you, Mr...? The pain is worse than the original vertebral fracture." "If the pain is that bad, I'll give you something to help you before the X-ray. Just a moment, please", said the doctor and disappeared.

"How did you manage that, my sun?" Juergen asked with a tortured smile. "A little politeness, a little threatening. I can be very persuasive when I want to be, and I wanted to be. There is something wrong with your back; we need the X-rays now. Firstly, we need to know what's going on in your back, and secondly, they could otherwise deny a direct connection with the physiotherapy if nothing is done until Monday. A patient can get up to a lot of mischief, especially at the weekend, right? " "I wouldn't have thought of that at all. You're right about the preservation of evidence. The pain is so bad that I can't think straight at the moment. Thank you for thinking for me and looking after me. And I said that this was not necessary." "It's okay. Oh, look, here comes the doctor with the medicine and then it's off to the X-ray."

I accompanied Juergen to the X-ray room. In this clinic, I didn't trust anyone anymore. Back again in Juergen's room, we had to wait for a while until a very pale and abashed ward physician entered to tell us: "The X-ray images revealed that three of the six screws securing the implant have loosened and two of them most likely provoke the nerve causing the pain."

"And what do you want to do now"? I asked quietly. This wasn't the time to lose your nerves or make accusations. What should not have happened had happened. Now, it was time to find solutions. "We will now keep Mr Schwarz as pain-free as possible with medication and then continue with physiotherapy on Monday to strengthen and build up the muscles. Not much has changed. The other three screws are tight." "So Mr Schwarz should continue to trust the physiotherapy in this clinic after what has happened?"

"What has happened anyway?" The ward physician raised his voice threateningly. "Were you with him during the physiotherapy? Can you judge it at all? Mr Schwarz could also have contracted the complications when he was alone in his room, or perhaps you even manipulated something yourself. Nobody can prove any of this. And now it's difficult to tighten the screws again from the outside with a screwdriver."

"I don't want to answer your outrageous remarks now, but we'll discuss everything with the head of the clinic on Monday. Before this conversation has taken place, nothing else will happen apart from pain medication. If you would now be so kind as to leave Mr Schwarz and me alone so we can discuss the matter in peace."

"You have chosen a feisty partner, Mr Schwarz", the doctor turned fraternising to Juergen. "Don't let her panic you. You can trust us. We know what we are doing." "I have had completely different experiences today. And my partner is not panicking or ignorant. Your refusal to deal with my pain speaks volumes about your competence. As there is no other doctor available, why don't you arrange the necessary pain treatment now and then leave me alone with my partner? We will discuss everything else with your boss. I assume that he has already left the house for the weekend?"

The doctor hadn't expected this. Like many other people, he had equated Juergen's Parkinson's disease with an inability to think logically and act independently. A few days ago, however, this man had been completely independent and fit, too lazy to walk but fit. And this wannabe doctor treated him as if he was stupid. Oh, Juergen

90

had done well. Less confident and no longer fraternising, the doctor replied with the door handle in his hand: "I'm going to the nurses' room now and will have the medication adjusted accordingly." "Great, don't let anybody stop you", Juergen called after him as he fled. The painkillers seemed to be working.

"Is it possible for me to take a look at your back? Perhaps I get an idea of how I can help you. Although I think it would be much better if you pulled the stakes here immediately and sought proper treatment." "You're welcome to have a look. But I'm not cancelling the rehab. I don't know what the consequences would be for me financially and what would happen if I were to need another rehab because of Parkinson's. Perhaps it would not be approved because of this." "What good is all this if the experts here rehabilitate you into a wheelchair?" I said rather drastically, but I had held back long enough now.

"It won't become that bad. Let's talk to the head doctor on Monday first. We won't let anyone else get close to me before then. You're right about that." By now, I knew when it was pointless to continue talking to Juergen. What he wanted or didn't want, that's what he wanted or didn't want. "Damn stubborn, know-it-all Virgo", I scolded him, his zodiac sign. "Stubbornness in human form. And then complaining when something goes wrong. Please, turn onto your side if you can."

He could. Juergen positioned himself very carefully on his side. You could feel the loose screws with your bare hands. How was I supposed to get them stable? Juergen slowly rolled back onto his back, and I fluffed the pillows to make him more comfortable. "Then I guess we won't walk around the clinic grounds tomorrow. I need your feet. I want to treat the reflex zones of your back thoroughly. Perhaps it will relax you." "And me too", I thought. "At the moment, I have no pain. Maybe it will recover a little; otherwise, we'll see on Monday. Don't be angry anymore. Oh, that feels good. I can feel it in my back, whatever you're doing with my feet." While massaging the reflex zones, I thought about what else I could do for him today. In my mind, I went through the operation area, the nerve pathways, and the muscles and then decided on a supportive craniosacral partial treatment. After all, someone had to take care of these screws.

Juergen, who would have loved to purr like a cat licking out a bowl of cream whenever I treated him manually, enjoyed the treatment again. The tension of the last few hours fell away from him. In between, I kept asking him if anything was hurting, but he just said: "You can't hurt me." "Don't challenge me", I replied with a laugh and continued. I only interrupted my treatment to look after June, eat something and then return to Juergen and continue the treatment. When the nurse arrived with the painkillers, Juergen said: "Please, put these on my bedside table; I don't need them at the moment." "But the doctor said…" the nurse began. "I don't take any painkillers if I'm not in pain. My partner treated me well, and I am doing well according to the circumstances. Thank you very much." "But now it's time for your partner to leave. No visitors are allowed at that time of day", she snapped back and left the room.

"How I hate this. As if we were small children." "My sun, you need a rest now. I promise not to do anything stupid and to wait for you tomorrow with any escapades. Maybe we can make it into the garden, and then you can get June so she can come and visit me, too. We will go somewhere where nobody can see us." "That's a good plan. Then I'll go now, even if I don't think leaving you here is good. Are we going to phone later?" "Absolutely. How did you manage that? I feel so much better." "It's a mixture of painkillers and my treatment. You are important to me." I kissed him and left the clinic, worried.

We made the most of Saturday and even spent much time in the clinic garden. The rest of the day, I treated Juergen manually and adjusted his homoeopathic medication to the new situation. "Now she is even massaging his feet. And she was strangely holding his head. She can't be completely clearheaded as if that would help. Total hippie weirdo, I tell you." I heard one nurse say that to another about me. I didn't mind their talking. The most important thing was that I could help Juergen, and I did.

We wanted to spend Sunday the same way as Saturday, and on Monday, we wanted to discuss the situation and the next steps with the clinic boss. As soon as I entered Juergen's room, I felt something was wrong. The joy that had been on his face yesterday had disappeared. Without greeting him, I immediately asked: "What happened?"

"They removed most of the stitches and somehow dressed the wound. It is burning and itching like fire." "Show me." Anyone seeking medical treatment must declare any existing intolerances, allergies and preexisting conditions. Juergen had done this correctly; his records showed he was allergic to all plaster forms. When I looked at his back now, not only was there plaster on it, but under and next to this plaster, the skin had turned a flaming red colour, and blisters of different sizes had formed as a sign of the existing allergy.

"Nobody can be that stupid anymore. Juergen, I have to hurt you now. They've stuck a plaster over the wound. Everything here is terribly red, and several blisters have formed. I'm going to take the plaster off and then treat the wound with my remedies before I tear the nurse into tiny pieces." "But I told them that I am allergic to plaster." "I believe you. Somehow, they must have realised that because this is a plaster for sensitive patients. They didn't believe that you were allergic to all kinds of plasters. But you said that you wouldn't allow anybody to touch you without me being there." I carefully removed the plaster. Nevertheless, Juergen groaned, which wasn't surprising given the condition of his skin directly over his spine. "I'm almost finished. I am so sorry."

"You don't have to feel sorry for anything. Ouch. I was stupid enough to let myself get carried away again. But Sophie, honestly, who would think that something as simple as pulling threads could go wrong? Ouch." "The plaster is off. Take a deep breath first. I now have to disinfect it carefully and then put gauze compresses over it, which I have soaked with homoeopathic remedies." How do you fix the compresses?" "Without other options, I'll fix them with gauze bandages. Do you want a loop or a knot"? I tried a joke. And it worked. Juergen laughed. "Oh, Sophie, that feels so good. The burning and itching is already subsiding." "That's good. Please, don't let anyone touch your wound again. It's sad, but they can't even do that. They also haven't removed the threads completely; material remains in the tissue." "You can't be serious. Can an inflammation develop there?" "Can, doesn't have to. But I'll take care of it. First, everything has to calm down from the allergic reaction."

After having treated Juergen's operations scar as best as I could, I went to the nurses' room and confronted the nurse. "How was I supposed to know that Mr Schwarz was sensitive?" she defended herself. "His documents, on which this is noted in red pencil on the cover page, could have been a clue." "Nowadays, almost everyone claims to be allergic to plaster. If you took all this literally, you wouldn't be able to do your job." Should I keep talking to this woman or explain anything to her? She wouldn't understand it anyway, and I didn't want to argue. One more point for to-morrow's conversation with the head of the clinic, tomorrow, some time or when-ever. "Juergen has to get out of here", I thought in an endless loop. But how was I supposed to get him to do it? He didn't want to, and he was stubborn.

So, being infinitely tired, I only said to the nurse firmly: "You won't touch Mr Schwarz again, and you won't treat his wound." "You are certainly not allowed to tell me that," she snapped. Yes, I am, and Mr Schwarz will be happy to tell you the same." The ward physician appeared, and when he saw me, he asked, visibly an-noyed: "What's the matter with you again?" "Have a nice day, too. If you would please accompany me to Mr Schwarz. That saves me further explanations. Just take a look for yourself at what this nurse has done." "If it has to be." "Yes, it must be."

He accompanied me to Juergen's room, where I removed a piece of the bandage so the doctor could take a look. "That doesn't look good at all. What happened?" He looked almost shocked. Juergen told him what had happened and that he wanted to leave the further wound care to me for the time being. "This is extremely unusual, but I can understand it under these circumstances. I don't have another nurse avail-able until tomorrow." "Could I please get some sterile instruments to remove the rest of the threads the nurse left in the wound? Don't worry; I won't do this before the wound has improved." "She did that too? Come with me; I'll give you everything you need. We had our differences, but I can only apologise for this matter now on behalf of the clinic. Do you need anything else?" "No, I carry everything else with me. Thank you very much." An apology, after all.

Around midday the next day, Juergen and I had an appointment with the head doctor of the clinic. Before I went to see Juergen, he had already refused a bandage change and a physiotherapy appointment. "Why did we discuss this with the doctor yester-day if they harass me today?" "I told you that you'd better leave this house." "And I've told you why I'm not doing so. Let's talk to the head doctor first."

We set off on our way. As we were together, Juergen was confident about journeying to the head doctor's office with his walker. As soon as we entered the office, I realised why the doctor hadn't made his way to Juergen with all his findings and acute complications.

"That's looking very well, Mr Schwarz. I've heard that you weren't entirely satisfied on your first day. Let's hear what's on your mind." So it sounded cheerfully from the desk behind which the head physician was sitting and, of course, remained seated. He didn't offer us a seat, not even Juergen. But I had resolved to keep quiet for the time being, and so I did. Juergen had insisted on clarifying how he should proceed. That was absolutely right. And he needed to take care of his things. For my taste, I had to intervene far too often.

"Yes, things are going relatively well now. My partner has done a great job", Juergen began the conversation. "Without her, I would probably still be lying in bed, moaning in pain, without any care." "Let's not dramatise things." I bit my tongue. Nobody was dramatising, and the wording for "we" didn't work at all. But I kept quiet.

"I am not dramatising. During the therapy, I told the very young therapist that I was in pain and couldn't do the exercises. She then helped and said it was because I still lacked muscles and the corresponding strength. I felt a crunching in my back and then cancelled the therapy for good. When I tried to get up from the treatment table the way I had learned in the hospital, the physiotherapist pulled me up by my arms. Then it crunched again in my back, and severe pain set in. That would become better, said the young lady and dismissed me. Somehow, I managed to get back into my room. Neither the ward physician nor the nurse were prepared to help me, and it was only after my partner", Juergen pointed his head towards me, "vehemently demanded pain medication and X-ray that they were willing to do both. The X-ray examination then revealed that half of the screws that secure the implant had come loose and were wobbling around happily."

"Nothing is wobbling around at all, Mr Schwarz. The screw connection has come loose. Well, that shouldn't happen, but the metal will be removed in one year anyway. Until then, you have to work intensively on your muscles. But that's what you're here for, and of course, you have to accept that you have to keep this area of your spine as still as possible." "I was very keen to do this, but the physiotherapist asked me to do exercises that had exactly the opposite effect, as my partner explained." The head doctor turned to me. "And how would you know that?" "Because it is one of my specialist domains", I answered briefly and concisely.

"Oh, excuse me, I didn't know you were a colleague", concluded the head physician immediately, and I let him believe that. That could only be to Juergen's advantage at the moment. Juergen thought the same, grinned at me briefly and asked: "And now, Doctor, what are we going to do?" "I will talk to our most experienced physiotherapist, and he will take care of you. Your case seems to be nothing for younger therapists." "And why did you let this lady experiment on me in the first place?" This was almost a full-blown tantrum for Juergen. I was delighted. He finally started to fight back. "I would have to ask the doctor who made this decision. But look, now everything will be fine. Take today off, and you can start with the full programme tomorrow. And next week, you can also go into the swimming pool."

"The nurse made sure this won't work when she tried to pull the threads out of my wound." "How can I understand that?" asked the doctor, somewhat confused. "Juergen, can I show the doctor your operation wound?" "Of course. I hold my shirt up so that you can open the bandage." While I was undoing the bandage, I explained. "Yesterday, as mentioned, the ward nurse tried to remove the threads. She left quite a lot of material in the suture and covered the suture with plaster, although Mr Schwarz's documents clearly state that he is allergic to any form of plaster. When I came to him later, the whole area, which the plaster covered, was massively reddened, and several blisters had formed. I then treated the wound myself and forbade the nurse to lay a hand on Mr Schwarz again. The ward physician was later prepared to provide me with sterile instruments to remove the threads, but he didn't want to do it himself."

The head physician first looked at me unbelieving and then at Juergen's back, which, although looking far better than yesterday, still looked more like a battlefield than a properly treated surgical wound. "You are sure that…" the head physician began. I interrupted him brusquely. "Do you believe I did this to my partner?" "Of course not. I will also take care of that." "And how do you want to take care of that?" I could no longer keep to my self-imposed vow of silence. "Mr Schwarz arrived on

Thursday. Within two days, the result of the operation was severely affected, with the outcome still unclear; the doctor, therapist and nurses refused help, to do an X-ray and give painkillers and the information on the documents about an existing allergy was ignored. I don't see where we can agree that Mr Schwarz continues to entrust himself to the incompetence of your co-workers. It seems to me that the only viable option is for you to pass Mr Schwarz to more competent hands and abandon this rehabilitation attempt at once. I would also feel much better if an experienced surgeon were to look at him immediately."

Juergen looked at me questioningly. The harmony between us was over; I could feel that very clearly. I found it increasingly difficult to keep my composure and not to take this head doctor by the shoulders and shake him until he finally admitted that none of this should have happened and that Juergen would be better off anywhere but here. And I also wanted to shake Juergen and ask him where his self-respect had gone, where his talent of getting to the heart of the matter was, his absolute intransigence, his strength, especially in illness, which I found so admirable.

"Of course, Mr Schwarz is in excellent hands here. You are of my opinion, Mr Schwarz?" The doctor continued without waiting for Juergen's reply. "I will personally ensure that only experienced staff looks after you, both in terms of therapy and care." I asked: "And what therapies do you want to prescribe? There really isn't much left that is possible and could justify a stay in a rehabilitation clinic."

"We will begin with physiotherapy. I will discuss the possibilities with our Mr... To start with, it's going to be half an hour of physiotherapy. That's a good beginning, isn't it, Mr Schwarz?" I heard this tone of voice from doctors several times recently. That's how they spoke to people they didn't consider equal. The tone you use when you think a person is far below you, perhaps even slightly simple-minded. Simply a Parkinson's patient. How often had I experienced in the last few weeks that someone who trembles is not taken seriously.

"Juergen, what do you think? Do you really want to stay here for half an hour of physiotherapy without being thoroughly examined and getting a competent second opinion? Wasn't it enough what has already happened here? It makes far more sense to leave the clinic and have an examination. I can look after you and find a physiotherapist to come to your house for these few exercises."

"Sophie, you have heard what Dr.…. said. Everything will be fine. Why don't you let him try first? It's not as bad as you make it out to be." This was how the man who had recently been screaming in pain spoke. I didn't know whether to be sad or angry. A knot formed in my stomach, in which these two feelings merged. Juergen turned to the doctor: "Let's hope the physiotherapist is good enough to convince my partner." He laughed. The head physician joined in the laughter and helped Juergen, who had sat on the walker seat because no other seat had been offered, stand up. "You see", he said to me, still laughing, "it's all not even half as bad."

"You know that this isn't true. But Mr Schwarz is the boss, not me. He is the one to decide. It is his body and his life. Have a nice day." I turned to Juergen and asked: "Shall I accompany you to your room, or is Mr … doing so?" "I think he has more important things to do." I would have loved to shout to him that I also had more important things to do. The knot in my belly became bigger and bigger. My children, my work, my life. But what good would that have done? So I helped him to get into his room, where I still managed to say goodbye to him, albeit much cooler than usual.

"I have to look after June now. Call when you know when your physiotherapy appointment will be. I should be there." "Why do you want to go already?" Juergen asked, astonished. "You stay longer usually. Yes, I will tell you about the appointment. But you don't have to be there." "Are you serious after everything that happened during your last physiotherapy?" "You are right. Are you angry? Why?" "Because I loved so much that you and the head physician laughed about my alleged overprotection. You have allowed yourself to be lulled into a false sense of security by someone who doesn't care about you and is putting your health at risk instead of leaving this place. This should be documented immediately and reported to your health insurance company. Nothing will ever change if people don't act against the mistakes of such irresponsible doctors. The doctor is only interested in the clinic's reputation. I don't want to argue; I need some peace now. But I didn't come here to witness such an unworthy spectacle; I'm not taking all this on myself. I wish I had travelled to Oberhausen." "Just because I'm not doing what you want? You said also that it is my body and my life. But that doesn't mean I don't desperately need you."

"Yes, to iron out the mistakes of the people you trust. It's good now, Jürgen. I want to clear my head with June. Get in touch. Maybe you'll think about everything again in peace. See you soon.'

I looked him in the eye for a long time, didn't kiss him goodbye, but turned away with tears in my eyes and left the clinic.

Chapter 22

I was tired and desperate, and I felt the little rest of my strength was pouring out of my feet to seek the ground. I fixed my gaze on the ground and the puddle of my remaining strength, which I thought to see before me. But these were tears that ran unstoppable from my eyes and dropped to the ground. I didn't even have the strength to sob or wipe my eyes. So, I just let the tears continue to flow. June laid her head on my lap. Her warmth and closeness helped me because my whole body was trembling.

"What's wrong with you"? I heard a voice behind me. Too weak to look behind me, I only asked: "Who wants to know that?" "It's me, James. Do you still not recognise me? Can I help you?" Nothing surprised me anymore. I didn't care where James came from, whether he was real or a fantasy, whether I was simply crazy. It didn't matter, nothing mattered. And so I began to talk to him.

"Help me? I don't think anybody can help me. I believed I would be able to help Juergen and felt that he trusted me. Never could I have imagined a situation like the one I'm in. This intelligent man allows himself to become the plaything of all medical staff even though so many mistakes have been made. Although he is not alone, he doesn't rebel against them and lets everything happen. And then I even get exposed, accused of being ignorant, of dramatising, while I am busy repairing the mistakes made by those supposed to be those who know. For heaven's sake, in what kind of scary film did I end up in, James? What have you done to Juergen? And with me also. I am only a shadow of myself and want to be with my children again. I want my own life back. Why do you and Juergen hold me captive."

"We don't hold you captive. You are doing that on your own. In contrast to many of those involved here, you have a conscience, a sense of honour, and dedication to the art of healing and the people who need it. In addition, Juergen is not just anybody for you, any patient. It is a horrible situation, and I am very shocked by what I have to witness. This is not medical art. I cannot explain why so many things go wrong in Juergen's treatment and why he ends up with such people. Have you read my essay

"The Hospital Pupil", which I published in the year 1800? In this essay, I have summarised what I consider indispensable as a prerequisite for entering the medical profession." "No, James, I haven't. Do you want to tell me about it? Why don't you join us, or don't you like dogs?" "Who couldn't like this dog?" James grinned, and strangely, his grin reminded me of Juergen. He sat down with us and began to talk. "I don't know how much you know about me as a person. I know you know very much about the Shaking Palsy, which was named after me at some point because I also wrote an essay about the Shaking Palsy. But about myself? What do you know about me?"

"I know that you were born the same year as Samuel Hahnemann, the founder of the homoeopathy, in 1755. And you died nineteen years earlier than he did. I always celebrated this as a triumph of homoeopathy over conventional medicine. Sorry, that is silly, I know. In addition, you are sitting beside me and talking to me. Perhaps I should be in one of the madhouses of your time. I know about them as well. And your father was a doctor in London, my favourite city."

"Homoeopathy. I never cared about it and still don't quite understand it. Perhaps you can explain it to me one day. Yes, my father was a doctor, and I have been fascinated by medicine for as long as I can remember. But not only medicine. I wanted to learn everything and to read—natural history, anatomy, physiology, chemistry, Latin, Greek, and French. And I painted, oh, I loved painting so much. How happy I was when my father finally began to train me to become a surgeon. Did you know that at the age of twenty, I was one of the first medical students at the London Hospital Medical College? For six months." James looked pensively in front of him, revelling in his memories. "I have also studied at James Hunter. Have you heard about this Scotsman, who is said to be the founder of modern surgery?"

"Yes, I heard of him". My tears had stopped, and I listened to him, completely mesmerised. "Wasn't he the man who obsessively dissected people and animals, even living animals? I remember best that he operated on people, constantly trying new methods, and dared to perform operations nobody else dared to do. When a patient died, he is supposed to have said: 'It is probable I killed him', only to dedicate himself to the next patient, or should I better say, victim. This is what I remember to have read in the book "The Knife Man" by Wendy Moore."

"Yes, that's the way he was. And you could learn so much from him. He was not afraid to try things out on himself and was driven to find solutions and explanations for things that could not be explained until then. But the times were like this. Everything was on the move—the industrial revolution. Your and my London grew and grew. The beautiful Hoxton neighbourhood where my family and I lived and where my father had his practice, with parks and good air, gradually became a part of the city where you couldn't dare to go out at night. It wasn't any better during the day, either. My reputation as a doctor protected me, and I looked after poor people who couldn't pay for my work. There was no sewerage system in large parts of the city. I don't need to explain what that meant. Because people couldn't afford the rent anymore, more and more people lived in the flats, and sometimes they slept in a kind of shift system. And the gin, what this booze has done. The poverty, the crime, the stench." James stopped for a short time, sunk in memories. He took a deep breath to gather himself and continued.

"I knew if I wanted to help people, I would have to know as much as hardly any other person. I would have to be better than I could imagine at that point. Never would I be allowed to stop learning. I would never be allowed to make a mistake because the consequences of my failure would not have to be borne by me but by the person I did it to, whether through negligence, ignorance or for whatever reason. Therefore, I had to fight all the sources of mistakes by learning. I didn't want to become like Hunter. I wanted to have his knowledge, but I didn't want to forget the human being I was treating. I didn't want to see only the body I treated but wished to be warm-hearted. As a proper doctor, you have to forget yourself. You have to be prepared to ignore your needs and be there for the people to help them as well as you can. In our hands lies the life of people. We must never forget this responsibility, but it must never make us arrogant because then we make mistakes, and we must avoid mistakes wherever possible. We must be aware that even if we have learnt a lot and even more, we still don't know everything and always must continue learning."

While James was saying this, tears got in his eyes, too. "It shocks me how many in my profession have forgotten all this. Perhaps they had never realised this at all. A good doctor has to be a good human being. He must be humble. The medical

102

profession requires complete dedication and the willingness to forget yourself. Nothing should be more important than the person who is treated and to learn. It begins with the education and even before that. In my time, young people started with their medical education to become doctors at fourteen or fifteen. Latin, Greek and French they had to master, at least Latin perfectly. They had to be capable of painting because only what you paint yourself can be fully grasped and internalised. Today, students only look at pictures in books or on the machines you call computers. Which medical student still paints himself while dissecting or afterwards to feel each structure? Of course, the sciences also have to be studied, in my time in Latin., Read, read, read, learn, learn, learn. Anyone who is not fully committed to his education and unprepared to sacrifice everything for it has no place in medicine. When I hear that medical students get together at the weekend to get drunk, they should give up their medical studies immediately. When they take their studies seriously, they don't have any time for such things. It is essential to know as much as possible so a doctor can always make the connection to the whole organism. If you want to relax, don't reach for beer and liquor but for a book, for example, about botany and always have a notebook and a pencil at hand because only when taking notes or making some sketches can you read and learn correctly. If money worries plague you during your studies, all free time has to go. The studies then take longer, so you have the opportunity to work, but you can never save on the content."

He had talked himself into a rage. But my heart opened. Yes, this was how it was meant to be. And countless people undoubtedly were and are of the same convictions. But what is the general situation in our healthcare system and universities today? No matter what convictions and knowledge a person in a medical profession has, how much of it have they to sacrifice for the profit of the organisation running the institution? How many people does a doctor in private practice have to treat in his surgery daily to cover his costs?

"What happened with Juergen's operation must not happen", James continued. "The surgeon has ignored the whole organism. He hasn't even asked a colleague who specialised in the Shaking Palsy for advice, but he stumbled over his arrogance. He had enough time; it wasn't a matter of life or death. Then, there is no time to ask for a second opinion, and the doctor has to rely solely on his knowledge and ability and act immediately. But in Juergen's case? There was enough time."

"It isn't better in this rehabilitation clinic, James. Do you think the physiotherapist is going to lose her job or is sent to further education because of the giant mistake that could have destroyed Juergen's life? I don't understand why Juergen is staying there. I would love to bring him to safety and to look for the right treatments and therapists in peace. His GP referred him to the recommended clinic, and from there, he was sent to this rehabilitation clinic. He usually always researches everything thoroughly and only wants the best, but he allows himself to be pushed around like this. He wants me to watch and immediately rectify any consequences of mistakes."

"Sophie, that's the fear. The Shaking Palsy causes fear and arises from fear. The person slowly loses control over his body, so he clutches at any straw. You are the most important person for Juergen, but you can't do operations; you haven't learnt this. Concentrate on helping him, not on your pain or your lack of understanding of his behaviour. There is still a lot more to come. Mobilise your knowledge, learn more and act. Be strong for Juergen so he can come back into his own strength. And if he realises that the knowledge of those treating him is limited and that no one can take his life and illness away from him, then at some point, he will transfer all the responsibility to you. Every person suffering from the Shaking Palsy should have such a person by their side."

"And what about me?" I asked timidly. "Didn't you listen? Willingness to forget yourself. This is what makes a good doctor. And please don't say you're not a doctor but an alternative practitioner. This is why I was talking about the medical profession."

During the whole time, I had sat quietly with June's head on my lap. After the flood of tears had stopped, I closed my eyes and focused entirely on the conversation with James. When I opened my eyes, I saw no James, but I could feel the weight of a hand on my shoulder. I turned around, but nobody was there. "Strange", I thought. But I felt strengthened and consoled. Two hundred years ago, a man had already written and demanded all this, which I thought to be a matter of course and, with me, most people. Juergen had just had bad luck for who knows what reasons. But there was still me. I now had to find a way through this jungle for him, help him believe in himself again, and regain his strength. There must be a reason why we met. "Come on, June, let's go. Both of us have to put Juergen back on his feet again. He has deserved it."

Chapter 23

"Good morning, Mr Schwarz and Ms, sorry, I don't know your name. My name is…, and I was introduced to your case and everything that went wrong. First of all, I would like to apologise for the mistakes made by my colleague, even if they are inexcusable from my point of view. I promise to do everything I can to reduce the consequences of these mistakes. And I am quite optimistic that we can achieve much if we work together."

The physiotherapist, who at first glance seemed very likeable and who I estimated to be in his early thirties, came towards us as Juergen and I were on our way to the treatment room. "Please come in first, and then tell me everything from your point of view and which problems you're having now so we can find solutions together. I have taken time until lunchtime, Mr Schwarz, to manage a proper beginning."

I watched as the physiotherapist registered Juergen's movements and posture with a trained eye and offered the proper support at the right time. "Thank you" was my only thought. "Thank you for Juergen finally getting the right help."

We spend two hours together. We analysed Juergen's situation step by step for two hours and worked out a detailed treatment concept. "It would be best if you could accompany Mr Schwarz to our appointments as often as possible so we can coordinate how you can continue the therapy back home", he said. Completely new tones. "That is no problem. Do I see correctly that Mr Schwarz has no other appointments, only the ones with you?" "Yes, that's true. They are probably afraid of making mistakes again or overburdening Mr Schwarz in the current situation. But that's perfectly all right. The three of us will manage."

We said goodbye until the next day, and I accompanied Juergen to his new room. In the morning, he had been transferred to another ward. I didn't know why, and Juergen and I didn't have time to discuss it until now. This room looked far more like a hospital room.

Juergen was utterly exhausted from the therapy and fell into his bed. "What do you think of this man?" he asked me. "As far as I can see, you have finally been assigned to a competent person. What do you think?" "I believe he is good, and I feel much better with him. Our exercises did me a world of good, even though I am utterly exhausted now." "I will leave and let you get a rest and return later. But can you explain why they put you into this room and this ward?" "They didn't tell me. They only said they could treat me better here and that I wouldn't have to go to the cafeteria anymore." "But you must move, you must walk." "Let's wait for one or two days. I only want to sleep now. Are you staying?" "When you're sleeping, you can't do much. Then, I take care of myself and the dog. I can be back around 3 pm. Is that fine for you?" "Of course. Thank you, my sun. You can't imagine how thankful I am. Yesterday, I thought you were gone because I behaved so stupidly." "I would never do so without telling you before. Or without shouting the information at you", I said laughingly. "Do you really believe I could behave so stupidly and irresponsibly, Juergen?" "No, but this thought simply came and didn't want to leave." I took him into my arms and held him tight until the fierce trembling that his body had been gripped by because of the exertion had subsided to the gentle vibration that had become so familiar to me.

"Just take your medicine before you go to sleep." "I would have forgotten it." "I know. I gave him his medicine, waited until he took it, kissed him goodbye, and left the room. Then I looked around the ward and saw that Juergen couldn't stay there. This was the ward for the care cases. I had to think of Juergen's words about how difficult it had been for him when he was in that clinic to get his medication fixed, to be confronted with people who were in the final stages of the disease. I could empathise with it. Nobody knows exactly how this disease will progress in the person and how bad or not it will develop. But the person needs all his strength and confidence to achieve the best results and enjoy his life despite and with the disease. In combination with all the other problems, such a confrontation was counterproductive. I saw a doctor and turned to him.

"Excuse me, please, I am Mr Schwarz's partner and would like to know why Mr Schwarz, capable of walking and not being a care case at all, was put onto this ward?" "I can't tell you this. I only know that he has an inflamed surgical scar and that the nurses on the other ward couldn't treat it." "Perhaps you understand that these

107

surroundings cannot be beneficial for his recovery, and I ask you to move him back again today. I already said that I am taking care of the treatment of the scar if the nurses can't do so." "Oh, he's only in his room, except when he goes to therapy. He'll manage. It's not so easy to transfer him back."

It was always the same. I said goodbye and went to my flat. Once there, my plan was set. Juergen would move in with me. We would go to the clinic for physiotherapy every day. I already treated the scar; this way, nobody could tinker with it anymore. For further exercises, which we could then do the rest of the day, I would discuss with the physiotherapist and Juergen. My treatments I could do far better in the privacy of this flat. But how should I make it understandable to Juergen?

"Do you know where you have landed?" I began the conversation. "What do you mean by that?" "They have put you on the ward for care cases." "I can't believe that. It's quite a nice room, although this nursing bed irritates me a bit." "Come on, let's walk across the ward so you can see for yourself." I held my hand towards Juergen. He hesitated. "Do I have to look at it? I told you how hard this is for me. It's enough when you tell me." "No, of course, you don't have to. I only thought in case you don't believe me." "I believe you. I only don't understand why they did so. I want my old room back." "While you were sleeping, I already spoke to the ward physician. No chance. Your scar would need treatment, and the other nurses couldn't do it, I was told." "What's all this rubbish?" said Juergen. "I won't let anyone, but you treat it anyway. What are we going to do now? This physiotherapist is excellent; you know my attitude towards cancelling the rehab. I am worried that I'll be left with the costs or that, if I need rehab again, they won't approve it if I drop out. Anyway, we almost managed a week here." "I have an idea", I said and explained my plan to Juergen. "Not bad, but if they kick me out, I can get the same problems as if I drop out myself." "They will not kick you out; you can believe me. They made too many mistakes, and they know it. Sending you to this ward is only one of them. Just tell me if you want to."

Juergen closed his eyes for a while and considered. Then he looked deeply into my eyes before answering: "I don't want all of this here. I never wanted it. But what possibilities do I have? Do you think I can manage to get to the flat?" "Of course, you can manage; if not, I will carry you." Juergen laughed briefly when he imagined this. "You can do a lot, Sopherl, but this could be too much even for you." "There are still a few hours until nightfall. I'll pack your bag now, and then we'll make off together with your walker." "Should we also steal a horse or a few apples on the way?" Juergen smiled at me, full of joie de vivre. "Not today, because of the bag I only have on hand left. But we can talk about it tomorrow." He kissed me, and together, we packed his bag.

"What will we say if a nurse wants to know what we are doing?" "Exactly what we are doing. That you move into my flat and only return to your physiotherapy. And that she should enjoy your lunch." "We can't do that", Juergen doubted. "And when she doesn't let us go?" "Mr Schwarz, let me worry about that. You are a self-determined adult, and this is not a prison. So keep your head up, chest out and move forward, soldier."

With these words, I opened the door. Juergen took a deep breath, stretched as far as his damaged back would allow, and left the room. We were on our way to the lift when a nurse approached us. "Mr Schwarz, you cannot go on a walk anymore. Soon, you will get a syringe against thrombosis, and it's time for dinner. We don't like it when the patients are not in their rooms." "But I go with my partner to her flat, have my dinner there and will stay there for the rest of the night. If you would please excuse me, the lift has just arrived." Juergen smiled at the completely baffled nurse and stepped into the lift. I also entered the lift, and as its doors closed, we laughed without restraint. "Like Bonnie and Clyde", Juergen burst into laughter. "Have you seen her face? Wonderful! A shame you don't have a camera in situations like this." Laughing and talking the way to my, now our, flat was shorter than we had thought, and as June welcomed Juergen as lovingly as only a dog can, all was almost right again in our little world.

"Do you think there'll be trouble?" Juergen asked as he snuggled into bed. "No, but if there will be trouble, simply leave it to me. You concentrate on your loose screws becoming tight, so you can finally show me the world. I didn't think you meant a rehabilitation clinic in the Black Forest."

"Sophie?" "Yes, Juergen?" "This is how it's meant to be. You by my side, and when I reach out of bed, there is June, and I can stroke her beautiful fur. It should always be that way." "Then we have to see how we can make it come true", I said and carefully cuddled up to him; I immediately fell into a deep sleep.

"You've caused quite an excitement", the physiotherapist greeted us the next day with a laugh. "Nobody has ever experienced something like this. A patient who grabs his bag and leaves. Splendid, simply splendid. Nobody else but me expected you to return. But somehow, I knew. And you did the right thing. I was stunned when I heard which ward you had been taken to. Shall we start with our exercises now?" And we started. Every day, Juergen worked intensely with the physiotherapist. He learned to lie down and get up, considering his loosened implant. Intensive exercises to build up muscles in the back and the legs were on the programme, walking without a walker and again and again the correction of Juergen's bent-forward posture, which had become very obvious since the operation.

"Do you know these machines where people used to put children who didn't want to sit upright in the past? I will build something like this for you soon with a chin rest", the physiotherapist threatened in jest, hitting Juergen's sense of humour exactly, which made him much more motivated to work through his sometimes painful and strenuous exercises than he would have been in a severe atmosphere.

After the therapy, we walked back to our flat, where Juergen rested while I went on a long walk with June. Then we had lunch, and afterwards, we went for walks, first in the park of the rehabilitation clinic. Then, when Juergen learned how to get in and out of the car, we went on a short excursion in the surrounding area with June. In the middle of the third week, Juergen dared to kick a ball for June again for the first time. Only once, but the beginning of new football games was made. In the mornings and the evenings, I treated Juergen's scar, and once a day, I gave him a massage of the reflex zones, which did him a lot of good. I also treated his back and chest daily, where possible, to relieve any tension. Juergen straightened up more and more, became more confident in walking every day and finally started to make plans for the future again.

"Sopherl, can we find a restaurant in this deserted area worth our visit? I want to invite you to dinner." "That is an excellent idea. I passed a rather trustworthy-looking restaurant with a large terrace with June. I didn't look at the menu, though, as I didn't think we'd go out." "Shall we try it tomorrow?" "With pleasure." "Sopherl, we'll have made it in three days, then we can finally go home." "Juergen, we'll have to talk about that in peace. I can't stay in Ludwigsburg forever. You know that. Have you made any plans yet?"

"It seems to work quite well with your children and ex-husband. It can stay that way until I can manage on my own again. However, I don't know if I want to do without you again." "Leave the bedroom eyes. Then you have to come with me to Oberhausen. It will not work any other way?" "I can't stay with you. What about my work, my stuff?" Juergen was shocked. "And what about my children, my work, my house, my pony, my cat and my life? Have you ever thought about this?" "Don't you like being with me?" "Juergen, that's not the point. We hadn't met when we were twenty, building up a life together, but only a year ago when each of us had his own life. When you want to bring these two lives together, the only way is to compromise. I've already done a lot, and even my children, although they don't even know you. But they will always be my priority. I can't see how you can get along on your own shortly. I think living in Oberhausen for a while will be the most sensible option. You've already lived in other cities of this world."

Juergen didn't seem to like the idea. His face darkened. I felt sorry for him because I had been thrilled to see him in a good mood. "I don't want to spoil your good mood. But sometimes, one has to be realistic. And admit it, I am very generous. I want to share my home with you and not leave you to your fate. And in addition, you can play football better in a garden than on a balcony." But my encouragement didn't reach Juergen. "But what about the children? What if they don't like me? I'm a stranger to them and an intruder." "We have to find a way to make it work—a lot of consideration, utterly open communication. Flat-sharing can only work in this way. I certainly didn't imagine it being like this. But now that's the way it is. We have to think about it in peace during the next couple of days, and we will find the right solutions." "Are you sure?" "What does sure mean? But what can we do? Hold our breath until you no longer have Parkinson's and no messed-up spine surgery? I can't hold my breath for that long. I prefer to look for solutions."

"Everything sounds so easy when you're talking about things." "Because it is easy. If you want to, you can always find a way. This doesn't mean that everything is going to work without quarrels and some bitching. I know my daughter well enough. But we have to go through this. Do you know another way?" "I could try to find some sort of assisted living for the time I need to become fit again." "My children aren't that bad, so you must do this. Or do you really want to?" "No, not at all. But you are right, I won't manage alone for a while. But I can't just impose myself on you." "Let that be my concern. Anyway, I can't stay much longer in Ludwigsburg or somewhere else without my children. It's impossible. Can you understand that?" "Yes, I can. I will think about it. But something different. Would you like to watch football? Germany is playing today." "Of course, you know I want to." That was the end of the topic for today. Both of us had to think about the problems on our own first. A football match as a distraction came in handy.

I knew that Juergen in no way wanted to move into my house. He didn't want to give up his independence, and I could understand that too well. My independence was essential to me as well. But life had different plans for us at the moment. I didn't even want to imagine the reactions in Oberhausen if I turned up with Juergen and his bag and baggage. It probably wouldn't be pure joy. I was sure my son would give Juergen a fair chance, but my daughter? Even if children knew why their parents had separated and that parents could find a new partner after a divorce, it was something completely different if he moved into the house without a prior time to get to know each other and if he had to fight with health issues. I still had some time to think about it and prepare it.

Chapter 24

The visit to the restaurant was a big success. A piece of normality was perfect for both of us. "I would love to drive back to our flat so you can drink a glass of wine to celebrate the day, but my back doesn't allow me to", Juergen said regretfully. "I don't mind at all. I very much enjoy simply being here with you, talking and having a good meal. That is far better than on the ward for care cases, right?" "That was simply an outrageousness. What do you think?" "I think there was a certain amount of spitefulness involved. But we've spoilt it for them. Do you want to go to the final consultation with the head physician tomorrow?" "In any case. I am curious to know if he says anything about my escape and what further treatment he will suggest. And I want to celebrate my last treatment with Mr.…. This man has helped me a lot." "He did indeed", I agreed with him. "By the way, as you requested, I've made an appointment for a control computed tomography with your wonderful surgeon. It's at the beginning of next week." "That early? I am astonished." "Well, not only one but three screws got loose. This worked. And his secretary is rather nice." "I can't believe we are leaving here in two days to see if Ludwigsburg is still standing." "Exactly. I will do some shopping, and then we wait for what the computed tomography will show. After that, we decide what we will do next. What do you think?" "I agree. That sounds well."

"I ordered this, especially for you," Juergen said as the sun set picturesquely behind the trees. "Only for you." I cuddled up in his arms and enjoyed his warmth and the sunset. He had proved his fragility, yet I felt safe, secure, and protected with him. Aren't we all fragile?

The farewell from the rehabilitation clinic's head physician was very frosty, as was to be expected. He advised an urgent appointment with the surgeon and a computed tomography. "We've already made an appointment. Until now, the last three screws are doing their job, but who knows for how long", Juergen said. "We did a good job of getting you back to normal after the initial discomfort", said the doctor with a touch of smugness that was entirely out of place here. I waited for Juergen to reply. He usually didn't miss such an opportunity. "We could have a good argument about the "we", but then I don't have the time to say a proper farewell to the only specialist in this clinic who has helped me. Take good care of Mr.... He is worth it. If you will excuse me now", said Juergen, got up and turned to me. "Sopherl, are you ready now, or would you like to clarify anything with Mr...?" "No, Juergen, let's leave to thank Mr... Have a nice day", I said to the chief physician, and we left his office.

The farewell to the physiotherapist was very warm. He provided Juergen with a lot of advice. "I know you won't follow them, but your partner will remind you. I want to apologise again for what has been done to you in this house, and I hope I could mitigate the consequences. It was an honour getting to know you." "The honour is all mine, Mr..." Juergen answered. Both men were deeply moved. "And my heartfelt thanks. You have done far more than something. Do well and look for a job worthy of you and your skills." There it was again, Juergen's smile as he shook the physiotherapist's hand.

There were tears in my eyes. Since Juergen had come to the clinic for the operation, he had never been shown such respect as he had just received, a respect that every human being deserves and that he must never lose just because he needs medical help. I could only say: "My heartfelt thanks and all the best to you". And I took the physiotherapist into my arms because I couldn't find any words. Then Juergen called: "That's it. Off to new shores." He took my hand, and we left the clinic holding hands. We put our luggage into my car, and June jumped onto her seat. I started the engine and opened the convertible roof. As I wanted to drive off, Juergen took my hand, kissed it and said: "Thank you, thank you, my sun. I wouldn't have got through it without you. And now step on the gas. Away from these inhospitable walls and off to freedom. Freedom at last." And I set off.

"I've never been so happy to arrive home because I only ever wanted to be out and about in the world. But now I feel this is the most beautiful place in the whole world", Juergen said with bright eyes. A deep sigh followed by a dark cloud spread over his face, making the glare fade. "Do you think I can do it again, travelling the world, free from doctors, hospitals, operations and bad rehabilitation clinics? Or was this the beginning of the end?"

I took both of his hands into mine and looked at him. "Please, look into my eyes now to see that I'm only telling the truth." Juergen did what I had asked him to.

114

"This, Juergen, was definitely not the beginning of the end. We will manage all that. It will last a while, I think three or four months, but then you will be completely fit to travel." "Why are you so sure about that?" Juergen looked at me, full of doubts. "I wish I had a bit of your optimism." "As simple as that, because from now on, I won't let anyone interfere with me anymore. Let's look at what's positive. Three of the six crews are still tight and have already held the implant for three weeks. Now, we have to make sure that it stays that way and that you finally become free of pain. I have already made a plan. I only need a prescription from your professor and a computed tomography. Nothing else."

Juergen looked at me questioningly. "And why only now? Why didn't you do it before?" "You can't be serious, Juergen." I tried to stay calm. Nevertheless, tears welled up in my eyes. "Have you forgotten that you didn't want to leave the rehabilitation clinic and didn't complain when the first operation didn't work? You allowed me to support you, and I did everything possible under the difficult conditions. Accusations against me are completely inappropriate." "Have I caused a lot of damage?" Juergen asked contritely. "Nothing that can't be repaired, but you could already feel much better. I want to concentrate on what lies before us, not the past. I only have to know what you want. When we have the appointment with the professor, I don't wish to witness how you let yourself be talked into the next nonsense, the next operation."

"A third operation? What makes you think that?" Sheer horror at this thought was written all over Juergen's face. "Because he is a surgeon, and a surgeon can only deal with a problem with a scalpel, at least if he thinks like this gentleman." "I can assure you, Sophie, I won't allow to be operated again under any circumstances. Can I now take you into my arms, or do I have to fear you will scratch and bite?" "Why don't you try it out?" I replied with a smile and snuggled into his arms.

Chapter 25

Seeing the waiting area of the surgical outpatient clinic, I was happy to have snacks and something to drink with us despite Juergen's teasing. It was just a mystery to me how Juergen was supposed to endure a longer waiting time on these chairs, which were not conducive to the back's health. First, we were sent to the computed tomography, which started without any waiting time. Back in the outpatient clinic, our patience was tested for several hours. Finally, we were granted access to a small room with an examination table, a desk with a desk chair and a small bandage trolley. Now we had to wait again. Juergen sat down on the examination table. After all, we could already hear the professor's voice through the thin walls, and we learned Mr M's femoral neck fracture was healing well and that Ms S's forearm fracture did not look good.

Finally, the professor rushed into Juergen's examination area with his coattails waving and said, in a voice that was undoubtedly audible throughout the ambulance, "Good afternoon, Mr Schwarz; what have you done with my beautiful operation?" At least he could laugh about his joke, but he stopped when he found out we did not share his humour. "We can't leave it this way, of course. It would be best if you had another operation, but this time, we have to operate from the front of your body. Then you are going to have a scar on your belly as well, but there is no other way to get it stable." Juergen looked at him, stunned. "A third operation? And what do you want to do exactly?" "Don't worry. We open your abdominal region where the implant is attached to the spine and secure the loosened screws from there. We can't do it from the back. Then you are restored in no time, and we will remove the implant in a year."

"So, another two operations because the first two achieved outstanding results. Not with me." Juergen's face had become red with rage. I didn't know him this way. "But it has to be done; how else do you imagine we can repair the damage? And what are you accusing me of?" "Sophie, can you please take over?" Juergen asked me. "I have to gather myself first." "What is your partner supposed to do? Be reasonable; the implant has to be fixed."

"Mr Schwarz and I are aware of this." My voice was calm, crystal clear, and sharp like a scalpel. "We only disagree about the procedure and will not discuss it. From you, I need a prescription for an orthosis that allows us to immobilise the lumbar spine as much as possible and an appointment for computed tomography in three months." Now, it was the professor's turn to redden in the face and be on the verge of losing control. "An orthosis? It's not been used for ages. This reduces the back muscles far too much. Today, operations are the only way." "We wouldn't have this conversation had the operation-way been successful. After two unsuccessful attempts, you can't seriously expect us to give you another chance. According to the motto, all good things come in threes. Would you be so kind as to issue the prescription now? Or do you expect Mr Schwarz to see another surgeon? Surely, you agree with me that he has suffered enough."

"Then Mr Schwarz has to sign a confirmation that he rejected my treatment and that I am not responsible for the results." "I think we better not do that because the current state wasn't caused by Mr Schwarz but his trust in you and the rehabilitation clinic."

"But there is something else", the professor began, not responding to my statement. "I found a note in your medical record from the billing department that you haven't fully paid my bill. The amount of € 249,78 is still due. If you were to pay this in the next few days?" Juergen already wanted to assure this, when I stopped him. "Excuse me, Juergen, but your health insurance didn't pay the total amount of this bill because the billing department made a mistake. They cannot charge for a certain item with such an operation. This is why you only paid what the insurance said was the right amount." "You are right, I remember", he said.

"But you are my patient, Mr Schwarz, not the insurance. We don't want to argue about such a small amount of money?" "With pleasure and very gladly in court also", I interrupted. "Operation failed, caused the patient unnecessary pain, billed incorrectly, and you seriously demand Mr Schwarz to accept all this without any comment and even pay for what is not legal? When this money is so important to you, we will be happy to offset it against the claims for damages that a court would determine against you. But you can also do without it and be happy that we'll leave the botched treatment alone because we have more important things to do. Just issue the

117

prescription and arrange the appointment in three months. We only need a computed tomography; we will not have to take your valuable time."

The professor grabbed the prescription pad without saying another word and then asked a secretary to make an appointment with him. "I want to know how you're doing. Should you decide on a third operation, please contact me. And never start an argument with your partner. You can't win it." He wanted to laugh cheerfully when Juergen said: "Please stop these bad jokes at my partner's expense. Throughout this difficult time, she has been the only one who never was wrong, recognised and respected her limits, and who is now forced to take over my treatment to prevent further damage to me. I will not come for a third or a fourth operation, but I will do what I should have done right at the beginning – trusting my partner. See you in three months."

Juergen leaned on me to get up from the examination table, didn't look at the professor again and left the room. "Sophie, are you coming?" "See you in three months", I also said, took the prescription and followed Juergen.

"Now we are free, at least for three months. And what are we going to do with our freedom?" Juergen asked when we left the hospital. "Looking for a good orthopaedic technician who has time as soon as possible."

Chapter 26

We found an excellent orthopaedic technician, and Juergen soon became more agile with the help of the orthosis. The pain that careless movements had caused didn't occur with the stabilisation the orthosis gave him. A calm everyday life started with a lot of exercise, manual treatments, and never-ending conversations. Juergen liked to tell me about his active time at the racing courses but also wanted to know more about me. "Your life has been far more interesting than mine", I laughed. "No, Sopherl, different, not more interesting. And the different things are always exciting for me."

His Parkinson's disease had utterly faded away into the background and was only noticeable when Juergen had once again delayed taking his medication for too long. It was still difficult for him to sit in a car for a longer time, so I could still not return home. I settled myself in Ludwigsburg and even bought an old bicycle after two overzealous Swabian traffic wardens asked me to pay a heavy fine for exceeding my parking time limit by precisely two minutes. Besides, I needed more training anyway.

"Juergen, we have to decide what to do. A couple of days have turned into two and a half months. I must return. I miss my children so much, and they also need me." "Why don't we look for a house and your children move here? I have already looked for houses, even with a stable for your pony and your daughter's pony." "Juergen, that is very kind of you, but I won't tear the children away from their familiar environment and their father. Or have you also made plans for him?" "It is so difficult for me to share you after all this time we had on our own. I also asked myself what would happen once we were there. You will be in your own life and I? What about me?" "Do you want to stay here and we look for someone to help you?" "No way. I now realise that I won't be able to look after myself completely for a while. But shall I barge into a family like that? 'I am Juergen, and I came to stay, and from now on, you have to share your mother with me?' If I was fit, I could introduce myself slowly. But I'm not fit now. I can't even drive a car at the moment. How am I supposed to get away when things get difficult?"

I looked at him unbelievingly. "Why should things become so difficult that you would have to leave? I will be there. Don't you trust me anymore?" What was going on in his head? It would never have occurred to me that Juergen might think he had to flee from my house because it could be somehow dangerous for him there. Perhaps there would be a dispute from time to time because a completely new sort of family had to develop, but what should have become so difficult that he had to flee? At that moment, Juergen was like a stranger to me, and I had thought of understanding him and getting to know him quite well during our time together. Then I remembered. Parkinson's disease is the disease of fear of losing control. I tried to look at things from Juergen's point of view. Of course, they hadn't met each other to protect my children yet. But my children had shown consideration for this man who was a stranger to them and had renounced their mother and their usual way of life. Was Juergen not aware of this?

I took him into my arms and held him tight. I felt these soft vibrations and held him even tighter. "I will never leave you alone unless you want me to, Juergen. Please believe me." Slowly, he released himself from my embrace, looked at me and said: "I would love to believe you so much. But I keep on asking myself why you should do so. My state is not a jackpot for a woman like you. And who knows, what else is going to happen." "Nobody knows that. But remember when we met, and you asked me if the knowledge that you are sharing your life with James Parkinson would change anything and I would prefer to leave? I stayed. Then I have two men at once – don't you begrudge me that?" A smile finally found its way into Juergen's eyes, which had previously reflected the whole world's suffering. "Aren't two men a bit much for a lady as delicate as you?" And the tension eased.

"There can always be conflicts. But they must be solved. What the children and I have already been through. And sometimes, even the sparks flew. But this doesn't mean one has to fear for one's mental or physical integrity. But, oh dear, do you like hot chocolate?" Juergen looked at me with wide, questioning eyes. "Hot chocolate? How do you come up with hot chocolate now?" "Because a dispute is settled with hot chocolate. At least between my son and me. My daughter is a bit more resentful, but she is a Virgo, so it's not her fault. But you will understand her; you're a Virgo, too." "In France, I am a Libra." "You", I laughed, "you are a bigger Virgo than most Virgos I know." Juergen was silent for a moment and smiled at me, his unique smile

I loved so much, and asked: "Sopherl, would you please make a hot chocolate?" "Why?" "Hasn't this been a small dispute?" "Not really." "But this way, we could practise having a dispute and the reconciliation with the help of a hot chocolate…" Now I smiled as well. "Okay, let's call it a dispute."

We agreed to give ourselves about a month before we moved to Oberhausen. This way, Juergen could become more robust, and I could prepare the children as much as possible. June became Juergen's walking coach. Only she convinced him that walking indeed had a right to exist, and he accompanied us on a short walking round almost every day. We trained all the everyday movement procedures, and finally, we looked for a remote car park, and after this long time, Juergen took a seat behind the steering wheel of his car. With a trembling heart, he confessed. I could see how his facial expression and posture changed as soon as his hands touched the steering wheel. Almost reverently, he set the automatic gearshift to 'Drive', slowly released the brakes and gently stepped on the accelerator. On this empty parking space, he tried at less than walking speed if and at which speed he could change from accelerator to the brakes. As he was satisfied with the results, he became more confident and faster. After almost an hour of exercising, he stopped. "There is no hindrance when operating the pedals, no pain, and the reaction time is as fast as it used to be. I can look in all directions without problems, even over my shoulder. The orthosis doesn't bother me at all; I can steer completely unhindered. Sopherl, may I drive us home, or do you want to drive yourself because you don't think I will manage?" "Are you sure?" I asked. "Yes, I am. And you know that I am very serious about it. I don't want to kill or hurt you or myself or anybody else." "Okay, but please tell me when I should take over and otherwise, please bring me home." And Juergen drove us back to his flat and said: "Now I'm ready to take on Oberhausen and its inhabitants. Perhaps we will have to make more breaks than usual on our way, but I will manage without any problems. Then, let's get into the adventure. Oh dear, me and children. I had reasons never to beget children, at least, none I know of."

"Juergen, the children already have a father. You won't have any educational job. You are my partner and become part of our household. That's all. They are already fifteen and seventeen. Get to know each other, and we will discover what will happen." "You always seem so relaxed and easy-going about what is a huge step. For you, everything is also different to what you have planned. How can you stay so calm?" "This says the man who proposes to me again and again. When you think this is already a problem, what did you think when you proposed to me? What does marriage mean to you?"

"That you belong to each other and stay together, being there for each other. But it's already becoming very one-sided at the beginning of our relationship. You have been doing far more for me than I did for you for weeks. I can hardly believe that you don't mind that. I'm feeling so inadequate. I tell you that I want to show you the world and you practise walking with me. That is far too early." "I also imagined it differently, but that's how it is now. We go through this time together and move on stronger as a result. In my life, nothing was like I had planned. I never wanted to marry or have children, and certainly not a divorce. These are just rough vital data. But life developed this way. I didn't want a situation like ours; I didn't even want a new relationship. But it is the way it is, and I don't begin to shout like a child until things change, but I act the way I think is correct and essential. I no longer drive myself crazy because what's the use of worries? Do they change anything, make anything more accessible, or prevent anything? No, no and no. So I don't worry, do my best and trust. I have promised to be there for you and that Parkinson's is no reason for obstruction for me." "Can you please promise me one more thing?" "You are funny; isn't it already enough?" I answered, laughing. "No, it is only enough when you promise to inform me immediately should anything change. If everything becomes too much for you, you don't like me anymore; you want to separate. Please be open and tell me as soon as possible so we can go on with dignity." "This, Juergen, I can promise you without hesitating. But please promise the same." "I promise. All this is very unusual for me. Until now, my life has only ever been about me. Now you've come into my life, and suddenly everything is different; there is a 'we'. So beautiful but still so strange."

I took his hands into mine. "Please be in the present; don't think of the past or the future. Be in the present and feel deep into yourself. How does this different life feel?" Juergen looked into my eyes for a very long time. Finally, he answered: "More beautiful than I ever could have imagined." "Let's do what we can to make it stay his way."

I prepared my children for my arrival with Juergen and made appointments with colleagues of mine for him so they could support his healing process with their therapeutic possibilities. Juergen managed very well with the orthosis and also during the nights when he wasn't wearing it. The fracture seemed to remain stable. How the bones recovered and what was happening with the screws the computed tomography would show us in a couple of weeks.

Juergen took his homoeopathic remedies and followed the instructions of the excellent physiotherapist when sitting down or getting up, lying down in bed or getting out of bed. However, except for short walks with June, he still insisted that walking wasn't necessary as long as cars existed.

Finally, the day of our departure to Oberhausen arrived. I packed our cars, and our mini-convoy set off on its way. How would it be? How would the children react towards Juergen? How would I manage to create space for Juergen in my house? These thoughts circled nonstop through my head, as they had done before. I was angry with myself for having hesitated so long to introduce Juergen to my children. But it had happened this way. Now, I somehow had to manage it. I saw no other possibility than living together. Still, the vertebrae injury prevented Juergen from living on his own. When the injury healed, we would see further. We will decide in a couple of weeks. The mobile snapped me out of my thoughts. Juergen's cheerful voice came out of the loudspeaker. "Sopherl, now I know what I have missed. Finally, on the road again. There are no problems to report. It's simply great. What about you?" "Everything is fine with June and me. Do you want to have a break?" "Not now. We can go for another couple of kilometres. Sophie?" "Yes, Juergen?" "Now I also believe that everything will be well. You are right. We will manage everything." "Yes, Juergen, we will manage everything.

Chapter 27

Soon, a new routine established itself. Juergen behaved very relaxed towards the children, which surprised him. He still didn't want to walk longer, but he began playing football with June again. Several times a day, June managed to lure him into the garden. It was challenging to say who enjoyed the game most, the man or the dog. It filled me with great joy to watch both of them, even though I kept a close eye on Juergen's movements, searching for insecurities in motion and standing, but nothing was to be seen, only his face beaming with joy.

"This reminds me of my youth. My parents had a Sheltie who also loved to play football. But I must say clearly that June is the far better football player", Juergen said when he returned to the house with June out of breath after a long football game.

"If I settle here," Juergen began, "I will need a neurologist for the prescription of my medication. Do you know a neurologist with the name of… I found him online; he should not be far away from here." "No, I don't know him, but I don't know many doctors." "Okay, I will make an appointment with him. Could you accompany me? After having had all these experiences recently, I believe it's far better to go there together. My trust is shattered." "That's absolutely understandable. Of course, I will accompany you, no problem. Just tell me when the appointment is."

As Juergen regained almost normal mobility and resumed his work and interests, I could also work peacefully and support the children in their activities. We all flourished.

Because an appointment with the neurologist was not possible for another two months, Juergen's doctor from Ludwigsburg agreed to send him prescriptions for the required Parkinson's medication by post for that long. Juergen had never taken the medication as instructed. "I've never stuck to a timetable, and I won't begin to do so because of some pills. I feel when I need the medication, I take it then and not at the time some doctor thinks would be right. They even told me to set an alarm to avoid missing a timely intake." "There are reasons for it", I began, and just as I wanted to explain them, Juergen interrupted me in complete contrast to his habit of letting everyone speak out. "I know, they explained it. I am in my body, so I decide. But Sopherl, is it possible that I need less dopamine?" "What do you mean by that?"

"As I said, I only take the pills when I feel that I need them or will need them soon. Now, I have been taking your homoeopathic drops and globules for quite a while, and more and more often, there are pills left at the end of the day. I wanted to ask you this for quite a while." "Yes, that's possible. Even when a lot of people don't want to believe it, homoeopathy really helps and all our other measures taken. Since when have you realised that you need less dopamine?" "It's a few weeks now. I began in Ludwigsburg after having returned from the rehabilitation clinic. But with all the excitement, I kept forgetting to tell you. I move far more than I used to be, just by playing with June. I haven't done that before." "Please continue to watch this; perhaps you can even bring yourself to do something more called sports. Can I convince you to go to a gym?" "Oh no, I don't want to become a Schwarzenegger. Perhaps we can discuss going running, but not as long as I still need the orthosis." "You love watching sports so much; don't you feel the desire to become active yourself?"

"You know, there are specialists for everything. I am a specialist in writing about sports. Athletes are the experts for doing sports." "Oh, Juergen, I can't laugh about this kind of joke because I know how important sports are for you. And I am a health specialist. Too many people have told me such remarks, thinking they were funny until life confronted them with the consequences of their rejection of sports. Then they didn't think it was funny at all. Your fracture of your vertebra might have been prevented, perhaps, with the help of enough strong muscles in your back. Even the dose of the medication can be reduced through sports, endurance-sports bodybuilding or even martial arts. You know how serious the effects of Parkinson's medication can be in the long run. The less you need, the better and wiser. I hope you will never regret being so stubborn about sports." "I am not stubborn. Let us wait for the results of the computed tomography. When the implant is save you can try to seduce me to go running. Watch out; I might run away from you." "As long as you return, I don't mind. The main thing is that you will be running."

We set up a workspace for Juergen with little effort, and within a short while, living together became so natural that it was difficult to imagine how it had been before when he was living in Ludwigsburg, and we only met occasionally. Juergen told me more about the exciting story of his life between the continents, always driven by rally car engines. There were so many anecdotes, so many stories. Although we laughed a lot, I always felt a touch of melancholy with Juergen. How much did he miss being on the road, the travelling, the roaring of the engines of cars and planes? How much did he suffer from no longer being part of this racing circus? How could I replace that for him?

One day, I asked him: "How sad are you that you're no longer travelling the world, always following the cars?" "Sometimes I arrived even before the cars", Juergen laughed. "But being serious, I can't tell you. It was a great, crazy time. What I don't miss is the pressure of deadlines. Rushing from the racing course to the airport and immediately preparing the story so it could be printed on time, only to rush to the next appointment. I also don't miss the discussions about what can be published and what not so you don't scare off advertisers. So many ingenious ideas were sacrificed for this. I miss travelling, but when I am fit again, I will show you the world, then we will travel, and if your children want to accompany us, they are welcome. Young people can't see enough of the world to learn. There is so much to see and learn when you're out and about. And it is problematic that so many colleagues don't contact me anymore. Out of sight, out of mind. Especially when close colleagues, who were also friends, seem to forget you – that hurts. But such is life. Whether through Parkinson's or any other life change, you will be forgotten once you are no longer even on the replacement bench of the racing circus or any other circus. You are not present in everyday life. Didn't this happen to you until now? The actors in the screenplay that is called Our Life change from act to act. Some manage to move on from one act to the next, but only very few. You have to live with it. But what I never had in my life before were a wife and children. This is a new adventure, and I am curious how it will turn out."

He took me into his arms. The orthosis pressed against my ribs, but I held him tight, too. "Sopherl, I always felt something was wrong with my body. Then I received the diagnosis of Parkinson's and first thought my world, my life had come to an end. But it always went on and on. I can still write, and now only what I want to write and when I want to do it. I want to look into the future, not the past. The future with you, although I can still not understand why you don't want to marry me. Yes, some things make me sad, but not so sad that I couldn't be happy anymore. And this is what I am here and now, happy."

Intermezzo

While telling our story, I almost forgot why Juergen and I wanted to write this book. It was meant to help people try different ways to live better with their James Parkinson's or any other disease. I feel that Juergen is patting my back, whispering into my ear, "Sopherl, don't forget that."

How could I forget anything from this intensive time? But there are no patent solutions that I could pass on. Let's start with homoeopathy. Every person needs different remedies. Hardly any kind of therapy is as individual as homoeopathy. It was an important foundation stone for Juergen's well-being and for needing less mediation. It helped to reduce some side effects of the Parkinson's medication and made some disappear.

I don't want to call our conversations therapies. But because I had to know so much for his treatment and, therefore, had a lot of questions regarding the symptoms, something developed that I would like to call a double trust. This helped him tell me many things he perhaps wouldn't have said to me as his partner, not wanting to hurt my feelings.

The consequences of the treatment errors in connection with the fracture of the vertebra made me introduce almost daily reflex zone massage, which did not only help the spine to recover but the complete man. Under this treatment, Juergen could relax entirely, and this is something challenging for a person who has Parkinson's. After the fracture had healed, Juergen received a cranio sacral treatment at least twice a week. It was to be seen clearly that this regular deep relaxation had a very positive effect on Parkinson's symptoms. The trembling became less; his voice became more robust and determined, and his posture improved.

I had massaged Juergen from time to time before when we lived apart. Later, I massaged him several times a week. His favourite massage was the Lomi-Lomi-Nui massage from Hawaii, a massage of the whole body for deep relaxation. Muscle tension in the area of the operation, as well as those tensions in the breast and neck typical for Parkinson's disease, lessened under this treatment. All this contributed to significantly easing the overall symptoms and led Juergen into a delightful balance he had lacked for decades.

The magnetic field blanket provided by a colleague helped us treat the damage to the implant. However, contrary to my assumption that it would only affect the fracture and the implant, we also realised that the positive effects affected the entire Juergen. His restless sleep calmed down, and his body regained its vigour.

Not to forget therapist June, who changed the sports refuser that Juergen had become over the years, passing into an enthusiastic ball athlete. No, he didn't run over a football field or did any headers and overhead kicks. Still, he ran over the uneven garden terrain, stood safely on one leg when shooting, and performed spins like a ballerina to get a ball, and no wind, weather, or sunshine could stop him from playing with June. His fitness improved, his mobility, reaction time, balance, and stability, and it was the pure love of life these two enjoyed whenever they could get hold of a ball. When packing our car for the journey, the man and the dog first put a ball into the car.

These things helped Juergen; it can be something different for another person. But it is essential never to let a diagnosis define oneself. You have a disease, but you are not the disease. Never allow a disease to control your life. This message was crucial for Juergen: "Never forget, Sopherl, leading a better life with Parkinson's or without, but in any case, leading a better life every single day."

Chapter 28

Juergen's tension grew with each passing day, which brought the computed tomography closer. "You feel better every day, and you need the orthosis much less. Why are you so nervous because of the examination?" I asked him. "What you are talking about is only a feeling. What will happen if this feeling betrays me and the facts show something else?" Juergen looked at me questioningly. "Would it help when I tell you that this is almost impossible as you are feeling so well and don't have any pain at all?" "Not really", said my sceptic. "I will be happy when I get the certainty I need to believe it."

I was sure the examination would show the complete healing of the fracture. I was a bit insecure about the condition of the implant. Would we have to get it removed because the screws were still loose, or the instability had aggravated so that it could cause any damage later on? I wanted to spare Juergen another operation. Up to now, he had been lucky that he had not suffered any severe after-effects from the anaesthetics. I didn't tell Juergen about my worries and always put them aside. "Do not create any self-fulfilling prophecies, Sophie", I told myself repeatedly.

"But we are only staying the planned five days. Can I rely on that?" I asked the evening before our departure. How would it be if Juergen was in his own flat again and the examination showed that he didn't need any more help? What would he decide?

"That's what we discussed. Of course, you can rely on it. I only want to gather a few things to bring here because I need them. What do you think? I like living together with you. It's not as tranquil as living alone, but it has a lot of advantages. Why are you looking at me so questioningly?" "Up to now, you haven't talked about your plans. That's why I'm a bit perplexed right now." "Oh, I assumed I had moved here permanently a few weeks ago. I understood it this way. If I got it wrong, I should better take my things back to Ludwigsburg instead of bringing more." Juergen looked very concerned, and I hurried to clear up the misunderstanding. "We should have talked about it more precisely. I also thought you had moved in permanently, but I was insecure. Have we agreed now and start the 'ant moving'?" Juergen smiled at me. "We agree, but what is an 'ant moving'?" "Very simple", I laughed. "Everyone takes as much as he can carry and starts running. This means for us that whenever we come to Ludwigsburg, we pack the car as full as we can." "That sounds like a good plan. But I want to keep the flat as a base camp."

"That is your decision, Juergen. I don't want to get involved in your financial matters." "Are you not interested in it?" "If you want to, we can talk about it sometime. But this isn't important for me. Let us enjoy being together and that our living together works perfectly. If I had been looking for a man to pay my bills, I would have decided on a different job." Juergen laughed. "That's a way to look at it. But when we're back, we should talk about a contribution on my part to the house and household costs. We should share them. Otherwise, I won't feel comfortable. I don't want to live at your expense. "It's nice that you want to talk about it. We will make a statement of costs, and I will tell you my bank account. Juergen?" "Yes, Sopherl?" "I like how easily we can clarify such things. There are no long discussions or arguments, as I know from many patients and others. That's great." "I'm thinking the same. And believe me, someday you will marry me. I have patience."

We arrived punctually at the hospital, where we had to wait for two hours before Juergen could get computed tomography. Sitting on the uncomfortable plastic chairs in the waiting area was difficult for Juergen, and in between, we strolled through the waiting area repeatedly. After the examination, we also had to wait, this time for the professor. After another two hours, we were called into one of the tiny rooms. This one had a treatment table, a bandage cabinet and a chair. There, we waited another thirty minutes. Finally, the professor arrived and greeted Juergen. "There you are again. Now we want to look at what has happened to the fracture your partner no longer wanted to entrust me. Oh, there you also are." He shortly looked at me and turned again towards Juergen. "I have to go to the corridor. There, I can look at the pictures. Afterwards, I will return." He said so and disappeared.

No, politeness wasn't one of his specialities, but this was unimportant now. We held our hands and waited for the judgement the pictures would show. Then, the professor's voice rang loudly from the corridor. "Ms Schwarz, or however you are called, please come at once to explain this." I let go of Juergen's hand, who looked at me questioningly and went to the device that showed Juergen's spine in detail. Tears of relief welled up in my eyes. Before I was asked a single question, I did what was most important to me. I called out to Juergen: "Everything is ok, Juergen, details later. But you can stop worrying."

"How would you know that?" the expert asked at once. "I can't interpret the tomography pictures in detail; this I must leave to experts. But I can see that the situation has stabilised rather than worsened. Would you be so kind as to explain the details or why you called me?"

"Because I want to know how you managed to do it. Not only has the fracture healed, which is unsurprising after such a long time. But it is impossible to have healed so entirely correctly without any surgery and also take a look at the transplant. The loosened and partially dislodged screws are placed as precisely as if I had just inserted them. This I hadn't expected. All this has been destroyed after the rehabilitation. Has Mr Schwarz had another operation somewhere else? I could understand that in his case. It was a bit turbulent." "No, he didn't have another operation. He wore his orthosis consistently and did a lot of exercises to strengthen his muscles. In addition, only naturopathic treatments were involved, which I can explain if you are interested." "That won't be necessary. I wouldn't use them anyway", he said while we returned to Juergen, who waited for us impatiently. "Would you please be so kind as to enlighten me? After all, it's my back you are talking about." He was thoroughly informed about the result of the examination. "Usually, such an implant is removed after a year. But I wonder if in your case it wouldn't be better to leave it if it doesn't cause any problems. It fits perfectly. Let us look next year, and we will decide then, Mr Schwarz. I wish you all the best and to you as well", he said and shook our hand for a goodbye.

We had made it. We left the hospital as fast as we could and hugged each other very long and tight. Huge burdens fell away from us. Our relationship had passed its first huge test with flying colours. We almost danced back to our car, holding hands. When we arrived at the car, we looked at each other and said simultaneously: "Leading a better life with Parkinson's". Then we picked up June and went on a beautiful long walk. To celebrate the day, Juergen accompanied us and even enjoyed it.

Chapter 29

It felt like the beginning of a new life. The vertebral fracture and its consequences, all the problems in the hospital and rehabilitation clinic, and the discrepancies that had, therefore, occurred between us belonged to the past. Every problematic situation had led to a deeper bond between Juergen and me. He, who had believed he could never trust a person, had been allowed to experience that such a person did exist for him.

Another person he could trust so profoundly was my son Jan. Take a car-fanatic teenage boy and an open-minded motorsports journalist, and the intimate bond is preprogrammed. But this bond didn't only depend on the roaring of the car engines; there was more. From the moment they met, they liked each other very sincerely. Juergen was there for Jan and Jan was there for Juergen. When I returned home, they often sat together, talking or making plans. Frequently, I withdrew so as not to disturb them because I knew how vital this men's talk was for them.

Each day, Juergen flourished more. He hardly needed the orthosis anymore. Someday, he put it into a wardrobe where it was meant to stay forever. He still strictly refused to go to a gym to work on his muscles. No matter how often and intensely I explained the importance of this for people in general and people with Parkinson's mainly, he stayed to his categorical no.

"Sopherl, I appreciate that you go to the gym and do your running. Really. But I've never been a muscle man and don't want to become one." "That's not the point. First of all, you have to train to maintain your muscles. If they grew a bit, that would be marvellous, but they shouldn't shrink in the first place. This doesn't happen because you're watching sports or praise me."

"But I still don't want to. Jan told me something he could do with me if I wanted to. He called it bodyweight exercises and talked about elastic bands. I have asked him to set up a training plan for me. He has become an expert on this." "You didn't tell me about that before." "We've just talked about it. I also could imagine frequently running with you if this is so important to you." "I would be glad if you did so because it is good for you and running together could be a lot of fun. But you should do it for yourself, not for doing me a favour or that I stop annoying you with it."

"I don't know you being this way, Sopherl. What's wrong with you? Are you angry with me?" "Yes, somehow. I only want you to become better and that we manage to keep Parkinson's under control. And I know how important sports are for achieving this. You're taking my remedies; you love my massages. But you don't have to make any effort for this. Don't try to calm me with any of these slogans. They make me furious. I am an expert in holistic medicine. I know everything Parkinson's can do and does if you don't set anything against it. That's why I am so stubborn and now angry." "And I know what I have to thank this stubbornness for. Okay, I will start training a bit." "A bit isn't enough. Every day, please. Do you at least want to try it?" "I will. And look, I already play football with June twice or thrice daily." "Oh, Juergen." I knew nothing more was to say or could be achieved about this topic today. I hoped Juergen wouldn't regret his attitude towards sports someday.

What Juergen missed, almost as much as a human being needs air to breathe, was travelling. This had been part of his life so much, and now it had disappeared from one day to the next. From country to country, from continent to continent, wherever there had been a rally about which he could or should report. After having withdrawn from his life in the journalistic everyday hustle and bustle, from being editor-in-chief and only taking on some freelance jobs, his travelling activities had entered a lull. He missed the sound of the aircraft turbines, hotel life, being on the move and the contact with the people engaged in motorsport. Unfortunately, the old saying 'out of sight, out of mind' applied to most of his professional companions. It hurt him a lot not to be part of it all anymore, being an outsider. Someone would frequently get in touch, and when he made contact, Juergen was never turned away. But I could feel that it was different from the past.

We went to some motorsports events Juergen had been invited to together. Over time, this also happened less and less often. Almost two months after the final examination of his back, Juergen received an invitation to a rally. I was very happy for him. However, when I learnt the circumstances, my protective instinct rose uncontrollably.

"Juergen, you can't be serious. You can't sit on the rear seat of a car travelling over hill and dale for hours with a fracture of the spine that has just healed. You recently complained about the potholes on Oberhausen's roads and said they weren't good for your back." "Sopherl, I don't know if I will ever get such an offer again. And I know, should anything happen to my spine, you will repair it."

He better hadn't said this. We had our first full-blown dispute. Emotions ran high. Until now, I hadn't known that you could also argue quietly. Juergen never raised his voice to shout, which I found extremely pleasant. I could become loud, but I wouldn't say I liked to do it. When singing, it was okay, but in a dispute – I wouldn't say I liked it.

"Do you believe one can repeat small or greater wonders as often as you want to? And do you also believe I don't have better things to do than repairing the consequences of your recklessness?" My eyes sparkled with anger. "You don't have to do it if you don't want to. But I also don't allow anyone to forbid me something, not even you." Juergen's eyes were sparkling with anger as much as mine did. "I don't forbid you anything. I appeal to your intellect. But that probably disappears as soon as someone waves with a rally. You know exactly what I have taken on myself to help you and heal your back. I had to do without my children and neglected my work to stay with you in Swabia for three months, and now you're throwing a sentence like that in my face and risking that it was all in vain? Think about it again."

"I don't have to do that; I already did so. The invitation didn't come at that moment but a couple of days ago. I am feeling fit enough, and I believe you are dramatising because you don't want me to go for whatever reason." "Why should I not want you to go? I know how important this is for you and how much you enjoy it. What are you insinuating? If I hadn't serious health concerns because of your back, I would wish you lots of fun, say 'see you soon' and mean it exactly like that. Perhaps I would ask you if you want to keep me informed about what's happening, but nothing else." "I don't believe you." "Says the man, who only believed me in hospital and rehab when the problems arrived. All this is hurting too much at the moment. Please leave me alone for now", I said and went to the forest with June to calm down.

I had forgotten to ask when the journey was beginning. So I was amazed when Juergen picked up his travelling bag the following day and set off with a quick "Bye, see you soon." "Stubborn Virgo", I thought, and at the same time, I hoped that his recklessness wouldn't be punished. I could understand what made him follow the rally cars' call, as he had done most of his life. What is better, renouncing for common sense reasons or taking a risk? Nobody can answer this question for somebody else. Leaving in a dispute I didn't like at all. But I couldn't change anything now, so I started my day.

The gentleman was relatively tight-lipped. He took the word short massage literally and kept his messages as brief as possible. "Arrived, back still intact." If he wanted it this way, I had to accept it. It would be better to clarify the situation face to face. This was what I thought, forgetting that everything can become worse. After three or four days, Juergen stopped writing at all, not even short messages. My enquiry remained unanswered. I couldn't take this as a bad joke much longer. When he didn't return when he said he would, pure panic arose within me. What had happened? What was going on with him?

Following an intuition, I called him on his Ludwigsburg telephone, not his mobile, and look, he answered. "Juergen Schwarz." "Sophie speaking." His voice became so cold that I started freezing. "Hello, Sophie." "You said you would return to Oberhausen today". I tried to sound as neutral as possible. "I am confused now that you are in Ludwigsburg and haven't contacted me for two days." "I thought I wasn't wanted in Oberhausen." "What made you think that?" "You wrote something that made me think that." What on earth had he misunderstood. I was overwhelmed.

"Juergen, please explain what that should have been." "Something like 'then I hope you have a lot of fun'. I could almost hear your overtone." "Which overtone?" "For me, this sounded like a booting out." "No, it wasn't. All I wanted for you was to have fun." "I didn't understand it that way. As I said, there was an overtone." "Do you believe me when I say this is not true?" "I don't know." I took a deep breath and tried to hold back the tears that began to come into my eyes, but it didn't work. In tears, I said: "That's not fair." More was impossible. The worries of the last few days, the first dispute, his not contacting me, that he had kept me waiting without letting me know anything – all that collapsed on me and inside me. I cried unrestrainedly. It was as if the tension of the entire past year was breaking through. "Are you crying?" Juergen asked, now having a bit more warmth in his voice and being embarrassed. "Yes" was the only thing I could utter. "Why?" "I can't speak at the moment. Just call later", I sobbed and ended the conversation. My phone began to ring at once, but I wanted to calm down first.

Almost half an hour later, I had cried out all the stress of the last few months and my sadness about Juergen's current behaviour, which I still couldn't explain to myself. I made a cup of tea for myself because tea makes every situation more bearable, and I dialled Juergen's telephone number. "I don't want a dispute", I began the conversation. "I want to understand why you are behaving this way now." I was completely calm now. "I also don't want a dispute", Juergen answered. That was already a start. "And why are you taking it this far? Why did you add an overtone to my statement that wasn't even there and didn't write or phone me anymore?" "I cannot tell you. There was simply the feeling that you didn't want me anymore." "Not yet." "Same with me." Juergen's voice lost the cold and the sharpness. He was himself again. I breathed a sigh of relief—a first step. I waited. The seconds felt like an eternity. Finally, I heard Juergen taking a deep breath as if he had to overcome himself to say the following.

"Sopherl, from an early age, I was used to being punished by withdrawal of love when I didn't function the way others wanted me to or if I had a different opinion— in my parental home and relationships. Either I did what I was told to, or I was ignored. In extreme cases, the relationship was ended. I don't know any other way. A few days ago, Sophie, I had never seen you upset. But I wanted to go on this journey, and I knew you were absolutely right with all your warnings. But I didn't mind. I was prepared to take the risk and believed you would never understand. I went too far, saying you could repair everything if something went wrong. Please believe me; I know exactly how much you have done for me and how much I have expected of you. I certainly didn't do that voluntarily. My automatism went off when you were so upset. Better go than being thrown out. I have that much dignity."

When I was sure that Juergen was waiting for my answer, I said, "I never wanted to throw you out. Why should I? I am myself, I am Sopherl. I am not one of these people who did all this to you. And I know all the dangers. Being the person who has to mend all the health troubles people do to themselves, appeasement slogans don't work with me. I was, and still am, aware of the importance of this event for you and that other events will also be essential for you. It was wrong to explode the way I did. We should have talked about strategies to minimise the risks instead. And, of course, I should have given you some homoeopathic emergency remedies, just in case something had happened. But I am also only human. But first, tell me whether the effort was worth it."

Juergen changed to his chatty tone, which I loved so much. I could listen for hours when he told me stories of his life, and there was indeed no shortage of them. "To begin with, I was cautious. For security reasons, I had taken the orthosis out of the wardrobe and wore it until bedtime. I thought this to be a good idea." He stopped and waited for my consent. "That was a good idea. Continue, please." "It was fun, but it wasn't worth all the effort nor the dispute. I never thought I would ever say something like this." Juergen stopped again. I waited. "Sopherl?" "Yes, Juergen?" "May I come home again?" "Please, come." "I want to get a good night's sleep first. I couldn't sleep because of our dispute and don't want to drive tired like this. But my bags are already packed. I packed them full of hope. As soon as I have slept, I will come. Is that okay with you?" "Absolutely. But don't change your mind while sleeping again." "No, definitely not. Good night, my sun." "Good night, my stubborn Virgo. Will you trust me one day?" "Every day one bit more, and today even two?"

Finally, he arrived. He had told me his estimated arrival time, and I managed to be home then. Why was I so restless? This man had travelled countless miles on the roads of the whole world during his life, and I knew he was a good driver. Or was the dispute making me restless even though we had settled it?

When Juergen drove up, I opened the front door. June ran to him, and he greeted her happily. Finally, he turned towards me, took me into his arms without saying a word and held me tight for a moment. "I think I've messed up. Can you forgive me?" "When you can forgive me that I behave like a broody hen shielding since your vertebra fracture. I didn't want to forbid you anything." "I know this. Some point was triggered in me. I am glad to be at home with my two women now. Do you allow me to come in?" I didn't answer but called June and went to the house. Then

I looked over my shoulder back to Juergen and asked: "What are you waiting for? Come in."

Chapter 30

A very relaxed normality occurred once the dust had settled from our first argument. The orthosis disappeared again in the wardrobe. Not regularly and not nearly as often as I wished, and it had been reasonable that Juergen accompanied me on my running rounds. The running did not cause Juergen any problems, and his most excellent fun was when he overtook me. Not without reason, I had a running shirt with 'I run as slowly as a snail, but I run' printed on it. But I could run for miles while Juergen lost endurance and fun after a mile and a half. When he ran ahead of me or turned round to tell me something and therefore ran backwards, no one could have imagined that man who had been diagnosed with Parkinson's many years ago was running here. He still needed his Parkinson's medication, but far less than before. His craniosacral and reflex zone treatments and massages belonged to our everyday life. Regularly, I adjusted his naturopathic and homoeopathic remedies. The necessary descriptions of his symptoms and feelings did not take up much space and were a matter of course. Gladly, my son and I listened to his stories about his times at rallies around the globe and his experiences as a journalist on all continents. These were stories from a different world, exciting, funny and sometimes sad. Juergen could describe situations wonderfully in written form and was a gifted storyteller, so we could never get enough.

And he was an encyclopedia on two legs. Who needed Google when Juergen Schwarz was in the house? We and our friends were fascinated by all the dates and events, names and facts this man had saved in his head. Everyone took him into his heart. No matter where Juergen and I appeared together, he was immediately liked.

However, people were always amazed at how well my ex-husband and Juergen got along. Sought and found is the saying. I often sat in our favourite pizza place with my two men over a good meal and a glass of wine and could have left them alone there. They never ran out of things to talk about.

Children and animals, and the fact that I was still building up my practice, didn't let us travel together as Juergen had wanted to, and he didn't want to travel on his own anymore. "I love being together with you far too much, and we have already wasted thirty years because we haven't met earlier. That's why we now have to celebrate having found each other and shouldn't travel separately all the time." It was Juergen who said this, whose freedom and independence had always been above everything when I asked him why he didn't travel without me because my hands were tied in so many ways. At least we managed to travel to training courses together. While I participated in the seminars, Juergen looked after June and the evenings we spent together. He then wanted to know in detail what I had learned during the day. He was interested in everything, and I was happy to be able to share it with him. Sometimes, we added one or two extra days to these trips to have at least a few days away from the demanding life at home. "Don't worry that we don't travel far now, Sopherl. To travel at all is important. The distance is not as important as you might think. There is something to discover everywhere. But not going on a journey of discovery is wrong."

We had been together for almost two years when, one day, Juergen asked me if I knew a good notary. His notary was a former fellow student in Berlin, and travelling there would be too time-consuming. He also didn't fancy the city at the moment. "Yes, I can recommend someone to you. He has been our family lawyer and notary for decades, even for my parents. Why do you need him?" "I have a few things to sort out. This vertebra story made clear how fast things can change. From one moment to the next, you dropped everything for me and fought for me with everyone. I was still able to say that I agreed with that. If that should ever not be the case, then I want you to be able to provide proof of power of attorney and look after me without them being able to get rid of you or hide behind the fact that you are not related or married to me. I don't want people to decide over my well-being who don't know what I want and for whom I am not important. I want you to be the one to decide. You proved that I can trust you unquestioningly and entrust my life to you. This is why I want to notarise that I am doing exactly that."

Of course, he was right about this, and everyone should take appropriate precautions. Nevertheless, the confrontation with this severe topic struck me like a bolt from the blue. At this time, I didn't want to think about where Juergen's Parkinson's might lead to and not about the fact that he was nine years older than me. I was only happy and relieved that we had overcome his vertebra fracture so well. I thought of

Juergen's liberated smiling face in the morning and didn't want to allow another thought.

"What's wrong, my sun?" Juergen asked worriedly. "I don't want to think about it; I simply don't want to," I said louder than intended. "You don't have to, but I. Then I will feel safer and better. Would you please make an appointment for me? And it would be best if you accompanied me. Then you would know everything and could object to things you don't want to, and we would never have to talk about this topic again." "Okay, you are right. Never have to talk about it again. Only living. Tomorrow, I will make an appointment."

A few days later, we went to the notary. Juergen requested, and the two gentlemen drafted all the relevant papers he would sign in a week. After everything had been listed for all conceivable eventualities, the notary looked at Juergen and asked him: "Why don't you simply marry this woman?" I cringed. It was getting personal, even though Juergen was the subject today.

"I am not the one you have to ask. For two years now, my proposals have been rejected by her." The notary asked me, "Why on earth do you not accept this poor man? He seems to be a decent bloke after all." He grinned, and then both men looked at me expectantly. I should answer.

"As you know, I have already been married. I have children. I don't want to. That has nothing to do with you. I know how difficult it has been for me to separate and file for divorce. And we had an amicable divorce, which was a simple official act. Nevertheless, I never want to go through something like that again."

The notary said: "Don't you already live together? Don't you already share a house, yard, table and, pardon me, bed? What would be made more difficult in case of a separation by a marriage? Everything else we can prevent with the help of a good marriage contract. A marriage would make a lot of things easier for you. You wouldn't have to carry any documents with you. You show your wedding ring, and you will be taken seriously, and nobody can rule you out. If I can advise you, especially because we have known each other for so long, to marry this man, don't make

142

it unnecessarily difficult for yourself and him. At least think about it one more time." We said goodbye after having made an appointment for the signature.

After leaving the house, Juergen took both of my hands into his. Behind us, the traffic rolled loudly past when Juergen looked deeply into my eyes. Contrary to his habit, he raised his voice to drown out the traffic noise and asked me: "Sopherl, my sun, do you want to marry me? It doesn't have to be in Vegas." I closed my eyes for a moment. Then I looked as deeply into his eyes as he did into mine and saw only love in them. And I answered: "Yes."

Juergen didn't say a word but took me into his arms and held me tight for minutes while the traffic still rolled loudly past. Very slowly and carefully, he let go of me, almost as if he feared I could fall over. "I hadn't expected this anymore. You make me so happy. What do you think about the 24th of March as a wedding dare? This is the day we met. This way, we only have to remember one date." There it was again, the smile in his eyes. Yes, it would become well. I made the right decision.

"When shall we tell the children?" Juergen asked on our way home. "I don't know yet. I have to process that myself. Please give me a few days." "Just as you like. After all, they are your children."

This didn't make it easier for me. How should I tell them? And what should the wedding look like? I didn't want any problems on this special day and knew that a wedding can easily cause problems even in the best families. Within a few days, a decision grew within me, and one morning, shortly after having woken up, I told Juergen: "I don't want to have anybody else but June at our wedding." Juergen looked at me and asked: "Are you sure? What about your children? Don't you want them with you on such a special day?" "I am sure. Of course, I would like to share this day with them. But I imagine it to be tough watching how their mum marries another man than their father. This could be asking too much of them or even hurting them. And I want to protect them from this. It will be different when we tell them about it after the deed. They didn't have to witness the wedding promise and everything else then. Nothing will change for them because we marry. Perhaps I am wrong, but I think it will be best this way. Do you understand what I am trying to say?" "I understand you very well. You always try to protect them. Do you believe they are so fragile?" "Souls are far more fragile than most people believe. Because I want to have fun, I don't have to force them to participate in something they don't want to or might hurt them. And I believe it could be overwhelming for them to decide for themselves because they don't want to hurt me. At least, I think so. Perhaps I am wrong. But I am pretty sure it's best this way for everyone involved." "Then it's a done deal. We also know the date. Now we only have to know where. Las Vegas is no option for the known reasons. However, going to the local registry office would not be appropriate for this occasion. After all, it's me getting married. That is something that I never imagined I could do." "Let's each do our research, and we will see which ideas we have."

There were many ideas. During my research, I couldn't get it out of my head that Juergen had wanted to fly with me to our wedding from the first day. There had to exist a dog-friendly alternative. Finally, I found it. In Wuppertal, the city with the suspension monorail. There, you could marry in the so-called imperial carriage. This would at least be a couple of metres above the earth.

"Juergen?" "Yes, Sopherl?" "I've got an idea. What do you think about a wedding in the imperial carriage of the suspension monorail of Wuppertal?" "Isn't that the vehicle from which the elephant lady Tuffi jumped into the river Wupper in 1950?" was Juergen's prompt enquiry. I was utterly amazed. "You don't only know about Tuffi but also remember the year she jumped into the Wupper? I give up. And yes, it's exactly this vehicle. Although Tuffi didn't travel in the imperial carriage as far as I know."

"That sounds excellent. And the imperial carriage is absolutely appropriate for us. How did you come up with this idea?" "I was looking for something in the air because you can't marry in Vegas, which would have made a flight necessary." "This is an extraordinary train of thought. But I like it extremely. From now on, you don't have to worry about anything else concerning our wedding, only rehearsing the correct answer. I take care of the organisation." "Are you sure? I mean…" I didn't get any further. "I am sure. I want to spoil you. I don't want you to have anything to do with it. You have enough on your plate. And I am looking forward to surprising you. May I do so?" "I appreciate it. It is only so unusual for me not to organise everything but be the one to be surprised. But I'm happy to embark on the adventure."

Juergen organised secretly, and it was great fun for him. Sometime later, I said: "Juergen?" "Yes, my sun?" "We haven't talked about names yet." "My name is Juergen; your name is Sophie, or what are you talking about?" Juergen asked, slightly irritated. I had to laugh. "Jester. When you marry, you must decide which name you want to carry. A double-name, or everyone keeps his last name, or one takes the last name of the other. This was what I was talking about." "Oh well. I want to keep my name, and I am used to it very much. What you want to do is your own decision. I don't get involved in that. Anything is fine with me. However, I think that a double name sounds rather unwieldy. But if you want it that way, no problem for me." "So you wouldn't mind if I took the name Schwarz?"

Now, the cat was out of the bag. I had been asking myself how to convey my wish to Juergen for days. "Quite the opposite." Juergen looked at me in amazement. "I would feel extremely honoured. But how did you come up with this idea? In your first marriage, you had a double name. I had assumed that you would keep your name now." "Back then, I wasn't quite ready to let go of my past by name. But it's feeling perfect now out for many reasons. It would be great to leave a lot behind, starting with a new name." "Listen very carefully now", Juergen asked me before pronouncing my new name sensitively. "Sophie Schwarz", he paused a moment, then he repeated the name. "Sophie Schwarz – that sounds nice, Sopherl. Wait a moment; we will write it down to see how it looks." He fetched a piece of paper and a pencil for each of us.

We both wrote my new name. "It looks beautiful. Please say it yourself, Sophie, with consideration." "Sophie Schwarz," I said very carefully. Then I repeated it a bit more convinced: "Sophie Schwarz." "How does it feel?" Juergen wanted to know. "It's feeling well, not unusual as if it's meant to be. It feels like it had always been my name. I feel extraordinarily fine with the name." "Then we will do it." Juergen took me into his arms. "And, Mrs Schwarz, should you want to change your decision concerning your name until the wedding, that is no problem for me at all. You should feel comfortable, no matter which name you finally decide on."

I snuggled up to him. I felt so safe, so secure, so understood. Nothing existed that we couldn't talk about. If one of us didn't understand what was bothering the other or what he meant, he asked and got the explanation. Everything was simply right.

A couple of days later. "Sopherl?" "Yes, Juergen?" "What about honeymoon? I'm just asking myself. Do you want to go on a journey?" "I would love to, but you know I can't now for many reasons. Can we postpone the honeymoon?" "Like all the other journeys we want to go on?" Juergen sighed. "Okay, that's the way it is. But I can kidnap you for one night, can't I? I mean, it's the wedding night. Shouldn't this be something special? At least that's what I heard." "Every night and every day should be something special." "Well countered, Mrs Schwarz." "Not quite yet, Mrs Schwarz", I laughed. "But I appreciate being kidnapped for one night. Where do you want to take me?" "Is the kidnap victim now seriously asking the kidnapper where they will be going to? I can't tell you that – where would the surprise be then?" Shaking his head, Juergen returned to his desk. I accepted it, even though I was about to burst with curiosity.

The big day arrived. We were asked to be at the suspension monorail station at one p.m. We arrived earlier. I had bought little flower arrangements for Juergen's jacket and June's collar. The florist, who had a dog herself, had put much effort into June's necklace decoration. I had feared that June would reject the unusual decoration. But I was wrong. She was very proud of it and seemed to know the importance of being our maid of honour. We climbed up the stairs to the platform, and there it was – the imperial carriage dressed up with beautiful floral decorations. Juergen had thought of everything. Soon, the registrar arrived also, and a man, dressed in a decorative uniform who introduced himself as our travel guide. He would tell us everything worth seeing and knowing about Wuppertal on our ride and would also be our witness to marriage. Juergen had thought of everything. We entered the imperial carriage, and the journey began. We learned exciting stories about the carriage and Wuppertal until the carriage stopped at the centre of the route. It was the time to marry. "Have you changed your mind, or are you sure?" Juergen asked, and there was a quiet fear in his voice. "I stand by my word", I answered. "What about you?" "Yes."

The registrar, with whom we had already had a good time during the journey, created a warm and welcoming atmosphere. Never before had she performed a wedding

146

ceremony like this, only for the couple and his dog. We were all touched very deeply. It was all about us and our promise. That was the right thing to do. We said yes to each other. For the first time, I signed with my new name. We had done it. We were Mr and Mrs Schwarz.

At other weddings, there is a lot of hustle and bustle after the deed is done. Everyone congratulates, there is dancing, and so much more that distracts from all the feelings associated with a wedding ceremony. We were married. We had promised the other person to share our life with him. We had already done this for over two years and experienced good and bad times. What was changed through a wedding? Nothing, and yet so much.

Finally, Juergen kidnapped me. We went to a beautiful hotel. In the middle of the room, a whirlpool was waiting. There was a marvellous menu accompanied by good wine and champagne. Juergen had really thought of everything.

Chapter 31

When we returned home the next day, we first told my son the news. "I already thought you would do something like that. You have behaved so mysteriously lately," he said, smiling. I looked contrite, as I had thought, having been careful enough so nobody would notice. "Don't worry, Mum, I am happy for you, for both of you and me." That was an absolute relief. "Can you understand we married on our own?" I asked nevertheless. "It is okay for me, honestly. But", he turned to Juergen. "You are my stepfather now, aren't you?" "I haven't thought about it", Juergen answered, and you could see clearly that he hadn't realised this until now. But I hadn't either. I thought that the status of our relationship only referred to us. So did Juergen. I was now eagerly waiting to see what they would make of it.

"So far as I am concerned, we can leave everything between us as it is. You have a father, and I don't have any ambitions to replace him. He is a nice man. You and I have been getting along very well until now, and I want it to stay this way. If you want to call me stepfather, you can do it. It's legally correct. But you don't have to do it. So, legally speaking, I am both a husband and a stepfather of two. I would never have dreamed of that. And you know what?" Juergen looked at us questioningly. "It's feeling great. I have a family of my own. But don't dare to call me anything else but Juergen. You have a father and a Juergen. How does that sound to you?" "It sounds good. So nothing changes between us?" "No, only if you want to." "I don't want to. I like it the way it is. Shall we go to a restaurant to celebrate this special day?" "We will do that", Juergen said, and I had no objections, only: "Before we leave, I want to tell Lena and Achim the news. For me, it is important to do it now and not postpone it." "Of course, do so", said Juergen. "I can understand that you want to tell your daughter at once, but why do you want to tell it to your ex-husband today." "Because we are friends, and you should share your happiness with your friends." "Yes, but do you believe he sees our wedding as happiness?" "We have clarified our topics. Maybe that's why it's so important for me to be completely open. I don't want him to get to know this from someone else, even if this were his children. He shall be informed by myself." "Ok, I can understand that."

As I had imagined, my ex-husband was genuinely happy. On the other hand, my daughter couldn't develop any absolute joy, so she reacted pretty much as I had thought she would: "Oh my goodness, are you serious? Do I have to wish you luck now?" We could both laugh about it.

June and I went for a long walk through the forest. I needed this now to process everything. I had never wanted to marry again. And now I had not only married but also had taken my husband's name. Everything went so fast. Hadn't Juergen and I just met? How short had the carefree time of our dating been? How quickly had we been approached by existential threats, as if life wanted to weld us close together before we could change our minds? How different might everything have developed if Juergen hadn't had his vertebra fracture and all its consequences? We would still be together, but married? I didn't regret saying yes. It was right the way it was. Mrs Sophie Schwarz. This name felt so familiar, more familiar than my previous one. Strange as I was only called this way since yesterday. I took a few deep breaths. This wasn't the first odd thing happening in my life, and as long as it felt good, I didn't want to question it. Once again, I thought of my son calling Juergen his stepfather. Juergen had become very important to him, and this made me happy. How different my life had turned out so far than I had dreamed, planned and imagined. How would it go on? What surprises did it have in store for me? "Come on, June, the men are hungrily waiting." With these words, I left the forest and went to my second wedding dinner.

The surprises were not long in coming. Difficult situations led to my husband's company having to file for insolvency. That was a terrible blow for all of us. Although we were long divorced and I had never been involved in his firm at any time, almost nobody stopped from making illegal demands on me and even threatening me. From one moment to the next, I found myself in a nightmare. Had I thought people would get help and support in such a situation, I learned quickly that this wasn't the case. Within a very short space of time, I had to make myself an expert in financial matters, insolvency law, corporate law and banking law to find a way through this jungle. Juergen, who had studied law, was stunned by what scheming was possible in a constitutional state. Although I had absolutely nothing to do with all this, they wanted to steal my livelihood and that of my children as well. But Juergen stood by my side like a rock in the surf, and when I was lying in my bed at night trembling with worries, he held me in his arms until I fell into a sleep of exhaustion. Sometimes he said: "My sun, trembling is my job. I can do it better than you. Do not worry so much; you will get out of all this. I am with you. I will not leave you alone as you didn't leave me alone."

And he was right. We made it. I swore my children should not miss out on anything because of their father's insolvency, so I worked even harder. "Sopherl, would you please take a break? And don't tell me you can't. You would immediately refute this sentence to one of your patients. You are a married woman now. Let your husband invite you for a holiday for a few days before you collapse." "Juergen, I want to stay financially independent, and the children are my business." "Okay, would you allow me to decide what I believe is my business and what not? And I have decided to invite my wife on holiday. Please think about when you can take a break." I've rarely heard Juergen speak with such a certainty before. Of course, he was right. How long had I been working seven days a week for significantly more than eight hours a day? I didn't know. And then there was this financial crisis, Juergen's fractured vertebra complicated by incorrect treatment and everyday life. I was really exhausted. Then I had an idea.

"Juergen?" "Yes, Sopherl?" "I am interested in a homoeopathic seminar in the south of Germany." Before I could continue, Juergen said: "I was talking about a holiday, Sopherl, not about a seminar." "I know. Please let me continue, okay?" "Okay, I'm listening." "The seminar will last two days. After that, we could perhaps go to Austria for two or three days. I would love to see the Grossglockner again, and I could practise driving mountain pass roads again there. What do you think about my idea?" "Four to five", Juergen answered shortly. "And what do you want to tell me with these wise words?" "Four to five days in Austria. And don't tell me that's too long. We have to travel there and back again. Then you want to become much smarter for two days, and you should also relax. This is what this whole affair is meant for. So four to five days in Austria." "Then I have too much loss of earnings. That's not possible." "Oh yes. Together, we can manage. Please don't be like that. I also had to learn to accept your help. Do you think that was easy for me? Heavens, you were and are my absolute dream woman, and I had to put up with you seeing me in a completely helpless state. Do you think that has been easy for me or I have enjoyed it? Now, I can finally give something back and compensate a bit. Accept my help, as I have accepted yours and still do. Or did you meanwhile stop helping me? Am I just imagining all the treatments and that you're looking after me?"

I felt as if I was waking up from an ecstasy. "I have never seen it like this. It is so natural for me to do all this for you. I must admit that taking is difficult for me; I am better at giving. My independence has always been the most important thing to me." "And this can stay this way. But you won't lose your independence by accepting a present or help. You are determined to take on what was previously a burden on two pairs of shoulders for your children on your own. That is very commendable, and I'm sure you'll make it. But only if you don't break down first. Isn't a husband allowed to help his wife, Mrs Schwarz?" I thought for a moment. Then I asked: "And what kind of help are you thinking of?" "I thought that I would pay for the costs of the journey, and if you don't have enough money for something at the end of the month, just tell me, and I'll pay the bills. That way, your loss of earnings won't matter, and I'll be happy having helped you." "This doesn't sound too bad. I know that you are completely right, but…" "I know what you are meaning to say. I don't want to take away your pride or your self-respect. As you always want the best for me, I also want the best for you, my sun. Isn't that why life has brought us together? Neither of us has to be uncomfortable or embarrassed in front of the other."

"I never thought it could be difficult for you when I helped you. Did I do anything wrong? Did I do too much?" "For heaven's sake, no, you did everything right. What would I have become of me without your intervention? I don't even want to imagine that. But it's about the feeling of helplessness. As a man, you want to impress a great woman and should carry her on your hands, and then she has to carry you. Our wedding brought together what belonged together, if I may quote Willy Brandt not quite correctly here. So, let us master our lives together. This is what I understand a marriage is about. What is the topic of the seminar?" " 'Homoeopathy in gynaecology'. Could be very interesting for me." "Then sign it at once and tell me the dates. I will organise everything else. Do you agree?" "Agreed. Juergen?" Yes, Sopherl?" "Thank you for everything, and thank you for setting my head straight. That was necessary. Thanks." "With pleasure from my heart", said Juergen, kissed me and began planning our journey.

Chapter 32

In the meantime, Juergen had become so fit that he could also drive longer journeys by car. So we packed our luggage in his vehicle, June sat down in her place, and off we went. After everything we had been through, I missed the ease and joy I usually felt when travelling.

"Do I have to talk to your boss again?" Juergen asked. I had to laugh. "Then you must talk to me. I am my boss." "I know. And you, in the function of a boss, don't let yourself, in the function of an employee, go relaxed on a journey. That is not fair. You have worked so hard, so allow yourself to be spoiled. What do you need? Can I do anything?" "Perhaps I only need some time to give me the permission and to let the tension of the last years go. Let us go on. It will become better." And it became better. With every kilometre and every hour, it became better. We had prepared everything well. Juergen had convinced me in his calm but extremely persistent way that I needed this break. And I was very thankful that he had done so.

Two days I spent at the seminar while Juergen was looking after June. The evenings we spent together. He chose a route to Austria, leading us through the Arlberg Tunnel. "Didn't you tell me that you don't like driving through tunnels? We can train this now. What do you think?" Juergen did not let up. Like I was helping him with his problems, he wanted to help me with mine. Although I didn't want to train, I agreed, gritting my teeth. After all, he was right. "Do you want to drive yourself, or do you want me to drive?" Juergen asked a few kilometres before arriving at the entrance of the tunnel. "I don't know how I am going to react. That is why I believe it's safer if you drive." "No problem", Juergen said and continued driving.

I thought about my childhood. This tunnel always stood between me and the long-desired skiing holiday. I didn't know why I feared tunnels so much as a child. When I was growing up, I still felt very uncomfortable in tunnels, so I avoided them if possible. But Juergen said: "You can only be free if you don't avoid things like that," and he drove into the tunnel. I waited for signs of fear as I had experienced as a child. But nothing happened. Everything within myself remained calm. When I saw the end of the tunnel coming, I asked Juergen: "That was all? I thought it was much longer?" "Well, fourteen kilometres, the longest road tunnel of Austria. It used to be the longest road tunnel in the world for a couple of years, but I wouldn't bet on it." "That sounds a lot, but I didn't have any problems at all. I waited for the feelings of fear or panic. But nothing. Next time, I want to drive myself. I'm feeling stupid now for not trying it before." "You have done it now, and now you are a bit more free. That's the only thing that matters. So the Grossglockner Road next. I'm already looking forward to it. The views you get there are marvellous." "I know. I'm looking forward to it as well." "No worries because of the mountain pass road?" Juergen looked at me enquiringly. "No, no worries, everything is fine. Thanks to my therapist Juergen."

Again, Juergen asked, "Do you want to drive, or shall I drive? "I felt how much he wanted to drive this road. My next training could wait. "Drive yourself; I can see how much you long to do so." "Right, but you need training." "We will train tomorrow. Now it's your turn."

Full of anticipation for the beautiful mountain world, we set off, but after a short time, we found ourselves in a thick fog. That was the end of marvellous views. The visibility reached as far as the front bumper of the car. That was it. Slowly, we felt our way ahead. Something happened to Juergen. This was his passion. Driving a vehicle, no matter under which conditions, in perfect peace and serenity made all insecurities and Parkinson's symptoms disappear. Here, he took over the helm with such naturalness that it filled me with deep joy, and I got a hint of what he must have been like in his active days. The fog enveloped us. That and the feeling of being utterly alone in the world – it was a beautiful feeling. We felt our way in perfect peace.

"Is everything okay with you, Sophie?" Juergen asked into the silence. "Yes, why not?" "Well, I thought you could find driving in the fog uncomfortable when you can't see where we're going." "Perhaps it is not too bad that I don't see the abysses so clearly at first", I laughed. "But seriously, I'm feeling fine. You radiate such a sense of security that I feel safe and sound." "Nobody ever said so when I drove. Women used to tell me off for driving too fast or showing too little consideration for them. I can almost hear the nagging that I would have had to listen to on such a foggy journey. I should stop at once and wait until the fog would disappear or turn around and look for a hotel or something like that. And you tell me you're feeling safe and sound. That is a balm for my troubled soul. I wouldn't drive if I didn't know what I was doing. I hope you know that." "I am very sure about that. You love your life too much to risk it. Look, there is a car coming in our direction." We faintly recognised the headlights of an oncoming vehicle through the fog.

"Some poor chap was probably forced to turn back," Juergen laughed, and he went on, highly concentrated. "I wonder how we shall find the road junction to Heiligenblut in this fog," I thought aloud. "I don't know. Wait and see."

We could see the junction easily because the higher we came, the more the fog disappeared. At some point, the mist had disappeared completely, opening up the view to the mountains of my childhood. "They are so indescribably beautiful," I said with tears in my eyes. "Yes, they are. And this is where you climbed around as a little girl?" Juergen was also moved. "Not exactly here. I can show you the mountains in Heiligenblut and tell you many stories if you want to listen to them." "If I want to listen to them? You're joking. Of course, I want to listen to them. How old have you been then?" "I am not sure, but I think I was eleven years old." "And at that age, you climbed mountains as high as those?" I could see from Juergen's face that he couldn't imagine this, having grown up in a big city like Berlin. "Of course", I replied. "There were no discussions allowed about this in my family. We went mountaineering in Austria for our holidays. No discussion. And it was great fun, at least most of the time. We also went on excursions or spent a day at a torrent or lake. But mainly we went to the mountains. We did not always go to the summit; it depended on the route my parents decided on. We had to get used to the height the first week after arrival. You will feel the difference tomorrow when we walk." "When I look at all this, I must confess that I want to walk. But tomorrow, we planned to go by car to the Edelweiss-Spitze, or not? Perhaps this impulse will have subsided by then." "We can drive there; I'm fine with that. I have nuts to feed the marmots." "Are they that tame?" "You'll be surprised."

We found a very nice hotel managed by a young Dutch couple. Our room had a big balcony with a direct view of the Grossglockner, Austria's highest mountain, which hid its summit in the clouds. With June, I went on a walk through the village. Juergen didn't want to accompany me. On the one hand, he wanted to relax from driving, and on the other hand, he wanted to give me the chance to indulge in my memories in peace. I did that extensively.

"You look as if you're still in the past", Juergen said when I returned. "What has happened?" He looked at me, a bit worried. "Nothing bad. Nothing seems to have changed after all these years—perhaps a new house here and there, but nothing that caught my eye. It's as if my father will come back from climbing the summit of the Grossglockner at any moment and empty a bottle of his favourite wine, Kalterer See, with his mountain guide, Sepp." Juergen took me into his arms, laughing. "Then I'll bring you gently back to the present." We remained this way for a while. It felt good. It was also good that Juergen had been the rock in the fog today, especially after the difficult time in the hospital and rehabilitation clinic or during his physical reconstruction at home, where he had been walking around with his orthosis for months. Seeing him now in his strength was beautiful. He was once again the strong Juergen I had come to know and love. The soft vibrations of the Parkinson's were part of him and didn't disturb me at all. We had made it.

Simultaneously, we looked at each other. Tears of joy filled my eyes. "What's wrong with you? Everything is fine now." "Yes, Juergen, everything is fine, and this is what I am so happy about right now. We have really made it. You are whole again and strong." I kissed him. "I thought the same while you were out and about, and I looked at this mountain. I am on the road again, not alone, but with the woman of my dreams, and with her, it's even more fun than on my own. Can a man be more happy? Without you, my sun, I would never have made it. I had given in or allowed them another twenty operations because I wouldn't have known better. You have performed a miracle." "Oh no", I replied firmly. "I haven't done that at all. I just kept an overview and used what I knew and had learnt. You accepted it, mostly anyway. So, at most, I was a kind of midwife to a miracle. A higher authority is responsible for the miracle itself, and I am deeply grateful to it." We held on to each other for a while; then, I asked Juergen: "Are you as hungry as I am?" "Oh yes, and it already smells so tempting from the kitchen. Shall we go to dinner, and you tell me all about your earlier time here?" "Too gladly. But then I also need a glass of Kalterer See or two."

We indulged in my reminiscences for a long time. "I still can't imagine that you were standing with these feet on top of these mountains and walked up there. You didn't drive. And your feet must have been much smaller then." "But Juergen, you know some exceptional athletes. Why are you so surprised I did something completely normal as a child?" "Presumably because it isn't anything normal for me. I always associate something like that with other people." "But I am another person." "No, you are my sun."

The next day, we drove the rest of the Hochalpenstrasse. The now apparent view opened up beautiful views of the mountains. Arriving at the top, I was looking for the supposedly eternal ice, which I remembered so well. I was amazed at how much the glacier had melted. So, something changed over the years, after all. I found the place where I had seen the marmots as a child and opened my package of nuts. We crouched down in the grass, and although June was with us, some marmots slowly approached us. "Do you know", Juergen began, "that in all the time I was busy with the vertebral fracture, there were moments when I no longer believed that I would be allowed to see more than a glimpse out of a window of the world again? And look at this now. It is overwhelming. Have you seen the wonderful flower meadows a bit more downwards?" "Yes, of course", I answered. "They are full of medical herbs. I used some of them for you. They were my introduction to naturopathy, the medical herbs. It is so sad that the meadows are being mown earlier and earlier where we live, long before the wildflowers and herbs have formed and dispersed their seed. Have you noticed that there are hardly any flower and herb meadows left? The insects can no longer find food. But if there are fewer of them, who will pollinate everything so that humans and animals continue to have food and herbs, which are such valuable remedies?"

We spent another few hours among the meadows, the mountains, and the marmots before we returned to our hotel. The next day, I dared to suggest a small hike. To my great astonishment and even greater joy, Juergen agreed. We hiked to a waterfall. In between, Juergen grumbled when it got a bit steeper. But he managed and was all smiles when he saw the waterfall. "That was worth it, wasn't it?" I asked. "You can argue about that now. Maybe one could have built a small road up here." Juergen grinned. "Of course, and once they built roads, they could have built one up to every summit. Why is walking so hard for you?" "I simply don't like it. It's taking so long, exhausting and doesn't make any noise like cars." "We can change that. I can start making noises when we're walking together." We laughed carefree and enjoyed being together, in nature and healthy. When we returned to the car, Juergen turned me around in a circle, then took me into his arms and said: "Leading a better life with Parkinson's." Still laughing, we drove off.

It was the last evening before our departure. We had dinner. "Juergen?" "Yes, my sun?" "I have an idea." "Let me hear it." "I would like to hold a seminar here in Heiligenblut and this hotel." "On which topic?" "The four elements – that's earth, air, water and fire. I have been inspired by the waterfalls, streams, and the fire island we discovered on one of our excursions. In addition, they have rangers in this national park. Perhaps they would like to support me." "It sounds like a good idea. And how would you like to organise the seminar?" "There is this room adjoining to the sauna. We could do yoga in the morning, matching the day's element before breakfast. After that, we would have breakfast, and after one or one and a half hours of talking about this element, we would go out into nature to feel the element – to a higher place for the element air, to a waterfall for the element water, to the mining tunnel up at the Edelweiss-Spitze for the element earth. We could have a bonfire on the fire island for the element fire. What do you think about it?" "That's almost a finished concept. When did this come to your mind? And yes, I think it's great. I would immediately take part in it. But for me, without yoga, please." "Of course, you can participate. When walking with June, I am always very creative. I discard most of the ideas. But some, like this one, survive this first phase. Do you think this could become a success?" "In any case. I am so convinced that we should talk to the hotel manager tomorrow if this would be possible at all and what they would charge." We went on talking and planning and couldn't wait until the following day but asked the manager the same evening. He was also enthusiastic about this idea and contributed some more good ideas. The only open question that remained was if the national park rangers would also join in. But we could live with that. A few days later, I received their commitment.

It was tough to leave the following day. We had waited for a journey for so long. "Sopherl, we have to do this more often. It's good for both of us. My whole life has been travelling, and I don't want to go without it. And look at yourself; you have flourished. We will have to look for solutions." "Yes, agreed, but…" "I don't want to hear a 'but'. I know all your objections and concerns. This is why I was talking about looking for solutions and didn't say that we hit the road." "Then yes, without objections and concerns." "Fine." The most beautiful weather accompanied us on our way back over the Grossglockner-Hochalpenstrasse and we enjoyed the journey and the weather to the full.

Chapter 33

Back home, we began to look for solutions and found them. It was mainly shorter journeys within Germany, but that didn't bother us now. The main thing was to travel at all. Sometimes, Juergen said that he missed the flying. But he didn't want to go alone, and flying with the dog was impossible.

Our happiness was only spoilt by the fact that both June and my cat Romeo had become seriously ill, and it was obvious that our time together would be more limited than we could have expected. We managed to delay the time of the last goodbye, but the knowledge that these diseases were incurable weighed heavily on us.

Juergen surprised me by participating in the dog walks more and more often and sometimes even in the running rounds. "I only want to find out why you have so much fun doing it", he said. He never told me if he had fun as well.

Our seminar in Heiligenblut was a great success. Jurgen didn't take part in the long hikes, which were too strenuous for June at this point, so both stayed at the hotel and played football. They could always manage to play football.

Some day, my daughter visited us and told us about a horse that was in terrible condition. She said we would have to help it as it was an extraordinary animal to her. I wanted to tell her I didn't have the financial resources to do that when Juergen joined the conversation. "What's wrong with the animal." What my daughter told us was heartbreaking. Calmly and matter-of-factly, despite all the emotions that the description had aroused in us, Juergen asked: "When and where can we go to see the animal?"

So we drove there the next day. Just like with my daughter, it was love at first sight with Juergen and the horse. An absolute giant of a horse stood in front of us, completely emaciated, eyes wide with fear. Juergen, who never had anything to do with horses, stayed calm and looked at the horse. "This guy urgently needs help. I have always wanted to adopt an elephant, but I have never done so. They enormously impressed me on my journeys; they are also made to suffer so much. But this guy isn't much smaller than an elephant, and I could always visit him to see if he is properly looked after. I can't do that myself. Would you do it, and could I trust you a hundred per cent?" He looked at my daughter.

A few days later, Mister Sunshine, as the horse was called, arrived. With a lot of knowledge, dedication, and love, my daughter nursed him up. Juergen was so glad about it. "I would never have expected that. Now, I have a wife, two stepchildren, and parts of a dog, a cat, and a horse. Nothing of this has more than one horsepower, but nevertheless, I am happy, perfectly happy."

Our search for solutions yielded even more results, so Juergen, June, and I set off to our own Tour de France, for which we had allowed ourselves three weeks. Juergen had lived and worked in Paris for a few years. He had wanted to be a foreign correspondent in the USA, preferably in New York. But his perfect knowledge of French meant he ended up working in France. Although he wanted to show me the country, he didn't want to return to Paris. "I've been there far too long and didn't enjoy it." I was okay with it because I disliked big cities, except for London.

We spent a dream time in France. As we had only decided on an approximate route, we stayed where we wanted and where we liked it. Starting in Burgundy, we went to the South and upwards again along the coast to Brittany, where we arrived on the day of the 24 Hours of Le Mans, the highest holiday in Juergen's personal calendar. In the morning, he called all the possible accommodations where we wanted to go to find out whether they could receive the TV channel broadcasting the 24 Hours of Le Mans. He found what he was looking for at the tenth hotel, and off we went. The journey there became our race against the clock, as traffic jams delayed our arrival time dangerously close to the start of the race. We arrived at the hotel ten minutes before the start. Juergen parked the car and ran into the hotel, where the concierge was already waiting for him, holding the key to our room in his hand. He had probably realised during the morning phone call how important the race was for Juergen and had been waiting anxiously to see if we would arrive on time. Immediately, Juergen disappeared into the direction of our room as he had warned me. I was just amazed by the speed at which he hurried up the stairs, ignoring the lift.

I knew from the last few years that Juergen wasn't responsive for twenty-four hours on the day of Le Mans. I checked in and looked after everything. When I entered our room, Juergen sat satisfied and happy in front of the TV. "I arrived on time for the start. Do you need me for anything?" "How could I dare to ask you for anything now?" "Are you not angry with me if I don't leave the room until the race has finished?" "No, as long as I can leave. No problem. June and I go for a walk now. Shall I bring anything?" "No, I will have anything I need when you and June return. Enjoy yourselves." He kissed me quickly and turned his full attention back to the race. Laughing, I left the room with June, explored Carnac with her and went for a long walk along the beach.

As the water lapped around my bare feet, I gazed into the vastness of the sea. "And James, what do you say now? You have become very quiet in recent months. You could almost think you're no longer there. But you're slumbering somewhere, I'm sure of it." "I never slumber, Sophie. This illness, which was named after me, also never slumbers. It calms down, but nothing else. Sometimes, it is for a longer while, then for a shorter while. But you and Juergen give it everything it needs to stay calm. Joie de vivre, sports, courage. You don't fight against the disease; you accept it as a part of Juergen. And you know that it isn't Juergen. How do you like to say: 'Lead a better life with Parkinson's'" I heard James chuckling to himself. "And this is what you're doing. You're leading a better life than most people who don't suffer from a chronic disease. I find that impressive."

"You are not alone in this, James. I am impressed by Juergen as well. He never complains that he has caught this disease. Only sometimes, he admits that he is afraid of what might await him. But then he says that nobody knows what to expect and that he even has a slight advantage with his diagnosis because he can already take precautions." "Yes, but what you are effecting with your homoeopathic remedies also impresses me. Samual Hahnemann and I lived at the same time, but I ignored all his research and inventions. That was a mistake, I have to confess now. But I wonder why my doctor-colleagues of today still ignore and even fight them." "I believe you must have experienced their effect because it is challenging for most people to imagine that such remedies might have healing power. After all, nothing remains of the original substance in the remedies. This requires an entirely different way of thinking than the one taught at our universities. Still. From day one of their training, naturopaths are taught how important it is always to recognise and respect their boundaries. That's right, absolutely right. But why isn't the same demanded of doctors? They and their knowledge also have limits. Every day, science discovers something new. Perhaps one day, something will be discovered that convinces the greatest doubters of homoeopathy. But it doesn't matter to me. Nobody is forced to be treated with homoeopathy. And who wants to may profit from it." "I have to confess, I would doubt as well if I did not experience the effects on Juergen."

"But none of this should obscure the fact that the Shaking Palsy will persist, that conventional medication will continue to have side effects, which may eventually become very apparent. This is why I have to be very vigilant. Sometimes, Juergen is too reckless for me with his steadfast refusal to exercise regularly or do something as simple as drink water." I worried very much about it because I know the importance of both. The last thing Juergen needed was another chronic illness, such as Diabetes mellitus type 2, for example, and I reckoned that was only a matter of time with his consumption of sugary drinks and ice cream. But for all the beautiful conversations we had and the plans we made, for all the praise he sang about me, these were two things I couldn't get through to Juergen.

"You are not responsible for him; he is responsible for himself. Never forget this. Taking over the medical care of someone you love is never easy. You don't just take responsibility then for the medical treatment. You quickly take responsibility for your loved one's actions as well, but you can't do that. Not even you, Sophie." "I know, but it's so difficult. It is so important for me that Juergen is well." "He is a grown-up man. You can't do more than to explain and give him advice. He has decided for himself and has to bear the consequences accordingly." "And this is one of the problems. He makes the decisions. This is completely right and important. But the consequences both of us have to bear because my life would also be affected by a deterioration of his condition. And, of course, he would ask me to dissolve the consequences. You saw it in the hospital and the rehab. That's what's bothering me. If bad decisions on his part lead to health problems, I'm not the person to tell him that he now has to see for himself how he copes with it because I had warned him. Of course, I would try everything to help him again."

"And that is all too understandable. But it's a trap you can't get out of, I'm afraid."
"I know. But at the moment it is great. And it shall remain this way forever, at least for a very, very long time." "I really wish you that. Juergen has had this disease for a very long time, probably forever. There is a tendency to see the medical diagnosis as the beginning of an illness. But most illnesses need more or less time to develop, especially something like the Shaking Palsy." "I think so, too. Juergen told me about his problems in his youth. It is essential for me that we could reduce the dopamine intake so much with all our measures. The side effects worry me more than the disease. But he can't do without the medicine." "How far could you reduce them?" "To about the half." "That is impressive. And gives hope. If nothing intervenes." "Don't think too much about the future. It's all about the now. And now, every moment is enjoyed."

June demanded my attention, and I was entirely back in Brittany with my feet in the sea and a growling stomach. "Let us enjoy every single day and be thankful, my girl", I said to June, and we strolled back to the hotel with relish, where Juergen was waiting for us.

"What have my ladies done for so long? I was on the verge of worrying." "And I thought you wouldn't realise anything because of the cars." "Not much, that's right. But that you are missing, of course. Are you also hungry?" "I'm starving." "Okay, let's choose and order something. After that, I will update you on Le Mans."

Within a short time, my personal motorsport journalist had informed me about everything I missed from the races when I was away with June, and that had been quite a few hours, embellished with stories and anecdotes from previous races and from his active time on the site. It was wonderful. At some point, June and I fell asleep. I knew Juergen would stay awake through the night until the end of the race in the afternoon of the coming day. To me, it was a mystery how he always managed to do so. Perhaps it was because of all his journeys with all their jetlags that he lost every day- and night rhythm; maybe it was Parkinson's disease, or perhaps the simple joy of motorsport made him forget almost anything else. As I cuddled up to him, nearly asleep, he whispered in my ear: "It's just perfect, thank you." Then he returned to the screen, and I fell asleep feeling wonderfully secure.

163

Chapter 34

We were sitting on a small balcony of a hotel situated at the beach and could see Mount Saint Michel in the distance. It was like a scene taken from a picture book about France. A quiet melancholy resonated in our mood because it was the last day of our Tour de France.

"It has been a wonderful journey for me. I appreciate you always being by my side so much. I could never imagine being so close to another person and not wanting to break free or be on my own because it would be too close. And now, thinking of Oberhausen and not being together with you all day long makes me sad." Juergen looked at me with sorrowful eyes, and I took his hand. "I miss my children and animals, but these weeks were precious. Just the two of us so intensely and carefree – we never had this before. It was, no, it is almost perfect. I guess we did the right thing by getting married after all, don't you think?" I knew my last sentence would make Juergen smile, and this was what he did. "I knew it from the first moment we met. You were the one who had been reluctant for so long. I knew at once that we both were meant to be together forever. And, of course, I was right." Juergen also knew his last sentence would make me smile and winked at me. "You were right, of course. How did I dare to doubt?" I laughed. We both then gazed pensively into the distance towards Mount Saint Michael. Only when it became dark and colder did we return to our room and then went on a walk with June.

Everyday life came, but the connectedness stayed. Even though we had already been through a lot together in the years before this trip and knew that we could rely on each other, it had been further proof and brought us closer together.

Chapter 35

One day after returning home from work, Juergen and Jan told me they had made a deal. "Which deal have you made? May I know it?" "Of course," Juergen said. "You are the mother. Jan is working on his driving license and has already passed his theoretical driving test in no time. And performance must be rewarded. This is why I suggested that I pay for twenty driving lessons. He won't need more than twenty lessons to pass the driving test. But should he need more lessons, he must not only pay for this lesson but also give back the money for one of the lessons I paid for."

Juergen was proud of his idea. "That's a reward and an incentive for even better performance all at once. You could call that perfect pedagogy." I had some doubts about that. "You know how expensive driving lessons are and that twenty aren't enough. I hear more and more often that children need thirty to forty driving lessons. They have to do so many compulsory lessons. That's not a good deal for Jan." "Yes, it is. I'm sure you've got driving practice centres in this area. I'm going to go there with him. But believe me, the lad will manage without my help. And then he's earned it twice over." "What do you think, Jan?" I asked. "Challenge accepted" was Jan's answer.

My son took his driving instructor into his confidence, who also accepted the challenge. Jan passed his driving test after twenty lessons. I didn't know who was prouder, him or Juergen. Then, my son received many driving safety tips and training from his stepfather. I was and still am very grateful to Juergen for that.

June's health deteriorated noticeably, and it became increasingly apparent that our time together was ending. We did everything we could to help her, but inevitably, the day came to say goodbye. My son and I held this wonderful dog in our arms when she died. It was terrible for all of us.

A few days later, I found Juergen and Jan engrossed in one of their men's conversations again. Only this time, I was asked to join them. "You love Great Britain and couldn't go there because of your dogs for many years," Juergen began. "Yes, that's true. Until some time ago, there was a six-month quarantine regulation for the importation of pets. It was cancelled at some point, but I couldn't go there for other reasons besides a dog having to stay in the car alone on the ferry. I didn't want to put June through that." "Okay, Jan and I thought that if anything could comfort you in this situation, it would be a trip to the UK. By the way, we're leaving in a week. Jan looks after the cat." "Is that all right with you, honestly?" I asked my son. "You also loved June so much." He confirmed several times that it was perfectly fine with him, so I agreed. Finally seeing the white cliffs again. We decided to travel along the south coast of Britain as far as Cornwall.

I was in tears when I finally saw the white cliffs from the ferry before me. All feelings mixed up within me: the joy of visiting my beloved Great Britain after all these years and the infinite sorrow that only June's death had made this possible. I missed her so much. But it was not only me who missed her. Juergen was also suffering. He took me into his arms without saying anything and held me tight. So I could cry out all the conflicting feelings inside me, safe in his arms.

Not far from Dover, we looked for our first hotel. There was no more walking with June in the evening, and I felt lost when we walked through the village without her. I was happy when we finally found a pub to have dinner, so I was freed from this situation. Juergen asked me if I would take over the driving the following day. I was astonished and alarmed. Until now, it had been a matter of course for Juergen to take over the driving on our journeys. We had never talked about it. I loved driving myself, and even more so after all this training, but it had been so natural that Juergen did the driving. I didn't know why. "Of course, I can take over, but why?" At least, I wanted to know that. Juergen hesitated for a moment, and it was evident that it was tough for him to say the following.

"Yesterday, on our way from Dover to this place, I discovered I'm not as relaxed as I used to be driving in left-hand traffic. I don't want to risk being completely overwhelmed by it. Maybe I have to get used to it again as a passenger." This hit me like a punch in the stomach. Juergen and driving a car was one. Fear crept over me. Was this the beginning of a physical and mental decline? Should our wonderful time, which had just begun, be over so soon? I firmly put all these thoughts aside. Now I had to be strong and give Juergen confidence, who had taken a lot of strength to make this decision and tell me. "If you trust me to do that, I will try. I have never driven a car in Great Britain, but I rode a bicycle. Please watch out as well." "We will train you as we did on the mountain pass roads and the tunnel, and when you manage it perfectly, I will take over again in a few days." I drove off. Juergen never retook the steering wheel during our entire stay in England.

Nevertheless, we had a perfect time. We hiked on the white cliffs, took long walks on many beaches and followed the footsteps of King Arthur in Tintagel. Juergen had never walked as much with me before – did he want to replace June's company? Certainly at first, as he later admitted. But he had developed a taste for walking and promised to walk a lot more in the future, even talking about hiking in the nearby Sauerland region. The fear that his decision not to drive on the left had triggered in me died down, but a tiny remnant remained.

Unfortunately, our cat Romeo also died not long afterwards. We were also deeply saddened by his loss. I didn't know how old he had been when I got him seriously ill. He had lived completely neglected at some riding stable and had been found there more dead than alive, and then he had found his way to me. How happy we had been when he recovered and got stronger every day. June, who had been only a few months old then, and he became best friends who slept snuggled up together and even shared a feeding bowl sometimes. This was too much for all of us, and again, Juergen suggested a journey. "How long has it been since you flew, Sophie?" "That's ages ago. Why are you asking?" "Because I will invite you and your son to London, flying is the most reasonable way to get there. I can do all the sightseeing I didn't have the time to do when I lived and worked there, and I can show you where I did this. What do you think?" "It's a great idea. Have you already asked Jan?" "Of course, and, also, of course, he said yes. There is too much dying here." "Far too much. And it is so empty without the animals." "That's true. But it's the way it is, and we must come to terms with this. Do you want a dog or a cat again?" "No, I can't imagine that at the moment. I've been through all this before and don't want to endure such a loss again. It hurts far too much." "It really does. Then let's try to enjoy our independence now. You've always been considerate of everyone. Now you'll be spoilt, and I'll finally show you the world."

And that's precisely what Juergen did and included Jan as a matter of course.

Chapter 36

We travelled, worked, expanded my practice, talked so much, made plans, and even realised some of them. It only became difficult twice a year when Juergen's favourite club, Bayer Munich, played against my favourite club, Borussia Dortmund, in the Bundesliga. But we navigated around this cliff elegantly and with a lot of fun. From time to time, Juergen joined me when I did my running, but he didn't want any regularity in his sporting activities, no matter how much he enjoyed his sporadic runs.

A routine blood test then clouded our joy. Juergen's blood sugar level wasn't just high. It was at dizzying heights. I hadn't known before that a human could reach such levels without falling into a coma. During our years together, we had countless conversations about Juergen's eating and drinking habits. Always without any result. Carbohydrates were his drug, whether in soft drinks or malt beer, or as ice at best as a whole family package, or as pasta, of which he could eat mountains at his favourite Italian restaurant. Even the results of this blood test, which shocked me so much, didn't bother him at all, but he took it more as a compliment that I could manage it without any noticeable consequences for him. This made it even more difficult to convince him that he had no other chance than to work on his habits. Together with him, I tried to find acceptable alternatives.

This complicated process conjured up many memories of his childhood and youth. Even back then, people had tried to talk him out of his beloved soft drinks or even forbid them. But it was not only this. Juergens' self-determination and his great love of freedom were two things that I appreciated about him from the very beginning of our relationship. With a diet adapted to type 2 diabetes, he felt massively restricted in both and entirely patronised. He was aware of the necessity, but bowing to it was an altogether different matter.

"I can understand that you don't like this diagnosis that adds to the Parkinson's diagnosis. And I don't want to give a lecture telling you that you could have prevented it in contrast to Parkinson's. But now the diagnosis is there, and you can't ignore it. How do you want to deal with it now? I don't want to argue with you about it, but you can't expect me to ignore it completely. Where is the use when I change the meals according to the necessary diet when you drink a malt beer or soft drink afterwards? I can't help feeling that your health and well-being are more important to me right now than to you. We discussed this differently."

"Oh, Sopherl, I know all this when thinking about it. But I don't want it. I don't want all of this. I don't want Parkinson's; I don't want diabetes. I don't want to say that I love drinking water when I long for a Coke, and I want to eat ice cream when I want to and not when some blood values allow me a spoonful. What's next? Can't you understand that I am fed up with all this?" Juergen, who almost always spoke in a calm voice, shouted nearly.

"I understand you better than you can imagine. Since we met, I have admired you for how you deal with your health problems and how little you allow them to restrict your joie de vivre and zest for life. When problems arise, and things can't be done the way they were before, we look for ways to solve them and achieve our aims differently. Where is the special problem with nutrition? Is it the famous straw that breaks the camel's back, and you say, 'I've had enough now', or is there something else?"

"If I knew it myself. But it's more or less a 'I've had enough now'. I have arranged myself with the Parkinson's. We had our problems at the beginning, but we have solved them, and I hardly feel restricted by him when I think of taking my pills and your remedies. I also enjoy the massages and all the other things you do. Of course, I miss the life at the racing courses but I definitely don't miss the stress of the editorial offices and everything that goes with them. But this diabetes is different; it's stealing too many normal things. Suddenly, I have to watch what I eat and what I drink and shall do without normal things. What is so terrible about having pasta with a Coke? Yes, I know, but why did I fight so hard that Parkinson's doesn't restrict my life when now diabetes does it even more? Everything inside me just rebels. I've fought all my life not to be told what to do and what not to do. And then some stupid blood value comes along and wants to bully me? Something inside me cries. I can't describe it. I am the master of myself and no one else!"

"And being the master of yourself, you can decide what you want. You can go on like you did before. Although this wasn't the most intelligent thing to do, we

169

discussed it widely. Now you can't laugh it off any more, can't ignore it any more. So take stock – what do you want? Do you want to discover new things you can enjoy as much as the old ones or perhaps even more, or do you want to die step by step from eating this sweet stuff? When self-determination and freedom are such high goods for you, why do you allow the Coca-Cola group and the ice cream makers to make you the slave of them and their products? It's time to free yourself." There was complete silence for a while. I could see Juergen thinking.

"There is something to the thought." "Let the thought sink in. Don't take the whole thing as waiver and prohibition but as a liberation." "At least this sounds much better, even when it doesn't feel better yet. But I still don't like water." "You don't have to like it; you should only drink it."

It would be a lie to claim that Juergen was happy to stick to diet plans. However, we managed to get his glucose values back to normal by intensively trying out what his body tolerated. He stoically endured every blood sugar test, and so we found out which products he tolerated best and which caused his blood sugar levels to shoot up. However, he didn't do any tests himself. This was my job, he had decided. Being confronted with this evidence, it became easier for him to change his habits, and the more the withdrawal of the sugary products progressed, the less he craved them. So also, with this diagnosis, we had found a way of neither letting it take away our zest for life nor falling into a victim mentality. Challenge accepted and mastered!

Juergen had always favoured personal responsibility, even during his illness. He never adhered to medication schedules. He refused rehab sports and speech therapy, driving his doctors to despair. But this took away the feeling of being at the mercy of others, of being ill, and gave him more self-determination. "If I have to live with such a diagnosis", he told me, "not knowing what is happening within my own body where a lot of things happen that I can't influence and that can destroy me well and gladly, I don't want to depend on anything else. It is awful enough to rely on this medication that I never wanted to take, and I am very thankful that they exist and help me. But I want to be the one who decides when I need them and also when I need a doctor. And I don't want my entire life to be determined by therapy appointments. I'd rather go for a run with you in between and do some exercises on my own or with you than constantly hang around in consulting rooms and be confronted with people who are at a much more advanced stage of the disease. That pulls everyone down. Why can't they organise this better? In addition, how should I be able to travel with so many therapy appointments? I prefer to improve my reaction time by playing car racing games on the laptop rather than stuffing blocks into holes. They put me off with this at the rehab clinic. I prefer dancing with you. And so much more. I want to live and not subordinate everything to this illness and only do things because I'm told that I have to do them because of my Parkinson's. I want to do everything with and despite Parkinson's, and I want to do it with you. I know many people, probably the vast majority, see it differently and think I'm crazy, but I don't care. Being conformist has never been my thing, and, like you, I've experienced how unhappy I was when the majority applauded and said that what I did and how I behaved was good. Nothing sensible ever comes out of it. Because the majority of people don't want self-determination or personal responsibility. But I want that, and so do you. Let them believe I am crazy, although I prefer being called eccentric. I take it as a compliment. I was often told that I was unreasonable because I decided against the safe way of jurisprudence—another word you can use to hunt me down: reasonable. And look where my supposed unreasonableness has taken me. I've seen almost the whole world and was happy, at least most of the time. If I had spent my working life in a law firm or court of law, I wouldn't have seen almost the whole world and wouldn't have been happy. So, my unreasonable decision turned out to be a reasonable one. It's the same with all these 'unreasonable' decisions we made during the treatment of my vertebral fracture. Imagine I would have undergone another operation. According to his latest plans, he would have immobilised most of my spine. How should I do yoga now? Okay, you can laugh if you want to; I know that I don't cut a good figure doing this, but it's fun, it feels great, and I don't do it out of therapeutical reasons, not because I am a Parkinson's patient, but because I am Juergen, and because I want to do it and enjoy it. And it's better for me than all the rehab sports they tried to force on me. Those things might be right for people who want that and aren't as self-determined as I am. But there are also people like me who want to go their own way. Sometimes, Sopherl, I want to shout out very loudly that they should leave people alone with all this standardised stuff and better encourage them to do much more they enjoy. With the help of medication and research, more and more has become possible, and a very liveable condition can be maintained for longer and longer. People should enjoy this. And now I also have diabetes. I'm not going to let him dance around my nose, either. Yes, I realised I was overdoing it with the sugary things and the pasta. But look at everything we discovered in the last few weeks; now I have super blood values. It would be more difficult if you didn't take so much care of me and didn't have so much patience with me, but I would still be free and in control of myself. That is so important, the freedom, and that the doctors see you as an independent and self-determined person, not just as a patient and a diagnosis. I deal with everything completely differently than someone else. You can't just lump everyone together. How many people would be helped if treated individually and left the way they are? Right from the beginning, when I knew it was Parkinson's torturing me, I did research on the different kinds of treatment, which might be the best but also the worst case scenario, and made plans on how to cope with it. I did the same with diabetes now. I also hope that no more illnesses will occur. Often, I have the feeling that as soon as they have a diagnosis, many people relinquish responsibility for themselves and are no longer the individual XY but just the patient with the XY diagnosis. And I think that's terrible, really bad."

Juergen paused in his monologue. Yes, that was precisely what distinguished him from many others. He did not surrender to his illness, nor did he fight it. He had made his peace with it. It was allowed to exist, but it also should allow him to live as best as possible.

Chapter 37

There were hardly any noticeable changes that made me begin to worry. Juergen seemed more introverted. He came up with fewer ideas or suggestions about what we could do and where we could go. He seemed more tired overall. And this was the most significant warning sign for me: He often asked me to take the wheel. That had previously been an exception because he was far too happy to drive himself. I didn't want to ask him at once because I had learned if something was bothering him, he needed time before he wanted to talk about it. So, I initially sat back, observed and worked out a new homoeopathic medication based on the symptoms I noticed, which I then also discussed with Juergen. He was then able to confirm my suspicion and also that he feared a Parkinson's aggravation could be on the horizon. By joining forces and using the new homoeopathic remedies, we managed to stop such an aggravation. Juergen's strength, joy and zest for action soon returned. But he still left the steering wheel to me more often than before.

"You look depressed," I heard the now familiar voice of James Parkinson say. "Don't I have every reason to be?" I replied angrily. "No, you haven't. Everything is fine, as far as it is possible. You can see that your remedies are still having an effect and that together, you are stronger than the disease." "But for how long, James? Don't tell me to concentrate on the here and now because nobody can look into the future. That's all well and good; I know it myself. But sometimes it's also tough to live under this sword of Damocles." "Why do you find it harder with Juergen than with yourself? Do you know what will happen to you? Nobody knows what his future will look like, and Juergen's future doesn't have to look worse than the one of any other person who doesn't have a chronic disease. That's a misconception. And you know that too if you are honest and think about it." "Of course, you are right, but that doesn't make it easier." I wasn't in the mood for understanding and acceptance. On the contrary, I was angry, sad, stubborn, and even more. Of course, I knew all that James was saying myself. But it didn't comfort me now, and it didn't make the fears that wanted to break through retreat.

I angrily snapped at James: "What good should this do me? Am I never allowed to be weak, sad, helpless, or angry? Am I not even allowed to give in to all these feelings and cry without you know-it-all interfering when I'm alone with myself?" Everything was quiet for a while. Tears were running down my cheeks, and I just let them go. Then I clenched my fist and punched the nearest wall with the rage and the absolute helplessness I was feeling at the moment. Yes, Juergen and I had achieved a lot. But how much longer would we be able to do so? And was Parkinson's his only problem? What about the side effects of the medication without which Juergen couldn't live? How long would my remedies have a positive impact? James wanted to say something, but I went on scolding. "Don't tell me any nonsense like carpe diem or live every day as if it was your last or something like that. I am not in the mood for such stuff. First of all, I have to free all these emotions. Then I can think about all this again. But now I have to scold, rave and weep." "Do so, and tell me when it's the right time to take you into my arms." I snorted angrily and continued to pound the wall with my fists until they hurt. I shouted out my anger and my despair because I felt so powerless. What do we humans have under control at all? After a while, I calmed down and looked for a handkerchief to wipe away my tears and blow my nose. Still sniffling and defiant like a child, I said: "Now you can take me into your arms."

Chapter 38

Juergen's crisis was over. My crisis, with all its doubts and feelings of helplessness, anger and despair, was also over. Although Juergen claimed that celebrating his birthday was completely unnecessary because the only person who should be praised on this event would be his mother because she had done all the work at his birth and couldn't be around, he was always pleased, when Jan and I considered it necessary to convince him, that the fact he had been born and become part of our lives was a fundamental reason to celebrate.

I couldn't afford a bigger journey for three at this time, but I could take Juergen to a foreign country for his 60ᵗʰ birthday because the Dutch border was not far from where we were staying. I planned a day in Nijmegen for Juergen, Jan and me, and it turned out to be a beautiful day. At the end of the day, we went to Juergen's favourite restaurant in our neighbourhood, where our birthday group grew even bigger. There, he treated himself to his favourite pasta dish to celebrate the day. In the meantime, his body could handle such a meal again without causing any problem as long as it remained an exception. And despite all the initial difficulties of the diet change, I knew it would remain an exception because Juergen's essential diet was now absolutely healthy, and he enjoyed it very much. However, he had wholly delegated the shopping to me. He said he did so because it had become too complicated for him and, after all, I would know better what was right and tasty. He had no desire to work his way into it. I didn't know if Juergen had cooked a meal in his lifetime. As long as we knew each other, he never did so. From his stories, I knew his cooker use was limited to heating prepared food. "Sopherl, there are experts for everything, and I am not an expert on cooking. For this reason, I respect people who can cook well a lot, and when they feed me, I am deeply grateful. By the way, have you planned something delicious today, or can I take you out for a meal?

My work started to take off, and Juergen was delighted with my success as if it were his own. But we also managed to be out and about and travel because this was Juergen's absolute elixir of life, and I loved it just as much. Even though he felt very comfortable in our house, you could always tell he was becoming restless when no journey was in sight. It didn't matter whether we were travelling to the nearby

175

Sauerland or a faraway destination. His travelling bag was always filled with the most essential items for the next trip.

Then, two things happened that abruptly ended our light-heartedness. On his 61st birthday, Juergen missed a step and fell. With some help, he could get up again immediately and move around without pain. We breathed a sigh of relief. No fracture, no more surgery, not that, please. A few days later, I heard a soft banging at the front door and then Juergen's timid call: "Sopherl, could you please come? Something is very wrong here." At once, I rushed to him. He had fallen again. He didn't know how it had happened. But he couldn't stand up and complained of severe pain in his hip. That could only mean one thing – a fracture of the femoral neck and, therefore, most likely a hip replacement operation, precisely what Juergen didn't need. I carefully explained my suspicions to him, and there was now no other option but to have him taken to a hospital by ambulance. He would have to be examined there and possibly operated immediately. He agreed, and I called an ambulance. Quickly, I gave him a homoeopathic emergency medication, packed up his Parkinson's medication, and we were ready. Then, the ambulance arrived a few minutes later. They carefully took Juergen onto a stretcher and drove off to the clinic. I followed them. "Don't think, don't worry. Keep a cool head, and stay objective. You can feel later", I told myself as I drove after the ambulance.

My suspicions were confirmed at the clinic. The fracture was also displaced, so the only option was an operation to replace the hip joint. I was overcome with cold fear. I had also been worried during the spinal operations, but only to the usual extent. But now it was completely different. I pointed out Juergen's Parkinson's disease several times, as this was very important for the anaesthetic, but I was only reassured succinctly. Perhaps I overdid it out of concern and because of the harrowing experience. When Juergen was pushed into the operating theatre and smiled at me encouragingly, I managed to smile just as much. But then I broke down crying after the doors had closed behind him. I knew that this was the end of our time, which we had labelled: 'Leading a better life with Parkinson's disease. Now it was going to become really difficult. I knew this with a certainty that I didn't know where it had come from. As always, I tightened my back after I had run out of tears and accepted the challenge. Besides, it was just a feeling, I consoled myself.

Chapter 39

"Sophie?" "Yes, Juergen?" "Do you want to marry me?" "Yes, Juergen, I want to marry you very much." "You are making me very happy, my sun", mumbled Juergen and fell asleep again. I had been told that the operation had gone very well and that it would only be a little while before Juergen would fully wake up from the anaesthetics. I had been sitting at his bedside for several hours and had just received the twentieth proposal, which was not to be the last one that night. Every now and then, he would wake up briefly from his doze, ask me if I wanted to marry him and then sleep peacefully once I had accepted his proposal.

I remembered Juergen's last operations and how long it had taken him to wake up from the anaesthetics then. This had been significantly shorter. Worries arose in me. I was aware that every operation is different, but I didn't feel good about this situation. Again and again, I had to tell the nurses that Juergen needed hydration; a doctor hadn't been here for all these hours. Some more hours passed, and Juergen woke up and proposed to me to fall asleep again. At one point, he was afraid in his doze. I gathered from his words that he thought being on a train to Glasgow from which he could not escape. I provided him with the necessary post-operative homoeopathic remedies. I hoped and prayed that what I feared most would not happen, that Juergen wouldn't fall into a postoperative delirium and, from there, into a state of dementia. For people in advanced age, this is a very feared side effect of anaesthesia, and often, a fall that results in an operation is the beginning of a life in dementia and a nursing home. Unfortunately, this also applies to people who have Parkinson's and need appropriate medication. I prayed that Juergen would be spared, not this brilliant mind, not this life-hungry man. And with each hour that passed with Juergen staying in his doze, my worries grew. After roughly eight hours, a doctor came for the first time, who was also astonished that Juergen still wasn't fully awake. When I asked him what we could do, he said we would have to wait. I knew this, but I had hoped for a different answer. At least the doctor ordered better monitoring of the fluid intake, which was only complied hesitantly and grumpily when I pointed it out. At some point, against my apparent protest, I was sent home. I was told that in this hospital, it was not customary for relatives to stay overnight, except for small children, and Juergen was not a child anymore. They laughed inappropriately. "We'll take good care of your husband", they said. This half-hearted attempt to cheer me up and instil confidence in me was a complete failure. "For this, something must have suddenly changed in your care and nursing concept within the last few seconds", I blurted out before I could hold it back. I made one more attempt to be allowed to stay with Juergen, but I was sent away like a naughty child. I went home full of worry. A new nightmare had begun.

When I arrived at Juergen the next day, he sat awake in his bed, smiling at me and drinking apple juice. I was gripped by anger and horror before I could be happy that he was awake and in a good mood. "Who has given you the juice? Please give it to me. You can't drink this. You know that this is pure sugar." "But it tastes great, and the nurse said I deserved it after the operation." "After this operation, you deserve something better and not something that is going to kill you." At this moment, a nurse entered the room and smiled at me. "You see, your worries were completely unnecessary. Your husband is awake, and you can see how well we look after him." "Do you call it taking good care of a person with diabetes when you give him apple juice?" "My goodness, why are you making such a fuss? He wanted something to drink, and when we asked him whether he wanted juice, tea or water, he wanted juice. If the blood sugar level is too high, we inject insulin to bring it back to the right level, don't we, Mr Schwarz?"

I took a deep breath. All this couldn't be true. Was there no clinic in this country where people with expertise and a sense of responsibility worked, or did Juergen have a talent for falling into the wrong hands? And firmly but as calmly as possible, I said: "I really don't want to discuss this now. But it would be very kind if I could speak to the doctor in charge and then to the professor as soon as possible. And before that, no drinks or food which do not correspond to my husband's diet. Thank you." We had spent weeks working on the proper diet for Juergen—so many hours of talking. I had the feeling it had all been in vain.

During the day, I was informed that Juergen couldn't be offered a diet suitable for people with diabetes because it was a weekend. Furthermore, I was told that it was the usual procedure to use insulin injections in case the blood sugar rose too high, no matter how the patient had been treated before going to this hospital or how he might be treated afterwards. Perhaps this was the usual procedure in every hospital,

I didn't know. And I couldn't change it. On Monday, the so-called diet specialist at the hospital came to talk with Juergen and me about his diabetes and inform us about the correct nutrition. What she told us was such an outdated knowledge that it left me speechless. So I cautiously asked: "But you already know that completely different recommendations have been made for at least twenty years now?" Oh, how could I have forgotten that you are not allowed to criticise anything during a stay in a hospital and that everything, the so-called specialist utters, is to be accepted as pure wisdom? "Do you want to doubt my qualifications?" the lady immediately replied in a huff. "If your recommendations are serious, I can only say yes." That made it clear that we weren't going to be friends. However, it was also impossible to prevent Juergen's diet from being anything but healthy during his stay here. When the so-called diet specialist left us, she told us we could contact her with further questions. And that was enough politeness.

However, I was even more concerned about Juergen's general condition and what was meant by nursing care in this house than about his diet. For example, he could not get up on his own to go to the toilet. Unfortunately, the nurses didn't respond to our request for help at all. Instead, they offered to provide him with adult nappies for a few days – I will never forget the horrified look on Juergen's face. So, I took on helping him instead of discussing principles, which would obviously be fruitless here anyway. Did all patients and their relatives put up with these conditions? As the wound care did not meet the usual standards either, I turned to the nursing service management. They told me they were sorry about this, but they were already short of staff and had cases of illness exceeding the usual level. But they would talk to the ward manager. If it was still possible, Juergen's care got even worse after that. I turned to the medical head of the hospital. He was also regretful but couldn't do anything for us regarding care. It had been different in the past, but since the hospital had become part of the …company, that was no longer the case. He could only do something about purely medical issues; everything nursing-related belonged to the nursing service management, which was directly under the management of the …company, whose motto was cost-cutting, regardless of the consequences for patient care. The doctors were slowly running out of ideas, he said, because the results of the operations would also be massively jeopardised. However, he promised to send me an experienced male nurse, whom he trusted entirely, to look at Juergen. He couldn't do any more. At least he tried. I was very thankful, and his openness showed his concern about the conditions. But showing concern wasn't enough? Why doesn't anybody fight against this?

He not only kept the promise to send a male nurse but also sent a senior physician who began his medical career as a male nurse. I even happened to know this man. They were presented with precisely the same wretched state of care that I had described to the medical director, and they were horrified. I don't want to go into details now, but it made them turn red with anger. "This no longer has anything to do with cost-cutting measures. This is a complete failure on everyone's part and will have repercussions. But this won't help you now. We'll get started ourselves first. What do you think, Mr Schwarz, if we treat you now according to all the rules of the art of nursing? After that, I'll speak to the ward manager, but I can't promise I'll achieve anything." Then he turned to me quietly.

"Do you love your husband, Mrs Schwarz?" "Why do you ask?" "Get him out of here immediately and bring him home. They either kill him here or make him a care case. Save him. Of course, I am not allowed to tell you this officially, but get everything you need to take care of him at home until he is back on his feet and bring him away from here. We are not discussing minor mistakes here, but dangerous negligence." "My husband was supposed to stay ten days post-operatively. What can happen if I take him with me? I don't have any nursing training." "To do this, you only need normal humanity. I'll also explain everything else you need to know while working. Please, Mrs Schwarz, get him out of here." I could see how serious he was. "Promised. With police force if necessary." The doctor still looked at me doubtfully. "My wife is earnest. It's better not to mess with her. She's my bodyguard, and I trust her completely." Juergen had been able to hear our quiet conversation. Now he asked: "Are you sure you want me to go?" "I would much prefer you to be transported lying down so soon after the operation. But yes, anything is better than staying here", was the answer. "Well, then we will do so, and I thank you very much for your frankness."

It was already evening, and I couldn't contact the professor. We would have to survive one more night. I had provided Juergen with everything he needed, brought him food he could eat without causing any problems and water. The only thing I was worried about was that he kept falling into a daze occasionally. But I couldn't take care of this now because the stressed nursing staff always found enough time to send me home. I thought of other countries where it was perfectly normal for relatives to visit their loved ones in the hospital and help care for them if they wanted to and could.

I was there early the following day and made an appointment with the head physician at Juergen's bedside. He entered the room cheerfully and told us how well the operation had gone and that they were already planning Juergen's transfer to a rehabilitation clinic. Juergen asked: "Without asking me? I call this very presumptuous. As I have had horrible experiences with rehab clinics, I thankfully decline. But before we go any further into the subject, I would like to refer you to my wife, who would like to discuss significant matters with you on my behalf and is much more competent than I am. I'm also still very exhausted and occasionally confused by the anaesthetic. But I can assure you that my wife speaks entirely on my behalf, and we discussed everything in advance."

"We can talk about the rehab later. Please tell me first what you want to discuss with me." He turned to me attentively, and I began explaining. "First, I want to ask you to imagine that everything I will describe to you in the following, as objectively as I can, would happen to your wife or another person close to you whose well-being is essential to you. I ask you to be honest when you tell me what you would do in such a case." "I will be happy to do that." So, I described everything that had happened in the days since Juergen had been admitted to this clinic as unemotionally as possible. I concluded my remarks: "That's why I want to bring my husband home today, where I can and will give him the best care and attention. I have already taken care of physiotherapy, which will come to the house first, and have already ordered everything I need from a medical supply store. It will be delivered today. It would be very kind of you if you prescribed the ambulance transport. Otherwise, we would cover the costs ourselves." The head physician's amiable and open face had become increasingly petrified during my explanations. I was already preparing myself for a tantrum when he turned to Juergen and me again in a friendly manner and said: "Please excuse me for about ten minutes. I need to clarify something, and I'll come back immediately." "No problem, I can't run away yet", said Juergen, and despite the dire situation, he made us all smile: Juergen and his sense of humour.

"Please tell me what you have organised for me, my sun? And when did you do it? You stayed here until the evening?" Juergen asked curiously. "You fell asleep again and again. I took advantage of these times to talk to the medical supply store, order the things we need, and organise a nearby physiotherapist who will come to our house as long as needed. It's going to start the day after tomorrow." "But this time, you will watch every appointment, please. Something like what happened in the rehab for the vertebral fracture won't happen to me again." "Of course, I will be there if you want to and also if you don't want to because I've really had enough."

At this moment, the door opened, and the professor returned to the room carrying a paper stack. "Your words have affected me deeply, and I know what happened to you is unforgivable. I wasn't here for a few days, but this can't be an excuse for what happened to you, but that doesn't help you now. I have your discharge papers here because I understand that you want to leave after all that has happened, and I don't dare to ask you to trust us again. This would be ridiculous. Here, I also have all the prescriptions and certificates you need, so no costs are incurred for your care needs. Just hand them to the person of the medical supply store who delivers them to you. In this bag are all the medicine and instructions on taking them that you will need in the next couple of days so you don't have to go to your GP for a while like you otherwise would have to do. You have to concentrate only on your recovery and care. Something like what you have experienced here must not happen, and I can only sincerely apologise for this. That doesn't make it any better, but please believe me when I say how affected I am. At 1 pm, the ambulance will arrive to take you home. Dear Mr Schwarz, all the very best to you, and since everything went so wrong here that was beyond the control of the surgeons, I wish you a completely complication-free recovery, even more than I would otherwise. I would also like to express my sincere thanks to you for not keeping these grievances from me but for revealing them. That doesn't happen often. And I can do nothing about it if I don't know."

We thanked him and said goodbye. We both felt a great relief. At the same time, however, I was placed under immense responsibility. I hadn't learnt nursing, but we would manage that together, as always.

But this hospital stay still had one highlight in store for us before the ambulance arrived. A lively and cheerful physiotherapist came into the room with a 'how are we doing today' attitude, who obviously hadn't been informed about Juergen's departure. She introduced herself and then asked Juergen: "So, Mr Schwarz, what do we want to achieve with our physiotherapy? That you can sit upright in your bed again?" Juergen and I looked at her in utter disbelief, and Juergen said: "I hope you are joking. You can't be serious." "Why?" the lady asked astonished. "You have got Parkinson's, and you are 61 years old. You can't have been able to do much more than sit before the accident." It was rare to see Juergen angry, very rare, but now he was furious. At least, it was very close to what you could call furious. "Fortunately, I have to prove you wrong. The day before my accident, I went running with my wife, which we enjoy doing together regularly and want to continue doing. We also travel a lot, and I am still entirely in control of my senses. So, doing physiotherapy with me would obviously overstrain you. But you don't have to worry –I will leave this bleak place in around one hour. I have some excellent advice for you – be sure to educate yourself further about the diagnosis of Parkinson's disease and realise that this diagnosis is not synonymous with severe mental disability and the inability to move. And I will, we all very much hope, continue to be spared that completely forever. Now, if you will excuse me, I would like to prepare for my departure." Juergen said so and turned his back to the physiotherapist. I was glad that Juergen had defended himself this time because I wouldn't have stayed so calm after all that had happened in the last few days.

Chapter 40

We coped with the situation much better than we had feared. Not being in a hospital but at home lifted Juergen's spirits and mine. But despite the rays of hope, it was clear that the anaesthetics had left their mark. Again and again, Juergen fell into a kind of doze and had difficulties concentrating, and the man with the infallible, phenomenal memory could no longer remember many things. It was also entirely unusual for him to be really argumentative at times. The man, who had always preferred to watch and report on sport, found it very difficult to do it himself. I remembered this from his last injury. But now it was combined with his new tendency to quarrelsomeness, which didn't make it easier. Also, it became increasingly difficult to convince Juergen to drink enough. You could tell very quickly when he had drunk too little because then the side effects of his Parkinson's medication became apparent – still decently, but this wasn't a good sign at all. One day, I found the infallible lure for Juergen.

"You have told me recently that you would love to travel to New Zealand or the USA. Do you still want to?" I asked him the other day. "Oh yes, I would love to, but this is impossible at the moment, and, who knows, perhaps forever", he sadly said. "I wasn't talking about leaving at once. But it should be possible in two or three months. Of course, you would have to train intensely to achieve this. Jan and I could help you. What do you think?" "Do you honestly think this could be possible? I have given up my hope", Juergen replied, resigned, but there was a spark of hope in this resignation. "Of course, this is possible. You received a new hip joint to use it. You are only too lazy to train enough. And you would have to drink far more." Juergen looked at me suspiciously. "And that's not a trick of yours? Aren't you holding the sausage before my nose and then pulling it away again? You've never been on a long-distance flight and told me you're not keen on it either." "This is true, but I would do it for you." "That would be amazing". Juergen's eyes shone. Then he said abruptly: "Florida. I want to go to Florida." "Not to New Zealand? I would have guessed that because you always said it was your favourite country." "You are right, but now I want to go to Florida, I don't know why. It will be great. All the things I can show you there? What do you think, would Jan like to come with us? This boy is doing so much for me and would love to go to America. May I ask him, or don't you want me to?" "This is a wonderful idea, and you would even have two body-guards this way." Juergen laughed. "That's true. Then we'll do it. When do you think I'll be fit enough for it?" "Let me think about what you need for this. You must be able to walk better. But this you have to practice anyway. It would be best if you survived a long-distance flight. The seats on a plane might be a problem. But we will find a solution for this. Driving a car will be a problem, but I can do it. And I know that airports offer a service for people who can't walk properly and help them get into the plane and out of it. We would have to register this in advance. You would have to accept a wheelchair for this, but that's all. Can you think of another obstacle?" "No, you thought of everything. This sounds feasible. So we can begin making plans. When do we start, next week?" Finally, there it was again, the rascal in Juergen's eyes." "Nonsense. You won't be fit enough that fast. You have to make up for the consequences of your laziness. What do you think about February? This is in three months. This should be long enough for your training and for me to get used to the thought of going on a long-distance flight." "February sounds great. This is what we will do. And I will train harder. I know it will cost you quite an effort, your first long-distance flight. But believe me, you will love it." And, of course, he was right once again.

And, of course, Juergen didn't exercise as intensely as I had wished for, but a lot more than before, especially with a lot of fun and an aim before his eyes, which was worth the effort. Day by day, the last remnants of the anaesthetic's after-effects fell away, and his zest for life increased to the same extent.

The day before our departure, I was getting a bit restless – I had never been in the air for so many hours, and then there was also the question of how Juergen would cope with the flight. I was filled with a mixture of anticipation and slight doubts about whether I had made the right decision to take the trip. When the plane lifted off the ground, I looked into Juergen's face, beaming with happiness, and any remaining doubts were gone. No matter which problems might arise, this happiness was worth it. While the hours before take-off seemed very long, the flight went by in my sleep, and we landed in Miami faster than I had expected. From there, we went to the only hotel we had booked in advance. We wanted to do everything else spontaneously.

We spent two marvellous weeks in Florida, and whenever Juergen needed any help, someone was there immediately. This was something I had never experienced in this form in Germany before. Juergen was in full bloom, happily showing us everything from Miami to the keys, from the Everglades to Cape Canaveral and, of course, the Daytona racetrack. Of course, we couldn't miss the opportunity to drive over the beach by car in Daytona. None of us felt like flying home again.

Despite many beautiful experiences, marvellous journeys and successes on Juergen's road to recovery, we couldn't ultimately find our way back to lightness. Something was missing that we couldn't grasp. Juergen seemed a bit tired at first, sometimes very absent-minded, and we had to keep reminding him to drink something. We didn't give up, but it became increasingly clear that we faced tough times. They were more demanding than I thought possible, but we got through them together. Our most important goal was to enable Juergen to live in dignity and in the company of people who truly loved him. At some point, it became clear that there would be no more improvement. But I absolutely refused to accept this and hoped for a miracle until the end because where there is life, there is also hope. And I fought.

Chapter 41

Despite all the difficulties, we had planned another journey. Juergen wanted to show me Dresden. The bags were packed; I had bought a folding wheelchair and loaded it into the car so Juergen wouldn't have to walk too far when he wanted to show me the city. As always, before a journey, I went to my pony. We wanted to leave early the following day.

When I returned from my pony, Juergen was wholly numb and unresponsive. His right arm was limp. I picked up the phone and called the ambulance. "Please come immediately. My husband has had a stroke."

The young assistant doctor initially suspected a gastrointestinal infection in the so-called stroke centre, i.e., a hospital specialising in strokes. At that point, I looked at him in complete disbelief—valuable time passed before he realised his mistake. Intubation was already necessary, but the doctor refused to perform it because he wouldn't know what Juergen wanted. Once again, I fought against a person in a white coat for Juergen because I knew his wishes precisely. That was why I was supposed to be at the lawyer with him when his will was drawn up and why I knew that he had expressly requested life-sustaining measures. This the doctor didn't want to believe. He even tried to send me home to get Juergen's will. Again, valuable time passed until I finally convinced him that his young career as a doctor would end in these minutes if he didn't do what Juergen wanted, which I knew so well. Juergen was then transferred to a university hospital.

That night, I was allowed to stay in the intensive care unit with Juergen. There was no change whatsoever, not even the next day. On the second night, they wanted to remove me from Juergen's bed with police intervention if necessary because relatives were only allowed to visit the intensive care unit for half an hour a day in this house, and they had already been very accommodating to me. I negotiated that I would give in to the violence but would be back tomorrow at 7 a.m. and, would demand entry by force if necessary and would stay with Juergen all day. They agreed to this. I left Juergen and the clinic with a weighty heart.

When I arrived the following day, Juergen was taken for a brain death examination. Now I knew why I had to leave the night before. They had probably feared that I would not have allowed this examination. Why hadn't they spoken to me openly? I didn't stand in the way of facts and necessities. I just hadn't wanted to leave my husband alone in what was probably his last hours because I knew how much people feel even in a coma and how vital the support of loving people is for them.

When Juergen returned to the intensive care unit, I was asked to come into the corridor, where I was told that brain death had occurred and that I could either agree to the ventilation being switched off or it would be done against my will by court order. Before making this decision, I wanted to see all the findings and the computer tomogram images. I was again told that I would certainly not be able to understand them, but if I wanted to, I could come into the nurses' room with them. The images of the interior of Juegen's head shocked me. It was much worse than I could ever have imagined it. It was more than clear that life was no longer possible. I consented but asked for a little more time to give my daughter the chance to say goodbye to Juergen. My son had driven me to the clinic and was already with me. From that moment on, they became very kind to me and gave us all the time we needed.

Until Juergen's last breath, I held him tight and sang all the songs he had loved to hear from me. He passed away entirely peacefully from his far too short, infinitely fulfilling life, and a gentle weight settled on my right shoulder.

I don't know how long it took me to get myself to leave the bed and the room. It was a very long time. The weight was still on my shoulder. That was the only thing I realised. My son escorted me out of the clinic, and there, as we stood in the open air, I felt the weight lift from my shoulder. I felt the touch of a kiss on my cheek, and then I knew I had carried Juergen's soul to freedom.

Chapter 42

I couldn't imagine that someone other than me should lead the funeral service. How was I supposed to sit silently while someone who didn't know Juergen gave a speech? I was initially met with scepticism when I expressed my wish, but then I received all the support I needed. I told everyone he could contribute to Juergen's farewell. Two people wanted to – a companion of Juergen from his time as an active journalist wanted to give a speech, and a patient of mine, who had got to know and appreciate Juergen at one of my seminars in Heiligenblut, wanted to sing an Irish song for Juergen.

I felt a deep need to celebrate and honour Juergen in a way that was not necessarily usual, as he had also not lived his life in the usual way. I had enough time to prepare everything because I didn't get any rest or sleep anyway. My children made a newspaper containing many photos from Juergen's colourful life and all the farewell texts, except for the speeches. I learned that a funeral service should only last half an hour and that our programme would exceed this tight time frame. After some back and forth, I was allowed to book double the time, and they even agreed to give me the last appointment of the day if I needed longer than the allotted hour. I was very grateful for that.

The farewell preparation had given me a task with which I could do something for Juergen, but after it was over, there was nothing more to do for him. But being there for him, being with him, from shared joys to caring for him later, had been my purpose in life in recent years. A life in fast motion—eight years from meeting to the final farewell, a rollercoaster ride with all its highs and lows.

And I remembered the words Juergen once said to me: "Sopherl, no matter what is going to happen, enjoy your life. I have enjoyed mine to the full. It would be nice if you didn't forget me and also if you were a bit sad. But not for too long and not too much, because life is too beautiful and the world is too big for this. Discover everything I couldn't show you anymore and even more. Sopherl, live and love."

Epilogue

We had the idea for this book in the last weeks of Juergen's life. We wanted to write about our time together, how we had enjoyed it, the struggles we had endured, and how every single minute had been worth it. Juergen wanted to encourage all people living with Parkinson's disease not to submit to this disease or any doctors and therapists. Nobody should ever give up but should keep searching until they find people who can and want to help. Nobody should ever organise their life around an illness or even identify with it. This message was essential to him. Juergen was always the traveller, the journalist, the motorsports enthusiast, and so much more. But one thing he never was. He was never Juergen, the Parkinson's patient.

Even if we could not provide a happy ending in the sense that Juergen was spared problems and death in the long term, there is still a happy ending. Juergen was happy until his last moment and was even granted his wish to die either on a journey or while preparing for a trip.

We had talked about this book a lot, and Juergen managed to write one page for it. I then was left with the promise I had made him that I would definitely write this book and publish it myself. No one should ever again adapt anything he had written to the ideas of others. How far-sighted. But it sounded much easier than it was. For him, writing had been part of everyday life; for me, it was a dream I had never fulfilled. I fought with myself, wanting to stick to our original agreement of splitting the writing between us. But Juergen could no longer do his part of the work, and I could never replace him. I first took refuge in researching James Parkinson, the time in which he lived, and studied many of his works, and how he touched me when speaking about his demands to a person who wanted to become a doctor. I walked through Hoxton, the part of London where James had lived, even though his house and consulting rooms no longer exist. There, I sat with homeless people, some of whom had overcome their homelessness through social projects and some of whom had not. Everyone has his reasons. But above all this, there was also a little bit of the spirit of James Parkinson, who was so committed to helping people throughout his life and work and realised that people with shaking palsy did not belong in one of the 'madhouses'.

In the seven years that have passed since Juergen set off on his great journey, I have started again and again until I finally knew how I wanted to write our book. I also hope that the people who read it will find strength and support on their way and never let anything take away their zest for life, no matter what illness or fate they have. Please never forget – you can lead a better life, with or without Parkinson's.

In the Dark Areas of My Logic
by Juergen Schwarz, December 14th, 2016

It was a creeping process, initially unnoticed and easy to keep secret at first. Nobody but me noticed anything.

It came quietly. I realised it late, but at first, I had no trouble disguising my own inadequacies in handwritten language.

But there was an unstoppable threat of danger. But I still had enough time: I was a journalist, but nobody realised the threatening fate. I learned how to write on a Monica typewriter and switched to computers during my time as editor of the Springer Foreign Service.

At the beginning of the process, I was 33 years old and had high hopes of becoming editor-in-chief of one of the publisher's magazines.

Appendix

Interview With My Patient B.
October 16th, 2019

(At the request of my patient without giving her name and any other names)

My patient B. wanted to contribute to this book to emphasise that Juergen's experiences in the medical field are not isolated.

Schwarz:

Which symptoms made you go to a doctor before you knew that the reason for the symptoms was Parkinson's disease? Which complaints did you then have?

Mrs. B.:

The whole left side of my body didn't do what I wanted. When I tried to go through it, I was thrown against the door frame, and everything felt strange. My left hand didn't function as usual. When I tried to put on a shirt, the left hand wasn't of any help anymore. The left side of my body was weak and not as functional as my right side.

Schwarz:

Did you go to a GP or a specialist first?

Mrs. B.:

It went on for years. I had these strange symptoms unclear to doctors for years. I went to an MRI, but nothing could be found at all. The problems were supposed to be psychological; everything was fine physiologically. The symptoms became worse. I struggled with depression and felt so misunderstood.

Schwarz:

How old have you been then?

Mrs. B.:

Oh, when did it start? That isn't easy to say. Twenty years ago, at least.

Schwarz:

Before anyone has even had the idea to take a closer look at the possible cause?

Mrs. B.:

Yes.

Schwarz:

And who then realised that you had Parkinson's?

Mrs. B.:

I went to a neurologist, who sent me to R. There, a special examination was performed, and it was diagnosed. The countless previous MRI and CT scans had not yielded any results.

Schwarz:

So it took so long, twenty years, until somebody had the idea to look for Parkinson's?

Mrs. B.:

Yes, exactly. I always felt misunderstood. I felt terrible and was always told everything was alright. I went to a psychologist, and they pumped me full of medication.

Schwarz:

Psychotropic drugs?

Mrs. B.:

Yes, yes.

Schwarz:

For a longer while?

Mrs. B.:

Yes. Then I went to the GP in between, who said I shouldn't take it. Then I stopped taking it (i.e. the psychotropic drugs) again. There were always episodes. I was feeling fine for a while, and then something happened, for example, with my mother-in-law, and the symptoms began again. I've always been made small. My husband didn't pay any attention to me, nor did he believe me. He was always on my mother-in-law's side. I was told to stay calm and not start a fight. I kept all that inside me for many years. That was probably a reason.

Schwarz:
Were you offered any therapies or none at all?

Mrs. B.:
No, nothing, only medication.

Schwarz:
Only psychotropic drugs? Has rehab sports or physiotherapy been recommended for your left side?

Mrs. B.:
I always asked for a prescription for physiotherapy because I have had neck tension for years. But I only received a prescription for six, perhaps twelve physiotherapy appointments, and then it stopped again.

Schwarz:
Who had the idea to look for Parkinson's disease?

Mrs. B.:
This was my physiotherapist. He noticed I was crooked on the treatment table and said, "There is something wrong." Then I went to a neurologist, and they diagnosed it all.

Schwarz:
So it was the physiotherapist's idea, not a doctor's, that something different than psychological stress could cause your problems?

Mrs.B.:
Yes, the physiotherapist who knew me for years. He said: "We're not getting any-where here. There's something wrong." And I still realise that I am still lying, some-how crooked.

196

Schwarz:
But it has improved, as I saw during your last treatment.

Mrs. B.:
Yes.

Schwarz:
And how were you told the diagnosis?

Mrs. B.:
The neurologist did so.

Schwarz:
And how did he tell you?

Mrs. B.:
He said it right to my face, like this: "You're having Parkinson's." I ran out of his consulting rooms crying three times until I said, "I'll never go there anymore." It was without any sensitivity. And he said: "You'll get along until you retire." I didn't know anything about it at all. Then I had pressure above my eye, which he said had nothing to do with it (i.e. Parkinson's). All of the symptoms I tell you about, where you say it's all related to it. For this neurologist, nothing was related at all to Parkinson's. He prescribed medicine, and that was all. Thereupon, my GP prescribed my medicine because I couldn't cope with the neurologist. And it isn't easy to find another specialist. Most of them have an admission freeze for new patients. Now, I have found a neurologist who just opened. She is super friendly, we can talk about everything. But she also only says: "Yes, you're looking well. You're doing great, and take your medication." It's always only about medication, prescription, and anything else is difficult. You're out again in two minutes."

Schwarz:
When you were told your diagnosis, did anyone explain to you anything about Parkinson's disease?

Mrs. B.:
No, not at all.

Schwarz:
Nothing about what to expect?

Mrs. B.:
No. As I said, the neurologist was very uncommunicative. He said it to my face, and then I had to leave. He said: "I prescribe you something." But with this medication, I wasn't feeling any better. I only had to take the R. in the morning and nothing else. Then I went to I., a clinic specialised in Parkinson's. I worked as a dental assistant. The trembling started when assisting with treatments, and one day, the left hand no longer cooperated. My daughter took care of looking for a clinic. After some telephone calls, I could go to I. There, I was given M. also, and I could move my left arm again, which had become impossible before.

Schwarz:
You couldn't move your left arm anymore before going to I.?

Mrs. B.:
No, nothing worked at all. I was shuffling when I walked. As I said, my left leg and arm could no longer keep up. I got one tablet, and one hour later, when the doctor entered the room, I could move my arm and walk again. It was like a bit of wonder.

Schwarz:
I can believe that! Have you been told what side effects the medication can cause?

Mrs. B.:
No, not at all. No.

Schwarz:
Nothing at all?

Mrs. B.:
No, no.

Schwarz:
Did they tell you anything about other possibilities for therapy? Physiotherapy, Bobarth-Therapy, speech therapy, occupational therapy or some others?

Mrs. B.:
I went there for a while, but I was told that my symptoms were too weak. I could do everything they asked me to do when I had taken my medication; before that, probably not. But with the medication, it was okay.

Schwarz:
How long did you have to wait before you could go to I.?

Mrs. B.:
That went pretty quickly. The waiting times at other clinics were very long, but I was admitted to I. just two weeks after my daughter's phone call.

Schwarz:
But was the suggestion to go to a clinic made by your neurologist or your GP?

Mrs. B.:
No, no. Only my daughter suggested that. It was all her initiative. She always saw me and said, "It can't go on like this. Something has to happen. You have to go to a specialised clinic."

Schwarz:
Did anybody there tell you about the medication's side effects or what else you could do at home?

Mrs. B.:
They didn't even mention sports. I learned all this from you, and this is so important. No doctor said so.

Schwarz:
Is your blood controlled regularly?

Mrs. B.:
When I ask my GP, she looks it up and says: "It's time to do it", but the neurologist never says so.

Schwarz:
Are the liver values, for example, checked regularly?

Mrs. B.:
No, only when I say: "We should control the blood again. "Then the doctor says: "Yes, you are right, we will do it.

Schwarz:
Is it done regularly, every quarter or half of a year?

Mrs. B.:
No. You have to tell them. I tell my doctor what I want, and she does so, but she does not suggest anything on her own.

Schwarz:
How long after I. did you come to me?

Mrs. B.:
It wasn't long. My daughter told me about you, and then I got in touch with you straight away.

Schwarz:
Did you receive any mental help from the doctors to be able to process the diagnosis and illness?

Mrs. B.:
No, not at all. On the contrary. You were pulled even more down at the neurologist's.

Schwarz:

What do you mean by that?

Mrs. B.:

Well, the neurologist said: "You'll manage until you retire and then…", something like that. I don't even remember what else he said. I left him crying three times. He behaved like a bull in a china shop. My GP said: "You shouldn't go there again. That is not good for you." I was reassured then. She gave me my prescriptions. But she couldn't tell me anything about my disease. It's all about getting my medication. With everything else, you're entirely up in the air. I only know this through you; the doctors don't give you any information or support.

Schwarz:

What are you personally doing differently now than before the diagnosis?

Mrs. B.:

First of all, I am reassured. On the one hand, it's a terrible diagnosis, but on the other, you're reassured that there is a reason for all your problems. You were always made to feel like a malingerer. "What has she already been having again?" And you go to a thousand doctors, and again, nothing is wrong with you. You began doubting yourself. Sometimes, you thought something must be wrong in your head.

Schwarz:

At the beginning of 2019, you went again to a clinic specialising in Parkinson's.

Mrs. B.:

Yes, exactly. I had heard about D. and its good reputation. It took me several attempts even to be accepted there. My GP gave me a referral and a letter. It came back immediately because D. wanted something from a neurologist. But I didn't have a new neurologist at that time. When I found a new one around October 2018, I brought my concerns to her. She gave me the referral, and I got an appointment.

Schwarz:

What experiences did you have there?

Mrs. B.:

It made everything worse. It didn't help me at all.

Schwarz:

What was done with you there?

Mrs. B.:

They didn't listen to you. They just pumped you full of medication. Every day, more medication. I was then supposed to take something different every hour, and it had the worst side effects.

Schwarz:

Which side effects did you have?

Mrs. B:

I was nauseous in the morning, listless, walking was difficult and broken, and I had vision problems, dizzy, tired, and sweating; I always saw black dots in front of my eyes, my left hand was twitching, and I cried for no reason. I began to cry when my daughter phoned for no reason. I was completely overwhelmed with feelings and emotions; cold shivers ran down my spine, my heart was pounding, I was irritable and distracted, my ears were ringing, and my feet were swollen. I was no longer myself at all. I had problems sleeping through the night; my mouth was dry, and it was so dry that I could hardly speak. I drank, but my mouth was dry again as soon as I swallowed. When I closed my eyes, it was like turning the pages of a book. It was an extraordinary feeling. And I had cramps in my hand. And I felt miserable because I had to take so many tablets. I was already thinking about what it would be like in a few years if I were already taking so much now. I couldn't sleep. Then a doctor came and said: "Let them give you a good sleeping pill." And I only thought, another pill? Of course, I didn't take one. But I was miserable as a dog. One day, I left the clinic. And I couldn't find my way back to the clinic. It wasn't far away, but I had sweat outbreaks and couldn't find my way. I was no longer a human being. I didn't care for anything then. I wanted to jump out of the window. I didn't know what to do anymore. In I., they had found out that I didn't tolerate two medications. And in D., they gave me this medication, although I had told them before that I couldn't take it. They were on my bedside table, and I had to retake them. And I got the same symptoms as in I. But the doctor said: "The medication can't cause that. I will send you a psychiatrist." Then I thought: "Wonderful." When I spoke to the psychiatrist, I told him about my symptoms. He grinned and said: "You don't need any more medication now." I thought he understood me but couldn't behave as he wanted to. And then I called you when I didn't know what to do anymore. I didn't know whether I should stay or go. Then I remembered to get you on board, and things started to improve again. They had driven me completely crazy.

Schwarz:
Did you have the impression that the problems you had with the medication were taken seriously by the doctors in the clinic?

Mrs. B.:
No, not at all. As I said, I was given the medication that I didn't tolerate again, although it was in the reports from the I. clinic. It had been tested there, what I tolerate and what not. And they gave me exactly what I didn't tolerate. I wanted to know what other possibilities I had. The answer was: "You have to continue taking this." I was feeling so terrible from one day to the other, and more patients had the same experiences. They said: "You leave this place in worse conditions than you entered it." It was awful.

Schwarz:
Did the other patients experience that they were listened to?

Mrs. B.:
No. Everyone said that they had to take more medication every day. It was the same with my roommate. She then stopped taking the pills the same way I did. I felt misunderstood. And it's all about the money. I wanted to discharge myself, but they said: "No, it's not easy." Because it was about the physiotherapists and the occupational therapists, they had contracts with health insurance companies. It's for fourteen days per patient, so you must stay for fourteen days. It seemed to me that it was all about the money, that they were getting it, and you, as a patient, were not taken seriously.

Schwarz:

Was the physio- and occupational therapy helpful for you?

Mrs. B.:

Well, they were helpful. They were very friendly. We had sports, but we also talked a lot. That was nice. I always had my appointments in the mornings. That was very nice, and I could go for a walk in the fresh air in the afternoons. I always went outside in the afternoons to see and hear something else. In the clinic, there were many seriously ill patients in every room. They brought me mentally down.

Schwarz:

Where these Parkinson's patients, who were in far worse conditions than you?

Mrs. B.:

Yes. Very seriously ill patient. And also MS-patients (i.e. multiple sclerosis). On my arrival day, a very nice doctor welcomed me. I had a good feeling, and I could go into my room in the late afternoon. A short time later, a nurse told me I had to leave the room at once because my roommate had a multi-resistant hospital germ. I was sent into a storage room, where I spent my first night. Without any explanation, I was left there. I was afraid of being infected, but I didn't get any further information from the nurse. They put me into this room and left. Half of the night, I phoned my daughters. I also wanted to know if I was infected; I was baffled. Just having arrived, being excited, and then something like that, nobody explained anything. The next day, I was told that no other room was available and that I would have to stay there. But then there was another room for me. My roommate there was seriously ill with MS. She was a very elderly lady. She was very nice, but she moved around the whole night, she screamed, and the doctors came in. They opened the door, switched the light on and closed the door. I didn't find any peace. My nerves were on edge. And then I was told: "Let them give you a sleeping pill." And again, I thought: "Wonderful."

Schwarz:

What was the doctors' recommendation when you were discharged?

Mrs. B.:

Well, I had reduced the medication myself, but the doctors didn't know about it. I wanted to try out the medication my way, but I couldn't tell the doctors about it because I needed their prescriptions—a conflict. I couldn't tell the doctors the truth, and they, of course, thought that I had got used to the medication. This was somehow stupid. I wanted to discharge myself, but I was put under such pressure that I stayed the rest of the days. They threatened me that I wouldn't get any reports and no further rehabilitation. You could say I was threatened.

Schwarz:

They told you that you wouldn't receive a report for your doctor if you left early.

Mrs. B.:

Yes, yes, that was precisely what they said. Again I thought: "Wonderful". The whole time there, I was under the worst tension and nervous.

Schwarz:

Did your stay there improve the treatment of your Parkinson's disease in any aspect?

Mrs. B.:

Not at all. It didn't help me; on the contrary. At home, I needed two weeks before I was almost myself again.

Schwarz:

And then you went to the Parkinson's outpatient clinic in L.?

Mrs. B.:

Yes, then I was in the outpatient clinic in L. I was positively surprised. I had an excellent conversation with a doctor; you could talk to him normally. That was super. When we left, we felt great. This doctor even explained some things. And we laughed. When I told him that I was looking after my grandchild and was so exhausted in the evenings, he said: "Oh, it's the same with my mother, and she is healthy. Don't worry about this." This was really good. He also talked with his boss about me. He had planned to come as well but couldn't manage to. So they phoned, and the doctor told his boss what he wanted to do, and the boss gave him an okay. It was perfect there.

Schwarz:
Would you say this was the first doctor to listen to and respond to you?

Mrs. B.:
Yes, that is true. I would go there again. But there may be another doctor in charge the next time. That's how it is in an outpatient clinic. With this illness, you are treated so miserably, so badly, and there, you feel understood and can talk and tell all your sorrows and questions. When you left, you felt like being newly born. That helps enormously.

Schwarz:
In 25 years, the first doctor with whom you felt taken seriously and who explained something to you?

Mrs. B.:
Yes.

Schwarz:
What helps you most to cope with this disease, the symptoms and the load?

Mrs. B.:
Sports, walking in the fresh air. I never thought it would because I wouldn't say I liked sports at all. And what else? It's distraction that prevents you from becoming hysterical about everything. You must think positively and look for something you enjoy to avoid brooding.

Schwarz:
What sport do you do?

Mrs. B.:
I go to a women's gym and do walking and rehab sports.

Schwarz:
Is this what helps you most?

Mrs. B.:
Yes, I think so.

Schwarz:
Have the Parkinson's symptoms become worse, or do they remain stable?

Mrs. B.:
Parkinson's remains more or less stable. There is always some ups and downs. When you get upset or excited, it's getting worse. I think I owe a lot to you that my Parkinson's disease remains so stable.

Schwarz:
I pass this compliment on to Samuel Hahnemann (i.e. the founder of homoeopathy).

Mrs. B:
But that's the way it is. I always say: "What would I do if I didn't have Mrs Schwarz." I also felt that I didn't know what to do anymore in the clinic. I would have jumped out of the window in the end. I did so many strange things. I reorganised my wardrobe, changed all the installations on my mobile and couldn't remember it afterwards. When I saw all this after stopping taking their medicine, I didn't know when and why I had done so. I wasn't myself anymore. You begin to become afraid of yourself. Honestly, I could have jumped out of the window at any time. I was so fed up with everything. I wasn't a master of my senses anymore. They had removed the window handles. There must have been a reason for doing this. You couldn't open the windows. They probably knew why. But it was like a psycho horror there.

Schwarz:
Did anybody explain these side effects to you?

Mrs. B.:
I still don't know them today. I have no idea.

Schwarz:

How are you feeling right now? How are you?

Mrs. B.:

As I said when we talked about it before the interview, I am fine. At the moment, I'm feeling a little down, but I hope to get out of it soon. But it's okay with the help of my medication. I have reduced the medication. That's working really well.

Schwarz:

It sounds as if you were feeling better after taking less dopamine.

Mrs. B.:

Yes, that's true. The more I got in the clinic, the worse everything became.

Schwarz:

So you only need enough to remove the movement restrictions and tremors, nothing more.

Mrs. B.:

Exactly.

Schwarz:

Do you think about your future with this disease?

Mrs. B.:

Yes, I do.

Schwarz:

What kind of thoughts are this?

Mrs. B.:

I fear that I will need care at some point and that I could be a burden to anyone. Losing my independence is my biggest fear. I fear not being able to do what I want to do or to drive. That would not be good for me.

Schwarz:

When you got diagnosed with Parkinson's disease, could you have imagined that you were feeling as good as you're doing now?

Mrs. B.:

I had hope, but I didn't know. The hope returned after I got the medication in I. I could suddenly move my left arm again. I was feeling like a newborn then. I thought, "That's impossible." And so fast.

Schwarz:

And during your last stay in a clinic, you were put on very high doses of medication even though you did not report any worsening of your symptoms.

Mrs. B.:

Yes, they didn't talk to you a lot.

Schwarz:

Can we say that the conclusion from the conversation is that nobody really talked to you or explained the disease and therapy to you, although you were in different clinics and to different doctors? You were not given much information about this disease, and there was no information about the medication, or what else could you do yourself to have a positive influence on the disease and its progression?

Mrs. B.:

Yes, nobody told me. The ideas and explanations came from myself, my daughter, or you. Everyone else always made me feel misunderstood. I have always said that I want to take as little medication as possible precisely because of the potential side effects. As much as necessary, as little as possible. If they give you more each time, you start to have doubts.

Schwarz:

Did the clinic not care that you did not improve under this treatment and that no positive change occurred? Were you simply dismissed after two weeks?

Mrs. B.:

Yes, they didn't believe me there.

Schwarz:

Were there several doctors in the clinic?

Mrs. B.:

Yes, of course.

Schwarz:

Did you also meet the head physician?

Mrs. B.:

Only during the head physician's weekly round. Ultimately, I just said: "I'm fine, and that's it." What else could I say? I just wanted to get out of there.

Schwarz:

What would you recommend to other Parkinson's patients?

Mrs. B.:

They should search until they find the right doctor, but that can be a long road. They should also look for homoeopaths, naturopaths, and therapists. These help with a lot of symptoms. I feel better if I have something and take or do something you recommend. It works really well. I don't know how I would feel if I only had my regular medication. Unfortunately, conventional medicine doesn't provide information about vitamins, minerals and other therapies. You get the medicines for Parkinson's, and that's it. And then they put psychotropic drugs on top of that.

Schwarz:

Thank you very much for your openness and the interview.

Mrs. B.:

It's with pleasure that I thank you very much for all your help. I feel comfortable, understood, and taken seriously by you—many thanks.

Schwarz:
You're welcome.

Oberhausen, October 16th, 2019

References

I cannot tell how many books and internet articles I have read in all these years about Parkinson's disease, the person James Parkinson, the different forms of treatment and history in general and the history of medicine. Unfortunately, I can't list them all here, but I can list the books I explicitly refer to in my conversations with James Parkinson. My special thanks go to the staff at the Cambridge University Library, who gave me access to an original book by James Parkinson and another book about his life in their rare books section. I spent an unforgettable time in the library reading them, which made me forget space and time and immerse myself entirely in the time and thinking of James Parkinson.

James Parkinson, "The Hospital Pupil or An Essay Intended to Facilitate the Study of Medicine and Surgery: in four letters", Aberdeen Medico-Chirurgical Society, London

James Parkinson, "An Essay on the Shaking Palsy", 1817. Dodo-Press

Arthur D. Morris, "James Parkinson His Life and Times", Editor R. Clifford Rose, Boston, 1989

Wendy Moore, "The Knife Man", Broadway Books, New York, 2005

Thank you

I sincerely thank the people who have supported and helped me over the years or who have just been in the right place at the right time and put up with me and all my doubts.

I thank my son, Jan Reichmann, simply for everything.

I thank my ex-husband, Achim Reichmann, for his precious help with Juergen during his last months and for meticulously proofreading the manuscript.

I thank Claudia Duschner (www.stimmewirktsofort.com) for my voice's reawakening, her patient listening, and support.

I thank Theresa Theiss (www.dessoirees.com) for her valuable tips and support with event planning.

I would like to thank the staff of the Munby Rare Books Reading Room at the Cambridge University Library for their help in finding the essential books by and about James Parkinson.

I thank the homeless people and the staff of the Tabernakel-Café in Hoxton, London, for their openness, help, and precious information about the present and past Hoxton.

And Juergen…